DEDICATION

For Kim,

MARK LOVE

Chasing Favors

A Jamie Richmond Mystery

Mark Love

Chasing Favors
Copyright © 2023 Mark Love
All rights reserved.

ISBN: (ebook) 978-1-958136-61-4
(Print) 978-1-958136-62-1

Inkspell Publishing
207 Moonglow Circle #101
Murrells Inlet, SC 29576

Edited By Rie Langdon
Cover art By Fantasia Frog Designs

CHAPTER ONE

How was it possible that almost a year had practically flown by? I'd swear it was just yesterday I was doing research for a character in an upcoming novel. That was when I pestered, pleaded, and gave a certain state police captain my innocent doe-eyed look in an attempt for me to ride along with a trooper during a patrol shift.

A year!

How the hell did that happen?

A year ago, I'd been safe and warm, happy in my cocoon of life. After all, I was surrounded by a small circle of good friends, had a nice cozy place to live in, and a job that I thoroughly enjoyed. And then boom! I witnessed the shooting of a state trooper and, then, helped solve the crime. Then my best friend got kidnapped and I was the one who figured out where she was being held captive, and came to her rescue. Next, my late father's art studio was discovered, along with a fortune in original works, which led to some crooks trying to rip that off. I sort of got caught up in that one too—and helped catch the bad guys. All of that happened in less than a year. There were times I felt as if danger and excitement were lurking around every corner.

And then there was Malone.

Oh boy! Malone.

Maybe he was the cause of everything that's happened to me.

"Jamie, are you talking to yourself?" he asked.

Speak of the devil. "Just enjoying a pleasant daydream. Must have mumbled something out loud."

I sprawled on the big sofa. It was so deep and plush, it had been known to swallow a person whole, so they practically disappeared. Or it could push two people together into an embrace. Probably only the top of my head was visible. Before I could even attempt to struggle out of the clutches of the cushions, he slipped in beside me, and then, I couldn't escape if I wanted to—as if any woman in her right mind would want to get away from Malone. He was handsome, tall and lean, with the most incredible blue eyes I'd ever gazed into.

"It's late, Jay. You should be in bed." Malone gently stroked my back.

"I like waiting up for you. Especially when you have the day off tomorrow."

He nuzzled my neck. "That's sweet. One of these days it may get old, and I'll find you sound asleep in bed, snoring away."

"I do *not* snore."

Malone stared deeply into my eyes. "Jamie, there are times you snore so loudly, you wake yourself up."

"That must be someone else. Perhaps our bedroom is haunted by a sleepy ghost. Or those noises you hear are when Ian is staying over." It was impossible to say this with a straight face, so I just snuggled up to his chest. "Will you wake me up if I ever go to bed before you get home?"

"Nah, I'll just make like a teddy bear and cuddle up with you."

The image of Malone as a bedtime snuggle buddy thrilled me. The idea of sleeping alone seemed foreign to me at this stage. A year! We settled quietly together; sometimes there was no need for conversation. Just being in each other's presence, curled up together, was enough. Truth be told, it was all I needed. I got the impression Malone felt the same way.

Here it was, the middle of October and Mother Nature was weaving her magic. The leaves on the trees were changing colors. The days were growing cooler and shorter. The kids had been back in school for more than a month. That meant Ian, Malone's unofficial kid brother, wasn't around on a daily basis. He was in his sophomore year at high school. About twice a week, usually on one of Malone's days off, Ian would be here for dinner and spend the night. I think he used us as an excuse to spend some time with Brittany, the pretty girl down the block he met last summer. They were an adorable couple. Malone was keeping a close eye on that relationship, as were Brittany's parents. Young love was so damn cute!

Malone was a sergeant with the Michigan State Police, overseeing the highway patrols on a western section of the metropolitan Detroit area. He worked the second shift, where the evening action was usually jumping. That allowed us plenty of time together in the daylight hours. When he was at the post, I focused on my own work.

A year.

This was the longest relationship I'd ever had. Not that there've been that many. Sometimes my quirky sense of humor or my lack of culinary talents or my job or my smartass attitude or my stubbornness scared a guy away. Or maybe it was a sense from me that the man just wasn't all he appeared to be. But Malone showed no signs of running for the hills. Could it be that I was maturing?

"As comfy as this couch is, I think it's bedtime," Malone whispered in my ear. "It's still warm enough that you don't need your flannel nightie."

"I do *not* own a flannel nightie."

"That's good to know. I guess the silk one would be just fine tonight."

I leaned back to look him in the eye, my nose brushing

his. "Are you sure sleep is what you have in mind?"

"Of course. Well…"

"Well what?"

Malone rolled off the sofa and pulled me with him. "Well, eventually."

***

Friday morning, Malone cooked brunch for us. Homemade Belgian waffles, topped with blueberries and rashers of crisp bacon on the side. Our plan was to run downtown to set up the studio. We had a few preparations to take care of for Ian. The kid would be coming over after school and would spend most of the weekend with us. It was a break from being at home with his mom, Terri, and his sister Caitlin.

The studio originally belonged to my late father. Peter Richmond was a successful sculptor who died when I was only seven years old. His place was in an old industrial building that had been converted into artist studios and galleries fifty years before. This past summer we'd discovered that his workshop and a supply room were still intact. That was when we'd learned of young Ian's own artistic talents. I had unlimited access to the studio and had taken to using it occasionally for my writing. Being around Peter's priceless works of art was inspiring.

"Did you talk with Terri yesterday?" I asked.

"Yes, she and Caitlin will meet us down there at six. Terri said it's been a struggle, keeping this a secret. What about Brittany?"

"I went down and visited with her parents. They're fine. We should get her home by midnight. Brittany thinks we're just going for the hockey game."

Malone had managed to get six tickets for the Red Wings game against the Boston Bruins. We told the kids only that we were going to the game and would grab some food at the arena. Terri, Malone, and I had been planning the surprise for quite a while now. It was all tied in with Ian's birthday, which is early next week.

On the way downtown, we stopped to pick up the last of the supplies needed. Malone checked each item off a shopping list that had taken on a life of its own. What had started out as a couple of things now filled a shopping cart.

"Terri insists on contributing to the expense," Malone said as we packed the last of the goodies into the back of his Jeep.

"And what did you tell her?"

"That she would have to discuss the issue with a certain stubborn redhead. I'm staying out of all matters financial. You just brought me along for the muscle." He gave me one of those low-voltage smiles, the kind that just touched the corners of his mouth and put a little twinkle of merriment in his eyes.

As an heir to Peter's estate, it turned out that there was more money available than I had ever dreamed of. While I wouldn't receive any funds for a few more years, it was something that had been lingering in the back of my mind. I earned a nice living writing mystery novels. Malone and I were comfortable sharing the expenses for the little rented house and any vacations or excursions. From the people who knew him best, I'd learned that Peter would not have hesitated at sponsoring a young artist's enthusiasm and talent.

"Do you think Terri will be offended if I don't let her pay for some of this?" I asked quietly.

Malone shrugged. "It's possible. She's working and doing her best to take care of the kids. Being a single mother with two teenagers is no walk in the park. I know Terri appreciates it when we spend time with Ian. But she may be concerned that he's taking advantage of your generosity."

"It's really not that much," I said. "I'm sure she's got other expenses that she could put that cash toward."

He was thoughtful for a couple of minutes. "Maybe you could take some money from her. Put it in an account for

Ian. Then when he needs more supplies, you can use those funds."

I glanced over as he drove through the late morning traffic downtown. "For a cop, you're a pretty smart guy, Malone."

"For a rich broad, you're pretty down to earth."

I slapped his arm playfully. "That's for calling me a broad!" We'd only learned about Peter's estate in June. Malone liked to tease me occasionally about the money. But it appeared to have no impact on his feelings toward me, one way or the other.

At the studio, we unpacked the supplies. Malone helped me arrange everything, so it didn't look like a jumbled pile of clutter. We took a few minutes to check the storeroom. After the collection had been evaluated, we'd wrapped most of the art in thick sheets of plastic, to keep the dust off it. Many of the sculptures had been returned to the heavy wooden crates Peter had built for them. There were a few sculptures left on display in the studio. Sixteen of our favorite artworks were currently touring the country, with celebrated stops in large cities.

"The kid will be turning cartwheels when he sees all this," Malone said.

"Hey, it's a combination of a birthday present and a reward for all his hard work during the summer. Think of it as a bonus."

"I just hope we're not putting too much pressure on Ian. Like we have high expectations for him to create something fantastic each time he's here."

"Malone, nobody is forcing him. This just happens to be an ideal spot for someone with the kind of talent that Ian has to learn how to sharpen his skills."

We were leaning against Peter's old drawing table, looking over the space. With the high windows facing north, there was plenty of natural lighting. There were two new easels, an adjustable drafting table, boxes of markers, pencils, charcoal, and brushes. There was a new, tall wooden cabinet with cupboards on one side to house sketch pads and canvases, and little drawers and cubbyholes on the other side to hold the various tubes of acrylic paint and other supplies. Several canvases in different sizes were stacked on top of it. A wooden stool with an intricate lattice pattern along the backrest was in front of the table.

Centered on the table was a large envelope. Malone walked over, picked it up, gave it a shake, then put it back in place. "What happens if he balks?"

"We're merely putting the offer on the table. Terri is on board and will support him whichever way he decides. Just like we will. And it's not like we're locking him in a dungeon and leaving him alone for weeks at a time without food or water or feminine companionship."

Malone wrapped me in his arms. "Man is not meant to live without feminine companionship." Then he kissed me for an hour. Okay, maybe it was only a minute or two. Either way, it left me breathless.

"You're absolutely right."

***

Malone dropped me off at home. He had a couple of errands to run before picking Ian up from school. I was working on the next book. This one was about an art heist and had many of the elements from our real-life summer adventure. As I switched on the computer, the icon indicated new emails. I clicked it. There was a note from Shannon, my literary agent, with an update about some promotions. Another was from a local bookstore, inquiring about me doing a reading and autograph session. But the next one rocked me.

It was from Randy. I hesitated. Maybe it wasn't the same guy. Maybe it was just some fan, someone who read one of the books, clicked on the website and wrote me a note to say how much he, or she, liked the book. It was a common name, after all. Not something unusual, like Nancielle or

Esmerelda. Yet somehow, I sensed that this was a specific Randy I'd met a couple of years before. The name was also a perfect description of his attitude toward me.

I opened the message and felt my palms turn sweaty.

Jamie,

I hope you're doing well. Congratulations on your books. I've read all three and see that your attention to detail and your active imagination are still working overtime. It's hard to believe it's been over two years since we met in South Haven. I'd like to think that was a magical time for both of us. It certainly was for me. We made quite a few good memories during your vacation.

I'm going to be in the Detroit area for a conference next week. It would be great if we could get together and catch up a bit. Maybe over coffee or a drink. There's also a little story I'd like to share with you. My phone numbers are below, both work and cell. Or you can just respond to the email.

Looking forward to seeing you.

Warmest regards,

Randy

I read it twice, the second time slowly, trying to see if there were any subtle hints or clues as to what had suddenly dredged up this romantic fling from the past. There had been some passionate, steamy interludes during that vacation on the shore of Lake Michigan. This was before Malone. Before I left my job as an investigative reporter. Before I started writing mysteries. Before giving up my cozy little apartment. Before…everything.

I was still trying to concentrate, to even consider drafting a response, when the side door of the house banged. Ian and Malone had arrived. I shut down the computer and pushed thoughts of a certain blond guy on a beach out of my mind.

"Hiya, Jamie!" Ian called as he zipped down the hall to the bedroom he used. The excitement in his voice was unmistakable.

"Is that the proper way to greet someone?" Malone asked, appearing in the arch by the kitchen. He winked and motioned me to join him.

Ian stopped in his tracks and dropped his backpack on the hardwood floor. He spun around, walked over, and wrapped his arms around me in a tender hug. The kid seemed to have grown another inch in the last week. Ian was now just a bit taller than my own five-seven.

"Good afternoon, Ms. Richmond. It is truly a pleasure, as always, to see you," he said.

I hugged him back. "It's a pleasure to see you too, smartass! What's got you so excited?"

"Are you kidding?" He released me and bounced a step back. "It's Friday! School is out! We're going to watch the Wings and Bruins!"

"Don't forget Brittany," I said.

"Yes! She called me last night. You guys are the best!" He grabbed his pack and tossed it in his room. "Maybe I should get a snack before we go? Lunch was like three days ago."

Malone pointed at the kitchen. "Have some fruit. We'll get dinner at the game. You've got time to clean up before we leave."

"That's sounds like a plan," Ian said.

CHAPTER TWO

Laughter must result in forward motion because the drive back to the studio seemed to fly by. Brittany was in rare form, joking and teasing not just with Ian but both Malone and me as well. She and Ian went to different schools, so although they talked and texted frequently, being apart for a few days seemed to draw them closer together. Brittany had confided in me that her parents were getting accustomed to the idea of her dating Ian. That meant the kids would probably attend duplicates of events such as homecoming, the winter dance, and many other social gatherings.

"I've got a green dress in mind for homecoming," Brittany said. "But you don't get to see it until that night. Of course, I'll wear it again when we go to homecoming at your school."

"Is it a long dress?" Ian asked. "Or something short? Because, you know, your legs really look good in a short dress. Ow!"

Malone started laughing. The rearview mirror was adjusted so he could see the kids. Brittany had jabbed a pointy elbow into Ian's ribs. "I'm sure Brittany will look lovely no matter how long the dress is. Don't you agree,

Jamie?"

"I do. Perhaps Ian needs to return to charm school for a refresher."

"Don't let him get any fresher," Brittany said with a giggle, "or my parents will want to be chaperones at every dance."

Brittany's presence kept Ian distracted as Malone pulled into the parking lot at the studio. Only as he switched off the car did the kid realize where we were.

"What's up, Malone? I thought we were going to the hockey game?"

"We are. Just had to make a little detour here. C'mon, we have plenty of time to get to the arena," he said.

I dug out my keys for the building. Brittany and Ian followed closely. Another car swung into the lot. Malone held back. The kids trailed me inside and down the hall to Peter's studio. I switched off the security cameras and unlocked the door but didn't open it yet.

"Are you still working down here, Jamie?" Brittany asked.

"Once or twice a week. It's peaceful and that makes it easier for me to concentrate. Plus I get to be around all those beautiful sculptures."

Past their shoulders, I could see Malone approaching, leading Ian's mother and his sister, Caitlin. Malone nodded. I put my hand on the door and pushed it open slowly. Ian automatically reached in and snapped on the lights.

"What the hell!" he exclaimed.

Terri was beside him now. She playfully yanked on his earlobe. "I didn't raise you to swear. Where did you learn such language?"

Ian spun around, realizing who was beside him. "Uh, I heard it from Jamie. But it's usually only when she's surprised. It's not like she says it every day."

"Most days," Malone muttered. He was doing his best not to laugh out loud.

"Let's all go inside," I said, drawing the others with me.

Malone had rigged one of the spotlights so that it was shining on the collection of goodies. Ian walked over to it in a daze. Brittany was holding his hand. On one of the easels was a sketch he had done of her during the summer. Another artist had put it in a frame and displayed it during a festival, to get some feedback. There had been multiple offers to buy it. The drawing was that good.

"Happy birthday," Terri said. "I know we're a little early, but this way, we can all be together to celebrate."

Ian was at a loss for words. That was a rarity for this teenager. He ran his free hand over the drawing table. I walked over to the cabinet and began to slide the drawers open, like a model on a game show, revealing the surprises inside. Brittany noticed the card and handed it to him. With shaking hands, he slowly opened the envelope.

Inside was a birthday card, signed by Caitlin, Terri, Malone and me. It was a funny card, with a little old lady on the cover. There was a smaller envelope inside. Ian's eyes flicked from my face to his mom's and then to Malone's. Hesitantly, he passed the envelope to Brittany.

"Please open this for me. Because I'm just gonna drop it."

Brittany gave him a quick hug and slipped a fingernail beneath the flap. She drew out another card and handed it over. Ian ran his thumb over the raised surface of the card. His gaze locked on mine. "That's Peter's trademark."

I nodded. "Seemed appropriate." The oval design included my father's initials. It was created with a brass stamp that he used to sign all his works. We'd discovered it during the summer's project. The stamp had taken up a place of honor on my bookshelf at home.

Ian opened the card. He read it, then passed it to Brittany. She glanced at me. I winked and asked her to read it aloud.

In recognition of this important day and as a way of thanking you for all your hard work, this card entitles you to private art lessons. You will have the opportunity to interview potential instructors. This studio is available for your lessons. If you so choose to pursue the study of art in college, a full scholarship will be awarded to you upon graduation from high school, provided you maintain a B average or higher. Congratulations.

Sincerely,
Vera Richmond
(On behalf of the Peter M. Richmond Estate)

"Holy shit!" Caitlin shouted.

Terri glanced at her, a wide smile on her face. "You too? Wherever did you learn such vulgarities?"

Caitlin wiggled a finger in my direction.

I shrugged and fought back a grin. "It could have been worse."

Ian went around the room, embracing everyone. Then he slowly looked in the cabinet, examining all the equipment and supplies we'd purchased. Terri dragged him over to the stool. Brittany had draped an arm around Caitlin's shoulders. The girls were almost the same height. Both girls were developing more curves than I'd ever have. Caitlin's dark brown hair hung beyond her shoulders.

"I've talked to your counselors at school. They have agreed that this could be considered a work-study program. Every Wednesday you will be released from school at noon. Then you can come to the studio to work on your art. The lessons can take place here at that time." Terri paused and placed both hands on his shoulders. "But if your grades drop even a little, you'll return to regular classes."

"How will I get here?" Ian asked, his voice thick with uncertainty.

"Jamie has graciously offered to pick you up at school and bring you here. You are not to disturb her, because she will be working. Jamie will bring you back home for dinner. Understood?"

The kid could only bob his head in agreement. I didn't think his eyes were focusing yet.

"However, and this is one gigantic however," Terri continued, "this is *not* mandatory. If you get bored with the art or want to pursue another career or field of study, you can. I refuse to be one of those parents living vicariously through her children, forcing you to do something you neither like nor enjoy. I think you are very talented. I'm proud of you. And your father would be too!"

Ian's arms went around her waist and he pulled her into a bear hug.

After a few moments, Ian climbed off the stool and proceeded to hug everyone again. Malone somehow ended up beside me. Ian clung to him for a moment, then stepped back, wiping happy tears from his eyes.

"Ready to go watch some hockey?" Malone asked.

***

Saturday morning found the three of us headed back to the studio. With Terri's approval, I had taken the liberty of scheduling interviews with a pair of local art teachers. They had been recommended by Odon Krippendore. Krip, as he preferred to be called, was an artist we'd met during the summer. His own studio and gallery were in one of the upper floors of the building. Krip was the first professional to see Ian's drawings and recognize the kid's potential. He was the one who'd framed that early sketch to gain some reactions from the public. Krip and Ian quickly formed a solid friendship. Krippendore had also been a close friend of Peter's. While my father's specialty was sculptures, Krip was a painter.

We'd had a little difficulty getting Ian moving that morning. Only the promise of fresh bagels, lox and cream cheese was enough of an incentive to get him out the door. Arriving at the studio, we spread the feast on the old drafting table, along with cups of coffee and bottles of orange juice.

"I really get to use the studio?" Ian asked around a chunk

of bagel.

"Don't talk with your mouth full," Malone chided.

The kid shot him a baleful look. But he stopped talking until he finished that bite and washed it down. "I get to use the studio?"

"You don't get your own keys," I said, "since you'll be riding with me anyway. We'll see how it goes."

"Can I use it on Saturdays too? I mean if you and Malone don't have plans. Because being around Peter's creations really sets the mood. It motivates me."

Malone winked at me. "One thing at a time. You may get tired of this place. Or have some other…activities that demand your attention on a Saturday."

"Can I bring Brittany sometimes too? I mean, she could be a model, like what Peter did," Ian said, trying hard to keep the excitement from rising so quickly.

"As Malone said, one thing at a time."

That seemed to satisfy him. We finished breakfast, chatted about last night's game. The Wings had won handily. All three kids were hoarse from cheering by the end of the night. Brittany and Ian had fallen asleep on the way home, curled up together. Krip was due to join us shortly. He would be introducing the tutors. It was my intention to have him stick around to see how these people interacted with their potential student. Ian wandered over to the space we'd set up for him. He kept looking back at me. Then he took a sketch pad from the cabinet, selected a few colored pencils, and settled in at the drafting table.

Malone made sure the hidden door to the storeroom was secured. Then he walked slowly along the line of sculptures that were displayed in the studio. No matter how many times I was here, my father's work left me in awe. I got the impression Malone felt the same way. He drifted over to the kid and looked over his shoulder. Malone nodded and said something in a low voice. Ian flashed him a grin but kept his focus on the sketch pad.

My curiosity got the better of me. I joined them. Moving

alongside Malone, I could see what Ian was working on. It made me gasp in surprise.

"I realized that since last summer, with everything that's been going on, I never had the chance to draw you, Jamie. And I should have." Ian leaned back and slid the pad over in front of me.

It wasn't exactly like looking in the mirror, but it was damn close. He'd found a shade of red that was a good match for my hair. The green of my eyes was there. The shape of the face, the nose, the chin and mouth, were right on. I was flabbergasted. He'd done this in less than half an hour.

"Nice job, kid," Malone said with a grin. "You have actually left her speechless! That doesn't happen very often."

I bumped Malone with my shoulder. "You did this so quickly?"

"This version. I've sketched you a few times at home from memory. But I didn't have all the colors available then like now. I'm sure it can be improved on," Ian said.

I noticed he was looking at the drawing, not at me. Ian turned it over and tucked the pad back on the shelf in the cabinet.

I leaned in and kissed his cheek. "That's very sweet. This is really how I look to you?"

"Jamie, you're beautiful," he said, blushing as the words tumbled out. "I'll bet Malone thinks so too."

"I think gorgeous is more appropriate," Malone said.

Now it was my turn to flush red. I left to freshen up and compose myself before Krip and the others arrived. When I came back into the studio, Malone was talking quietly with Ian. I edged up beside them to listen in.

"Krippendore recommended these people. But one thing to keep in mind is that they may have different styles of teaching. Different approaches. What's important for you is to be comfortable with someone. Don't feel intimidated. And remember, there is nothing that says you must choose one or the other. If they don't work out, we'll keep looking."

"But the estate is paying for this! I don't want to waste their money," Ian said. There was a tremor of nerves in his voice.

Malone glanced at me. "I'll let Jamie speak to that."

"The estate has buckets of money. And it has already been agreed upon that Peter would consider paying for your lessons to be money well spent. Think of it as an investment in your future. But there's one other very important thing to remember when you're meeting with these people."

"What's that?" Ian asked.

"Just be yourself. Malone and I will be right here. So will Krip. Don't be afraid to ask questions."

Before he could speak, there was a knock on the door. Krippendore had arrived with the first candidate. Malone walked over and let them in. Krip was acting as a gracious host and handled the introductions. With him was a man in his sixties, who had snow-white hair and merry blue eyes. He was short and bulky. He was wearing a suit and tie. I noticed his clothes were worn but relatively clean. I doubted he could button the jacket over his paunch.

"This is Professor Thomas Dombrowski," Krip said.

Dombrowski merely nodded in the general direction of each of us. "Friends call me Tom or TD. I save the professor part for when I'm in the classroom." His voice was higher than I expected. He kept his attention on Ian.

Krip handled the interview. Malone and I took a couple of steps back and listened. I recalled the details that Dombrowski provided. He studied art at Aquinas College in Grand Rapids and spent his career teaching the subject at several smaller colleges in the center of the state. Dombrowski had retired from classroom teaching last year.

We had allotted half an hour for each candidate to talk with Ian. I noticed the kid was paying close attention to everything Dombrowski said.

"Why don't you show Tom some of your sketches?" I

suggested.

"An excellent idea," Krip agreed.

From a portfolio, he and Ian arranged several different works on the drafting table. Tom Dombrowski took only a few minutes with each one, studying the amount of detail. He asked Ian a question or two but kept going back to the first sketch he'd done of Brittany, using just a couple of regular pencils.

"The shading here is good. Of course, I haven't met the young lady but she seems to have captured your attention," Dombrowski said.

"That's an understatement," Malone muttered beside me.

"Hush." I had to bite my lip to keep the laughter from bursting out.

Krippendore remained close to Ian's side. Together they listened to Dombrowski's comments. The interview went quickly. When Krip said it was time to wrap things up, Dombrowski nodded. He shook hands with each of us. It was the first time he'd acknowledged Malone and me. I noticed his grip was loose and flimsy. I glanced at Malone for a reaction, but I couldn't tell anything from his expression.

CHAPTER THREE

Wisely, Krip had scheduled the two instructors an hour apart. That way, if the conversation ran long, they wouldn't overlap or bump into each other. I didn't know how competitive these people might be. No sense creating any tension. During the gap between visits, I watched Ian and Krip move to one of the sculptures. The two of them were physical opposites. Youth was on Ian's side. He was getting close to five-eight in height and had started to add a bit of muscle tone in the chest and shoulders. He wore his sandy brown hair swept back and trimmed. Where Ian was thin, Odon Krippendore was stocky, with a full beard, mostly gray, that would be the envy of any department-store Santa. Krip usually wore his gray hair long, tied back into a ponytail. He could have been a hippie during the sixties. Maybe he still was.

Even though Krippendore professed to have no interest or ability to teach, I could tell Ian was absorbing every word. Krip didn't talk down to him. He treated the kid as a friend, someone with shared interests. There could be fifty years difference in age, but that didn't seem to bother either one.

"You look pensive," Malone said, appearing beside me as if out of thin air.

"Just watching those two interact. Do you think that happened with Peter as well? Bonding with another artist? Or another person?"

He shrugged. "It wouldn't surprise me. Everything we've learned about him, from Krip and Vera and Lincoln Banning, supports that. Even Judge Barolo commented on the strength of their friendship."

That memory brought a smile to my face. Dante Barolo ended up marrying Meredith Bell, who once modeled for Peter. My father had played matchmaker and introduced them.

"Who is the other prospect?" Malone asked.

"Erica Morehouse. She should be here any minute. What did you think of Dombrowski?" I asked.

Malone slowly shook his head. "Doesn't matter what I think. Ian's the one they will be working with. What's important is what he thinks about them."

Before I could respond, there was a knock on the door. Krippendore gave Ian an encouraging smile and went to let her in. I didn't know what to expect. Would she be old and stuffy like Dombrowski? My train of thought was derailed as Krip's laughter boomed into the room. The lady in the doorway leaned in and gave him a quick hug.

"This is Erica. Jamie, Malone, and Ian." Krip said with a wave of his hand.

Erica Morehouse was probably in her early forties. She was a lot shorter than me, with more curves than a sports car. Her blond hair cut in a short bob, she looked ready for anything. Erica was wearing jeans, sneakers and a black sweater under a gray leather jacket. She took a couple of steps into the studio, one hand extended to Ian, who was closest, and froze. Erica's eyes widened, first in surprise, then delight as she took in the sculptures around the room.

"Oh! My! God!"

Krip shook with laughter. "Apparently, I forgot to mention this was Peter's studio. My apologies."

"I will never forgive you. Well, maybe someday," Erica

said. She grabbed Ian's hand. "Would you mind terribly if we look at these lovely pieces first? Maybe you could tell me a little about them."

Ian glanced at me. I nodded. He'd done the tour-guide routine with others before. He could recite details about what materials were used, how long it had taken Peter to complete each piece, and the title. Ian had learned all this from the files my father had made for his work. Erica kept her hand on Ian's arm as he walked her through the studio. Krip followed a couple of steps behind, just listening in. Erica would ask a few questions about each piece, making observations. Ian responded. Eventually they came back to the drafting table. Erica climbed onto Ian's new stool. She studied the two guys and asked more questions. Her face was expressive, lit with enthusiasm and excitement.

"What's her background?" Malone asked quietly.

"Studied at the University of Michigan and the Cranbrook Academy of Art. She taught for about ten years at Cranbrook after getting her master's. Now she teaches part time, so she has more time for her family and to concentrate on her own work. Krip assured me her schedule would fit with Ian's availability," I said.

"Quite a difference between her and Dombrowski in their approaches here," Malone said. "I thought it was odd that he didn't even look at the sculptures."

"I did too. I mean, who does that? Walks into a room with these priceless works of art and doesn't even notice or acknowledge them?"

Krip opened the portfolio and set three of Ian's sketches on the table. Erica studied each one slowly. Ian was about to say something when she held up her hand. After a couple of minutes she motioned him closer with one finger. Together they bent over one of the drawings and talked quietly. Krip stepped back. He looked at me and raised his empty palms.

Malone and I just sat and watched. Erica and Ian quietly discussed each one of his drawings. After a bit, he opened the cabinet and removed the pad he'd used earlier. Erica studied the sketch, then looked over her shoulder at me, as if realizing for the first time that others were in the room. She patted Ian's arm, jumped off the stool and walked over to us. Ian and Krip followed in her wake.

"Forgive me. I got so caught up in the power of this studio that my brain failed to register you two sitting back here. I feel like an idiot!" she said.

"No apologies needed. I'm Jamie. This is Malone."

She shook hands with both of us. Her grip was firm. Erica had a smile that was infectious.

"This studio is impressive. It would be a wonderful place for your son to continue to hone his craft."

"Ian's not our son!" I said, feeling my face turn beet red.

"We're friends of the family," Malone explained.

"Close friends," Ian said sheepishly. "The best of friends."

Erica was laughing. "Well, now that I've made a complete fool of myself, let me apologize for making assumptions. But no matter what the situation is, this studio would be a great place for Ian. He's talented, with a lot of potential."

"We think so too."

She looked at the four of us. "Krip told me you're interviewing others to tutor Ian. It would be a pleasure to work with him. I do hope you'll consider me."

"Well, we don't want to make any rash decisions. It's important to us all that whoever we select be a good match for Ian," I said.

"Of course. How soon were you hoping to get started?"

"Ian will have time on Wednesday afternoons. From one until five. There may be an occasional Saturday as well."

"Wednesdays would be perfect for my schedule," Erica said.

"Let's start next week!" Ian blurted out.

We all looked at him in surprise. A stunned silence filled the room. Krip cleared his throat. "Maybe you should discuss this privately. I'll take Erica upstairs and show her what I've been working on lately."

"That's a wonderful idea," she said. Without another word, she followed him out of the studio. Krip closed the door behind them.

"We don't have to make a decision today," I said.

Ian was practically bouncing off the floor like Tigger in the Winnie the Pooh cartoons. "I know, but she's great! That guy, Lumpkowski…"

"Dombrowski," Malone corrected.

"Right, Dombrowski. He was more intent on telling me what I'd been doing wrong. He just wanted to lecture me. He kept saying "You shouldn't do this. You shouldn't do that. You should be studying techniques first. Five minutes after meeting him and I felt like I was disappointing him. But Erica—"

"Mrs. Morehouse," Malone corrected, "Or Ms. Morehouse."

There was no slowing the kid down. "She told me to call her Erica. And you saw the way she reacted to Peter's art. Erica was respectful. She gets it! Dombrowski couldn't even be bothered to look at them. That old man is just looking for a paycheck. He wants someone he can dictate to. I had teachers like that in junior high. Never learned anything from them."

Malone looked at me. He was doing his level best to suppress a grin. This was a serious decision. But it felt like an easy one to make. I reached over and took both of Ian's hands in mine.

"Breathe. She's still in the building."

"I know. It's just…she's more encouraging. Erica complimented me on the sketches. When she saw the one I did of you this morning, her whole face lit up. She's excited. Malone told me earlier about different teaching styles. Hers, I like."

"I understand that. But I need you to do me a favor," I said.

"Anything," he said anxiously.

"Take a seat. Close your eyes and just relax. Don't talk. Give me a minute to think about this."

"But Jamie…"

"What the hell! One minute! That's all I'm asking for." I pointed at the stool by his drafting table. Erica had hooked her purse on the back of it. In the excitement of the moment, she must have forgotten it.

"One minute," he grumbled. "But I'm counting."

Malone cuffed him lightly on the back of the head. "Go."

When the kid was out of earshot, Malone leaned close. "She does seem to be more enthusiastic than Dombrowski. And Krip recommended them. He's gotten to know Ian a bit. Do you trust his judgment?"

"I do. But I'm reluctant to decide so quickly."

"The kid might think it's cruel if you make him talk to other people. She really has set the bar pretty high," Malone said.

"I know. Maybe we'll do it on a trial basis." Ian was slumped in his chair, running a finger across the drafting table. "He's so eager to develop his talent. This must be what it would be like to see him on Christmas morning."

"Why do I get the feeling you enjoy torturing him?" Malone asked.

I smiled sweetly at him. "I never had a little brother."

He wrapped his arms around me. "You can be so bad."

"I learned it from you. But in a good way." I hugged him, then called to Ian. "Run upstairs and ask them to join us."

He leapt from the chair and disappeared. I wondered if his feet even touched the floor. Within five minutes they returned. Ian and Erica were deep in conversation. Krip hung back.

"We would like to have you work with Ian," I said.

"*YES!*" Ian jumped forward and hugged me.

"No reluctance on his part," Malone said with a laugh.

When Ian released me, I turned back to Erica. "Let's try

it for a month and see how it goes. You and I can work out the details related to payment. There are some forms that the lawyers will require you fill out."

"Can you start this Wednesday?" Ian asked.

Erica looked at her watch and her face lit up with a beaming smile. "Got an hour or two? We can start now. And this is on me."

Ian's grin matched hers. "If that's okay with Jamie and Malone."

"Think I'll make a coffee run," Malone said.

Krippendore threw me a wink and ducked out the door.

Erica and Ian moved to the drafting table. She took off her leather jacket and draped it over the back of the stool. Their heads came together. Ian flipped the page on the sketchpad. He listened intently as Erica spoke. I noticed her hands were involved in the conversation. She gestured quite a bit, emphasizing a point or two. Ian walked over to *The Lovers*, a sandstone carving that was on display. Erica lightly touched his arm.

"Don't rush. Take a few minutes and just look at what Peter Richmond accomplished," Erica said quietly. "Study the lines."

"It took him months to get this right," Ian said.

"So you understand there's no reason to hurry."

Their conversation continued in quiet tones. I'd have to send Krip a gigantic thank you note for recommending Erica Morehouse. If her lessons kept him this engaged, I was sure Ian's talents would blossom under Erica's tutelage. Watching them together made me consider her assumption that Ian was my son. Mathematically, I supposed it was possible for me to have a sixteen-year-old boy. I'd never seriously thought about being a mother and raising children. During the time Malone and I had been together, it wasn't a subject we'd discussed. It wasn't like either one of us was too old. Maybe having Ian around the house quelled any parental urges. I'd have to ask Malone about his reactions to Erica's statement later.

Knowing neither one was paying any attention to me, I pulled out my phone and went to my email account. For the third time, I read Randy's message. Should I ignore it? Send a sweet response, with a thanks but no thanks? Delete the message? Or would it be appropriate to meet him, just a casual conversation between a couple of people who'd spent a lovely week together two years ago?

This wasn't a decision I was ready to make on my own. Linda and Vince were having a date night, going to a fancy restaurant and then seeing a Broadway play at the Fisher Theater. I sent her a text about getting together on Sunday after Malone went to work. It would be just the two of us. She responded quickly and offered to cook dinner. Linda's culinary talents far outshone my own. I could have forwarded her Randy's email but decided against it. Tomorrow would be soon enough to get her reactions.

Malone returned with coffee for everyone, then drifted upstairs to shoot the breeze with Krippendore. I stayed in the background. Erica continued working with Ian. The kid was a sponge, absorbing every comment and suggestion. Two hours raced by. Time to break it up.

"We'd better call it a day," I said. "Seems to me a certain young lady is waiting for Ian."

The kid flashed a smile. "Pizza and a movie."

Erica shot me a wink. "Is this the girl in the drawings?"

"Yes, that's Brittany," Ian said.

Maybe it was just me, but I swore his eyes did a little sparkling happy dance whenever he mentioned her name.

"Go grab Malone. I need a minute with Erica."

He left the studio, making sure the door latched behind him. Erica pulled on her leather jacket and slung the purse over her shoulder.

"I've got your email address from the information you gave Krip. The attorneys will send you a contract Monday morning, spelling out the arrangements and all the necessary legal details," I said.

Erica nodded. "I'm excited to work with Ian. His

enthusiasm may kickstart my own efforts."

"That would be a nice perk."

"Jamie, I know we just met, but can I ask a favor?"

"Ask away."

"Would you mind if I brought a camera on Wednesday? I'd love to take a few pictures of these sculptures. I promise, this is just for my own collection. I might be able to learn something from Peter's work."

I hesitated for a beat. This was unexpected. "Let me think about it. I'll let you know before Wednesday."

"That would be great."

The guys returned. Malone distracted Erica while I activated the security cameras. I wasn't paranoid. But the events of last summer left me very cautious. Malone felt the same way. Together we locked up the studio and walked out to the parking lot.

***

Ian had conned Malone into driving him and Brittany to the mall in Novi, where they could get pizza and see a movie. Brittany's parents would pick them up and bring them home at ten.

"Can I hang out with Britt after the movie?" Ian asked sweetly.

"You've had a long day. Better make it early," Malone said.

"It wasn't that busy. How early?"

"Ten thirty," Malone said sternly. "We had to drag your butt out of bed this morning. Ten thirty is late enough."

"Come on! That's like five minutes after her parents pick us up."

I had to turn my head and cover my mouth to keep from laughing. Malone was obviously messing with the kid. Somehow, he could do that while keeping a straight face. Ian must have sensed I might come to his defense.

"Jamie, can you make him understand? I haven't seen

Britt all that much. She misses me. I miss her too! We don't see each other every day. I don't want her to forget me and start dating some guy at her own school and—"

Malone was quaking with laughter now. "Enough! If it's okay with Mr. Murphy, you can stay until eleven. And tomorrow your focus better be on homework. No video games, no girls, no football. Nothing but homework."

"Deal!"

I leaned over and nuzzled Malone's neck. "You're so tough with him."

He nodded solemnly. "I learned it from you."

***

We were curled up on the sofa. Malone had lit a fire and the birch logs were snapping and crackling. That was the only background noise we needed. It did add a little atmosphere as well. Good thing I didn't have a bearskin rug on the floor, or I'd have been conducting a lesson in the fine art of clothing removal.

"You seem a little preoccupied," Malone said, lightly running a hand down my back. We were nose to nose so it was easy to look into his eyes.

"Something Erica said keeps playing in my mind."

"Would that be when she thought Ian was our son?"

There are times when I forget how perceptive Malone could be. "It's an easy mistake to make. We are old enough to be his parents. Maybe she thought he was your biological son and I'm your gorgeous trophy wife."

"Trophy wife?" He leaned in and took my breath away with a kiss. Malone shifted onto his back, drawing me on top of him.

"Yes, a trophy wife. That's where the beautiful woman is obviously much younger than the man. Although sometimes they're not married. So I could be the trophy lady friend." I started giggling, a result of the way his fingers were tickling my ribs and the absurdity of what I was saying.

"I don't have any children, biological or otherwise," Malone said. "Ian's a kid I've known for years."

Ian's late father and Malone had coached Little League teams together for several years. When his father died in a car accident, Malone was already a familiar figure, someone who stepped in to spend time with Ian.

"You and I have never talked about having children," I said quietly. For some reason, now I couldn't look in his eyes. I wasn't sure what would be there. "We've just been enjoying our time together."

Malone slipped a finger beneath my chin and gently raised it until he could study my face. "That we have. Should we have a serious discussion?"

"Not tonight. Erica's comment just caught me by surprise."

"Me too."

He proceeded to find a way to keep my mind and body occupied. Time flew. Malone had the good sense to lead me to the bedroom just before Ian returned. I didn't want to give the kid any ideas. Chances are he already had plenty of his own in that regard.

CHAPTER FOUR

Sunday evening I went to Linda's for dinner. Malone was working. Ian was back home with Terri, doing the last of his homework. I made a detour at a little Italian bakery and picked up bread and cannoli. She'd prepared shrimp jambalaya. I helped put together a salad to go with it and warmed up some of the bakery's crusty dinner rolls. After dinner we moved into the living room. Linda flopped on one end of the sofa. Her dog Logan came over and put his head in her lap. She rarely went anywhere except work without him. Linda scratched between his ears. I took the other end of the sofa. I watched her while she was talking to the dog. If you looked up the definition of the expression drop-dead gorgeous, it would probably have her picture next to it. Linda has a luxurious crop of wavy black curls, with a face, body and legs that Hollywood would go crazy over.

"What's going on, Jay Kay? I haven't seen you this distracted in a long time. Problems with the new book?"

I never could hide much from Linda. Guess that's to be expected when you've been best friends since the second grade.

"I got an email the other day from Randy."

Linda's beautiful, dark eyes widened in surprise. "The cute guy with the boat? South Haven Randy?"

"That's what you remember? The boat?"

"I remember you had some fun on the water together. Seems to me he tickled your fancy." She comically wiggled her eyebrows at me. "Among certain other things."

Earlier, I'd printed out his message. Now I gave it to her. Linda read it over without comment, then folded it in half and passed it back.

"Did you answer?"

"Not yet. I'm not sure what to say. A tiny part of me is curious to see him, to see what this story he's referring to is all about. But the rest of me is running in the opposite direction. I don't want to screw up what I've got with Malone. My life is good. Hell, it's damn near perfect. About as perfect as I've ever been."

Linda looked at me closely. "Have you ever told Malone about South Haven? About the time you spent there with Randy. Or helping the cops catch those idiots who were breaking into people's homes?"

"No. It seemed like ancient history by the time we met. We never talk much about our pasts. What happens if I tell him, and it drives Malone away?"

Linda started laughing. She pushed Logan off her lap, then moved over and drew me close in a hug. "Jay Kay, does Malone think you were a nun who jumped the wall at the convent? Or that you were saving your virginity just for him?"

"Shut up." Her laughter was contagious.

"Maybe you could dress up like a nun for Halloween. A simple black dress, long sleeves, a white collar. And a black scarf to cover most of your hair. But make it sexy with some fishnet stockings and stiletto heels."

What an image she was painting. "You're terrible. Besides, nuns don't dress like that nowadays."

Linda settled back but kept her arm around me. "I'll take your word for it. But you do have options here."

"Such as?"

"Well, you could ignore the note. Just delete it. Or you could respond and tell Randy that you'll meet him for some coffee and put a time limit on it." She gave me a sweet smile. "And you should talk with Malone. I don't see him going away, unless he came home and found Randy tickling your fancy again."

"Linda!"

"I'm just saying. If the situation involved me, I'd tell Vince. We have talked a lot about our lives and experiences before we got together."

Logan was whimpering so she took him outside. Maybe she was right. Malone and I had always been pretty straightforward with each other. There had been a few surprises, but nothing we couldn't work out together. Considering everything we'd shared in the last year, talking to Malone was probably a good idea. The dog came back in and settled beneath the window. Linda returned to her position on the opposite end of the couch.

"Come to any conclusions?"

"Yes, and I have one more option. I'm going to tell Malone about Randy and this note. Then I'll offer to meet him for coffee. And you're going with me."

She started to giggle. "What am I? The chaperone? Will I have the key to your chastity belt?"

I flushed as red as my hair. "Hush! I just want your company. You were with me in South Haven. You should be with me now if I'm going to meet Randy."

"Maybe he's gotten fat and all his hair fell out."

"In two years? Seriously?"

"Strange things happen, Jamie. Maybe you ruined him for any other woman, and he let himself go."

"That's highly unlikely. But I guess there's only one way to find out."

***

I was sitting on the bentwood rocker when Malone came home. There was just one lamp, on low. It was growing cool outside. I still wore the jeans and sweater from earlier in the day. Fur-lined moccasins kept my feet warm. He paused in the archway to the kitchen. Malone was wearing boots, jeans and a black leather jacket. Simple stuff. So why did my heart do a little stutter-step at the sight of him?

"Hey, Jamie," he said softly.

"Hey, Malone. How was the shift?"

He shrugged. "Pretty calm for a Sunday night. Maybe all the crazy people got their kicks on Saturday and were in recovery mode before the week starts."

I got up and met him for a long hug. "If you're not too tired, there's something we should talk about."

"Are we continuing the talk we started last night? The one about kids?"

"Hell no! This is something else!" Somehow that was the furthest thing from my mind right now.

"Sofa or bed?"

This was not a bedroom conversation. I steered him to the plush sofa and we sat down together. Malone didn't crack a joke. He merely slipped an arm around my shoulders and kept me close.

"You sound serious, Jamie. Is everything all right?"

"I'm fine. It's just something has come up. More accurately, someone has come up. It's a guy I met a couple of years ago. Before there was an us."

Malone didn't say anything. His face was calm. His eyes locked on mine for a heartbeat or two. Then he did this kind of magic trick, where suddenly I'm no longer sitting beside him. Now my legs were on the sofa and my buns were in his lap with my arms around his neck.

"Malone!"

"Yes, Jay?"

"I really need to tell you about this."

"I'm listening. Just thought this position would be more comfortable. Let's hear about this mysterious guy from your past."

Now it didn't seem like such a big deal. I explained about the vacation Linda and I had taken in South Haven. Malone was letting his fingers drift through my hair. He didn't interrupt when I told him about the fling with Randy. He was more than a little surprised to learn about the home-invasion ring that the three of us had helped the local police catch in the act, which led to arrests, convictions and the return of most of the stolen property.

"Did you think I'd be upset to hear this tale?" he asked.

"I wasn't sure how you'd react."

"Jamie, we've both been with other people before we met. It's not like Bert sealed you in a vacuum jar and kept you out of reach of any men."

Bert was my stepfather. He was also a captain with the state police, and Malone's boss. *Yeah, I know. It's complicated.* Very little in my life was nice and easy.

"If he tried that, Linda would have smuggled in a glass cutter. And you weren't exactly living in a monastery, studying Zen and contemplating the meaning of life," I said.

"True. So are you saying this Randy guy is back in the picture?"

I gave him the printed copy of the message. This wasn't easy to accomplish, since the paper was in the back pocket of my jeans. It took a little wiggling to gain access to it. Malone didn't seem to mind. He read the note, shrugged and handed it back. I tossed it on the floor.

"Did you respond?"

"Not yet. I've been thinking about it on and off since Friday. Linda thinks I should meet him for coffee. If I'm going, she's tagging along."

"That sounds like a good idea."

I shifted just enough so I could look him in the eye. "Are you okay with this? With me meeting him for coffee?"

"Jamie, what we have together is very solid. It can certainly stand up to a chaperoned coffee date with an old vacation fling. Besides, I'll bet you're curious about that little story he mentioned."

"That goes without saying."

Malone was still playing with my hair. He knew it drove me crazy. Now he brushed it aside, leaned in and kissed my neck, moving up to that little spot right behind my ear. I was melting.

"Any other matters we need to discuss?" he whispered.

"You keep doing that and I'll be incapable of any lengthy conversation."

He didn't stop. Somehow Malone managed to stand up with me in his arms. "That's good to know."

***

Monday morning, I responded to Randy's message. Within an hour he answered back, giving me the details as to where he was staying and the hours of the conference he was attending. Randy suggested we could grab a drink in the hotel's restaurant. That wasn't going to happen. The last thing I wanted was to send him a subliminal message that I might rush into his arms and go up to his hotel room to pick up where we'd left off two years ago with a horizontal quickie. I hadn't mentioned Linda would be joining me. The hotel was in Novi, just around the corner from a large, outdoor mall. I suggested we meet at a coffee shop there, Monday evening at 6:00.

He agreed.

Linda had already been clued in. She wasted no time teasing me and wanted to let me know that she was drawing up specific guidelines that I would have to follow before my "coffee date" with Randy. She could be such a smartass!

I wondered where she learned such behavior.

Linda came over after school. It just so happened she taught at the same high school Ian attended. She was in casual mode, wearing navy blue slacks, flats and a lightweight red sweater. Even after seven hours teaching history to hormonal teenagers, she appeared fresh as a daisy, looking as if she had just stepped out of the pages of a fashion magazine. Linda studied me up and down as I came out of the kitchen.

"You are not wearing that!" Linda's hands were on her hips in what I considered the stern mama look.

"What's wrong with this? We're just meeting for coffee. Jeans and a sweatshirt are fine."

She tapped her foot. If she wasn't such a lady, a stomp would have been appropriate. "I refuse to be seen in public with you like that. Jeans that are old, worn-out and tattered. That sweatshirt is bulky enough that Malone could wear it. Are you supposed to be a bag lady? Perhaps a street urchin?"

"It's just coffee," I groaned.

"Yes, it's just coffee. In a public place. Where God only knows who you might run into. And your hair looks like two squirrels got caught in a tornado while they were trying to find a good place to store walnuts." She pointed to the bedroom. "Go! Right now."

Sulking, I did what she said. Linda gave me a nudge toward the bathroom. "A little makeup wouldn't kill you. Nobody says you can't look nice when you see Randy. At least, be presentable."

I scrubbed my face and ran a brush through my locks. At her insistence, after shedding the sweatshirt, I put on a little lip gloss and some eyeliner. Linda picked out a green silk blouse, dressy black slacks and a pair of short black boots. She nodded her approval as I dressed.

"You need jewelry. Where's that pair of gold hoops Malone gave you?" She rummaged around in my little jewelry box and selected the pair.

I slid the earrings into place. "I think you're enjoying this."

"Jamie, you spend almost every day in jeans. Why not dress up a little? It's not like you don't have some nice clothes."

Sometimes I hate it when she's right. We grabbed our

coats and purses and headed out to meet South Haven Randy.

Even though we got there about ten minutes early and the place was busy, Randy was already waiting at a four-top table by the front window. His face lit up in a charming smile as we approached.

"Linda! It's so good to see you. I'm glad you could join us."

"I wouldn't have missed it," she said, leaning in for an embrace and buzzing his cheek with a kiss.

Randy turned his attention to me. At my hesitation he waited a second, then extended his hand for a shake.

"Oh, what the hell," I muttered. I pushed his hand aside, stepped in and gave him a quick hug and a smooch on the opposite cheek.

"You look fantastic. Both of you do," Randy said, waving us to take our seats on one side of the table. He took our orders and went to fetch coffee.

"He's still cute," Linda said.

"I think his hair is thinning."

She pushed my shoulder playfully. "Maybe. But you've got to admit that he looks good."

"Fine. He's still kind of cute." She wouldn't let up until I agreed with her.

Randy returned a minute later with a tray of coffee cups and a small plate piled high with cookies. We each took one to nibble as he sat across from us.

"Congratulations on the novels, Jamie. I discovered them in Black River Books and was really impressed."

"Thanks." I blushed a little at the compliment. "Writing mysteries seemed like a natural progression from my days as a reporter. Some of the articles I wrote back then were great practice for developing characters and twisting plots."

"So tell us what's new and exciting in South Haven," Linda said.

Randy described some of the current projects the city was undertaking to expand its residential base and draw in more tourists. He was animated and comfortable, but his eyes kept darting back and forth between us. There was definitely something odd going on.

"The conference is for city managers from across Michigan. We're all learning about new grant opportunities from both the state and federal government. Some of it is dull and boring. But it's necessary." Randy paused to gulp down half his coffee.

"I would imagine connecting with Jamie and me could be quite the highlight for your trip," Linda said. That sultry voice of hers was working overtime. She bumped my leg under the table.

"Definitely. But there are a few things I should explain."

"Your note mentioned a little story," I said.

"That was my feeble attempt at intrigue." Randy fidgeted in his chair. "Maybe it was a stupid idea. Trying to make something out of nothing. But I'll never forget how the two of you helped Jared and the police catch those guys."

Linda gave him a sweet smile. "That was all Jamie's doing. My idea of a peaceful vacation does not include a stakeout."

"My one and only experience pretending to be a cop," Randy said. He winked at me.

"I seem to recall you were more interested in making out than you were in the surveillance of that neighborhood," I said.

"Can't blame me. You were very distracting." He flashed a broad grin. "You still are."

It surprised me to realize that his looks and comments were having absolutely no effect on me. Linda bumped my leg again. I glanced at her, caught the wink and chose to ignore it.

"That was two years ago. I'm sure there have been a lot of changes for you during that time. Just as there have been for both of us," I said.

Randy sat back and raised his hands in surrender. "You're absolutely right. I was merely recalling the memory of that night. A little flashback."

"So is there a story, or was that just fluff to get my attention?"

"Yes, there really is a story. At least I think there is." His bluster was gone. Now he looked worried sick.

CHAPTER FIVE

"Or it may just be my imagination playing tricks." Randy pulled a phone from his jacket and opened an app where the pictures were stored. He flicked through a couple until he landed on a specific one, then extended the phone to me. Linda leaned closer. On the screen was an adorable brown-eyed little girl, caught in laughter. Her dark hair was a jumble of curls.

"That's Gracie," Randy said fondly. "She's five."

"She's a cutie," Linda said. I nodded in agreement.

Randy made a swiping motion with his finger. I advanced the screen. Here was another shot of Gracie with her arms around a pretty woman's neck. Her hair was the same shade and mass of curls as the little girl. There was no hiding their identical smiles.

"That's Liz. We're getting married."

I almost dropped the phone. Linda snagged it, studied the screen for a moment and passed it back to Randy. He closed the app and set the phone on the table. There was an instant of hesitation before he could meet my eyes.

"When's the big event?" Linda asked.

"Next month. We're having a little ceremony the weekend before Thanksgiving. It's been in the planning stages forever. Hard to believe sometimes. But I'm excited about it."

"Congratulations! I'm happy for you," I said. "Tell us all about them."

In addition to his job as the city manager in South Haven, Randy played piano and sang a bit with a group of local musicians. They performed in a bar during the winter and one of the city's outdoor venues during the summer. Linda and I had witnessed such an event while on vacation. Last year during one of those outdoor concerts, Gracie had been at the edge of the gazebo's platform, spellbound. She'd been dancing and swaying with every tune. During a break she'd climbed the stage and run her fingers along Randy's electronic keyboard.

"Liz chased after her up there on the stage," Randy said, smiling softly as he told the story. "Gracie wanted to play. I couldn't say no."

"How did she reach the keyboard?" Linda asked.

"I had a stool back there. She climbed right up and started pressing the keys. As soon as a note sounded, Gracie started giggling. Liz couldn't stop apologizing, trying to get her off the stage." Randy gave his shoulders a little shrug. "I didn't mind at all. Gracie stayed right there with me when we played the next set."

"So music brought you together," I said.

Randy laughed. "Yeah, that was the beginning. It was a Saturday-afternoon gig. Next thing I knew, we were having pizza together. Then we went for a walk after the meal. Gracie was between Liz and me, holding our hands as if it were the most natural thing in the world."

"Congratulations, Randy," Linda said.

He beamed with pride. "Thanks. I'm a lucky guy. It wasn't long after that we began spending every weekend and most evenings together. Liz and I didn't go on a date without Gracie for three months. It just seemed natural to be together."

"You're telling us that this is part of your story?" I asked.

"Yeah. This is background. We've been so busy, what with my job and hers, that we've sort of overlooked a few things." Randy's face took on a sheepish expression. "And a few people. Like my mom. She lives back on this side of the state, over in West Bloomfield."

"You forgot your mom?" I asked, a note of incredulity slipping in. "What kind of a son are you?"

"I didn't forget her! I just couldn't visit her as often as in the past."

Linda made a disapproving, clucking sound with her tongue against her teeth. "You're a sorry excuse for a son. Ignoring your own dear mother. After all she went through, giving birth to you and everything."

"I wasn't ignoring her. Jeez, I forgot what it was like with the two of you. You can pummel a guy like a tag team in a wrestling match."

Linda reached over and patted his arm. "Relax. We're just teasing you. Go on with your story."

Randy explained that his mom had met Liz and Gracie several times and loved them both. She was delighted that he was getting married at long last, and that she would already have a granddaughter to spoil. In the last three months, every time Randy tried to plan a visit with her, she would give him a reason why she wasn't available. At first, he thought she was just giving him an out, so he could spend more time with his girls. But something didn't feel right.

"Mom has been on her own for a long time now," Randy said. "Dad died of a heart attack. Sitting there watching the news. He never said a word, just slumped over in the chair. After that, it was just the two of us. I finished my master's degree a couple of years later then started working in the metro area."

"If I remember correctly, it wasn't that long ago when you moved to South Haven," I said.

He nodded. "It will be three years in February. A headhunter recruited me. Mom was insistent that I take the job. It wasn't like I'd be working in Tokyo or Melbourne,

Australia. It's only three hours away. Besides, she still has her own job, her neighbors and friends."

"But you think she's avoiding you? That's your story?" I asked.

"There's more to it," Randy said. "Just give me a chance."

"Patience has never been one of Jamie's strengths," Linda said with a smirk.

Ignoring her, I folded my arms across my chest and leaned back. *I can be patient. Sometimes.* Randy caught the look on her face, took a breath and continued the tale.

"I surprised her two weeks ago on Saturday. Didn't call. Just got in the car at five in the morning and started driving. Got to the house a little before eight, rang the bell and banged on the door. The plan was to just show up, take her out to breakfast and catch up. She won't use one of the phone video-conferencing sites, so I hadn't really seen her in over three months. But nothing prepared me for what happened when the door opened."

Randy drained the rest of his coffee and carefully set the mug on the table. "It was a guy. He was wearing pajamas and a robe. Mom showed up right behind him. When I came in, he scurried down the hall and went into her bedroom. Into. Her. Bedroom!"

"Holy shit," Linda gasped.

"Exactly. The fact that she hadn't told me about him made me wonder what was going on," he said quietly. Randy's eyes were on the table now, his fingers brushing cookie crumbs into a pile. "It's been eighteen years. She was forty when Dad passed away. I didn't expect her to wrap herself in the shawl of widowhood and never get involved with another guy. But she could have told me. I would have understood. Hell, I encouraged her in the past. It was more upsetting that she'd been dodging me for three months than the fact that she's met someone."

As Randy grew quiet, I took a moment to consider my own mother's lifestyle. Vera has been married and divorced multiple times after my father's death. She's given up on matrimony and instead enjoys the attention of multiple gentlemen, particularly those who have a place in high society and don't mind footing the bill for her lavish wardrobe, accommodations, and travel. She's like a high-class gypsy. Or a bohemian hippie girl. Linda's mom lives in North Carolina now and has been in a healthy relationship with the same guy for years.

"Do you want to tell us more?" I asked softly.

Randy nodded. "His name is Nicholas Bellamy. Probably late forties, maybe early fifties, yet he was able to sort of retire early. He and Mom both attended a fundraiser for this nonprofit called K-9 True Companion. Mom has supported that for years. They were at the same table. Had a nice conversation over dinner, then started dancing together. Bellamy is suave. He doesn't overdo it, but there's just enough charm to have an influence on her."

"So he's a bit younger than your mom?" Linda said.

"Yeah. Maybe ten years. Maybe less. It's a guess. I mean, it's not like I asked for his ID to get a sense as to who he is."

"How did the rest of that morning go?" I asked.

Randy started to laugh. "It felt like I was the parent and caught them sneaking in after curfew. Or making out on the family room sofa. They got dressed and we went out to breakfast at one of our old favorite haunts. Mom kept blushing. Bellamy just seemed to roll with it. He was very attentive to her. Asked me all the right questions. I can't explain why, but something about him set my nerves on edge."

He explained that the rest of the visit was cordial. His mother kept touching his arm, grasping his hand, telling him how happy she was. Bellamy doted on her. Randy kept thinking it was merely his imagination. Maybe Bellamy was trying too hard to impress him. Or to show that his mother was being well cared for. The guy just seemed a little…off.

"Dad had a big insurance policy of his own. Plus there

was one from where he worked. He was a supervisor. Ran the equipment maintenance programs for the road commission for Oakland County. Mom lives in the same house I grew up in. That's paid for. She still works as the office manager for a medical clinic."

"You said Bellamy is semi-retired?" Linda asked.

"Kind of. He claims to have sold his last business for a nice profit and is looking for something new. Bellamy said he's a serial entrepreneur. Whatever the hell that is," Randy grumbled.

"I ran across a few of those when I was working as a reporter. That's someone who starts a business, gets it running successfully, then sells it and starts another one. Often the new business has no correlation to the previous one."

Randy gave us a reluctant shrug. "I guess that makes sense. Maybe it's all perfectly innocent. Do you think I'm overreacting?"

"Nobody wants to see their parents get hurt. Especially when she's been on her own for such a long time," Linda said.

"So, what is it you were hoping for here?" I asked. "Why do I get the feeling you were thinking this little family drama would trigger my interests?"

Randy covered his mouth with his left hand. His eyes widened and he had difficulty looking at me. *Busted!*

"You cute little shit!" Linda said with a laugh. "You figured this would get her spider senses going and she'd want to get to the bottom of this!"

Randy knew curiosity ran thickly through my veins. Digging for information, whether through research or interviews, was part of what made me so good at my job as an investigative reporter. Finding different sources, asking the right questions, observing the reactions of people interacting were all part of it. But I wasn't going to let him off the hook. I leaned forward, propped my elbows on the table, rested my chin on my hands.

Randy cleared his throat. His gaze went to Linda, then shifted to me. Now he turned serious. "It's my *mom*. Beyond Liz and Gracie, she's the most important person in my life. I just don't want her to have her heart broken or get swindled by some guy. She has dated occasionally over the years with friends and people she's known forever. I want her to be happy."

"What if she's in love with Bellamy?" I asked.

He swallowed hard but didn't answer.

"What if he feels that way about her?" Linda asked quietly.

Still no response.

Linda turned her head to look right at me. I shifted my gaze in her direction. Linda's expression was empathetic. Randy wasn't just some stranger we'd bumped into. He was a guy from my past. A guy I liked. Could I blame him for being concerned about his own mother?

"I'm not a cop or a private detective. What exactly do you expect me to do?"

"I don't know!" Randy's face showed his exasperation. "It was a stupid idea. Just talking about this with the two of you has convinced me. I'm an idiot!"

I reached across and grabbed his hand. "No, you're not. You're a son who is concerned about his mother. There's nothing idiotic about that. Stop beating yourself up."

"What if I'm making something out of nothing?" he mumbled.

"Then taking a closer look at this guy will give you peace of mind," Linda said. "And that's better than worrying about her."

"I don't even know where to start," Randy said.

I squeezed his hand. "Just leave that to me."

CHAPTER SIX

Old habits die hard.

Old skills rarely die. They may get a little rusty, but it doesn't take much to dust them off, give them a shake and coax them back to life. I dug a small notebook and a pen out of my purse. Linda noticed this, gave me a smile and went in search of more coffee and something more substantial than cookies.

"I can do a little checking. Some details may be visible on the internet, with business sites, organizations and social media. But I'm going to need more information from you."

Randy's head was going up and down like one of those gimmicky bobble-head dolls you got at a baseball game. "Anything you need."

"Don't suppose you got a picture of him?"

"That I do. I managed to get a few of him with Mom." Randy lifted his phone and went back to the photo album. He got to the right spot and handed it over. There were three shots of them.

My first reaction was they made a cute couple. She had the round angel face, like Hollywood's image of a cherub. Her hair was as white as freshly fallen snow, with some little traces of blond. She had pale blue eyes that seemed to glow.

The smile she flashed lit up her whole face. There was nothing phony about it. The guy was clean shaven, with dark brown hair shot through with gray. The hair was thin on top, but he combed it straight back, not bothering to disguise it. Clear brown eyes stared right into the camera. I've never been good at guessing peoples ages, but I pegged him early fifties.

"Send me those," I said, passing the phone back.

Randy keyed in my number and let technology do its thing. "What else can I tell you?"

"Start with your mother's name, the home address and where she works. Then tell me everything you can remember about that conversation at breakfast, especially anything about Bellamy's background."

Randy filled in the blanks for me. I scribbled down a bunch of notes. Linda returned with little salads, croissants and more coffee. She took great care of herself and wasn't about to consider two dark chocolate cookies with sea salt as nutrition. We took a break. Randy relaxed and seemed to be breathing easier.

"Can you tell me anything else?" I asked after the dishes were cleared.

He shrugged. "They met at that fundraiser. Mom's been involved with a couple of different nonprofits for years, working on committees, helping to raise awareness and money. She's done a lot of local events, mostly behind the scenes."

"Did they talk about any common interests? Anything they like to do together, maybe something new to your mom?"

"Nothing that I can recall. But I got the impression that Bellamy still has his own place. It wasn't like they'd moved in together. Although that could be something that happens further down the road," Randy said thoughtfully.

"Older people may not take things slowly when it comes to big decisions," Linda said. "They want to make the most of their time, especially if they've been on their own for a while. At least, that's what happened with my mom."

I sat back. All three of us had experienced the loss of our fathers, just at different times in our lives. Maybe Randy's mother was simply tired of being alone. There was a good chance that many of her friends were married, perhaps for thirty years or more and she'd grown bored being the fifth wheel, the odd person out when a group got together. Or thinking that friends felt sorry for her, since she didn't have anyone in her life.

"How long are you in town for?" I asked.

"The conference runs until noon Friday. Then I'm heading back to South Haven." His face took on a wistful look. "I miss the girls."

"Did you make any plans to see your mother while you're here?" I asked.

"No. I can't recall if I even mentioned the conference or not. Why?"

Linda turned to look right at me. "And what's going on in that cynical mind of yours?"

"Just thinking it would be a way to get a closer look at Bellamy. From an objective third party, of course."

"Am I missing something?" Randy asked.

"Call her. Tell her you're in town for the conference and you want to take her and Bellamy out for dinner tomorrow night. Pick somewhere nice. Tell her you'll make reservations," I said, closing my notebook.

"I'm obviously missing something," he said.

Linda started giggling. "Yes, you are. Jamie will be your date. She's an old friend you happened to meet up with. This gives you another chance to see your darling mother and her new beau. Two couples, having a lovely dinner."

"That's brilliant!" Randy said.

"Just don't overplay it. Don't tell your mom about me. It can be a nice surprise. I'll spend most of the day tomorrow digging into Bellamy's background. Then I can add to the research at dinner."

"You'll be my date?"

I wagged a finger back and forth. "Dinner date. Nothing more than that. You're engaged! I'm just a friend from days gone by. I will meet you at the restaurant. Don't get any ideas beyond that!"

"Jamie, I can't thank you enough for doing this. But you should know, Liz is the only woman for me."

"That's good to hear," Linda said.

"And she knows about both of you. We're close with Jared and his wife, Sara. Their daughters are pals with Gracie." Randy couldn't stop smiling; obviously, he was thinking about them.

"Pick a spot and make the reservations. Somewhere fancy that will give Bellamy the impression you've got money to burn. Especially when it comes to your mother," I said. "Nothing too casual."

Randy nodded. "There are a couple of places that come to mind. I'll call her as soon as I'm back in the hotel."

"Don't forget to call your girls," Linda teased.

"Not a chance."

***

Tuesday morning, Malone went to the gym after surprising me with breakfast in bed. We'd talked at length when he got home last night. He encouraged me to see what I could find out about Nicholas Bellamy.

"So this Randy guy wasn't trying to rekindle any passionate moments from that summer vacation with you?" Malone asked while sliding one solitary fingertip down my neck to my collarbone. We were reclining on the sofa. I was still wearing the green silk blouse and the slacks. I'd kicked my boots off and left them by the rocker.

"Not at all. I think the only memories that stuck with Randy were my stubbornness and the way I helped the cops figure out about the home invasions."

Malone exhaled gently on my ear. "I'm willing to bet he remembers a lot more than that."

"That's ancient history in the land of dating. And it was one week."

"Summer vacations are special. They deserve extra attention. He's probably got pictures of you in a bikini."

If it was his intention to drive me to distraction, Malone was doing a damn fine job of it. Now his lips were tickling a little spot at my collarbone.

"I don't want to talk about Randy." I moaned. "Or South Haven. Or summer vacations. Or...anything."

"No talking? Jay, that's so unusual for you." There was just enough ambient light that I could see his mischievous smile.

"You taught me a long time ago, that there are times for talking and times for love."

"So if you don't want to talk..."

The kiss was enough to deliver my message and shut him up. There was no more conversation.

Now well fed and dressed in jeans and a hooded sweatshirt after a good night's sleep and a hot, steamy shower, I fired up the computer. Time to start digging into the life of Nicholas Bellamy. Last night after our conversation with Randy, Linda and I kicked around a few possibilities. Naturally, Linda's curiosity was now percolating as well. After she left, I typed up my notes and filled in a few details that I recalled.

A search of Bellamy's name revealed multiple entries, some with photographs. It took a lot of time to narrow down the list. Fortunately, I had the pictures Randy had sent last night. I thought this would be the easy part. But none of the profiles listed were a match. Either they were in the wrong part of the country, too young or too old. I wondered if Randy had tried this himself.

I switched to some of the social media sites. On a hunch, I went to Facebook and pulled up Randy's mother. Allison Brooks smiled back at me. She was a lovely lady. There were dozens of pictures of her with friends or with Randy. More recently she'd included some shots of Liz and Gracie. There was one on the beach with the four of them from a Fourth of July picnic. Allison's expression was one of pure delight. Randy probably hadn't popped the question at that stage, but it must have been soon after that. I realized that she and Randy had the same smile, the same gleam in the eyes.

There was no information on her relationship status. Not surprising. Many women preferred to leave that blank and avoid being bombarded with messages from men and women looking for an instant friendship. Or a sugar daddy. Or long-forgotten friends. Or distant relatives. Or...whatever. I noticed there were no pictures of Bellamy with Allison. Maybe he was camera shy.

Shifting gears, I dug into Allison's background. There was mention of the medical clinic where she worked, along with a few photos of her and coworkers at social gatherings. I checked these as well, just to get a better sense of the lady.

I paced for a while, planning my next move. A cup of herbal tea was a good distraction. Reviewing my notes helped. Since Allison had met Bellamy at the fundraiser, that seemed like a good place to start. As with many nonprofit organizations, there was a listing on their website of recent events. Clicking on that gave me details, including the venue, and pictures.

The evening had been titled "Finding New Friends." I scrolled to the agenda. Held at a country club out in Oakland County, there was a gourmet meal, a silent auction, dancing with a five-piece band and a live auction. The silent auction was where patrons could write their bids on a clipboard and at the end of a designated time, the winner was announced. The live auction was conducted by a local celebrity, one of the reporters from a TV news station. There was even a list of the various goodies that would have been available for both types of auctions.

The live auction had fewer items. These were big-ticket prizes that would have drawn a lot of interest. There was a dinner cruise on Lake St. Clair for twenty people. Another opportunity was a private wine tasting event for ten. A dealership offered a two-year lease on a Tesla. A few more prizes were on the list. But the last one was a painting, a landscape signed by a local artist. I skimmed over the name, then jumped back.

"What the hell!"

Odon Krippendore had generously donated the painting.

Krip!

I've never believed in coincidences. Sure, they might happen on occasion, but what were the odds that Krip would be supporting the same charity at the same event where Allison would meet Nicholas Bellamy? Tingles of nervous energy shot through me. It was tempting to pursue this line of thought and track down Krippendore, but I only had a couple of hours left to dig up more on Bellamy. Because so far, I'd found absolutely nothing.

Randy didn't know the name of the business Bellamy claimed to have sold. He didn't even know what industry it was. There were too many possibilities. Bellamy could have been in real estate, he could have owned a restaurant, sold life insurance, been a stockbroker, an airline pilot or a record producer. Maybe he was a shoe salesman. Or a truck driver. Maybe he was the Wizard of Oz.

I tried variations on the spelling of his last name.

Nothing.

Flipped the last and the first names.

Nothing.

I checked every social media site that came to mind. He didn't have his own Facebook page. There was nothing on LinkedIn, the site for business professionals. Not a single, freaking site had anything to show that matched the guy in the pictures with Randy's mother.

So who the hell was Nicholas Bellamy?

Perhaps Randy was smart to be nervous about this guy. The more I dug, the more frustrated I became. It was possible that Bellamy hung out with a crowd who believed social media posts and such were beneath their status and were meant for other people to use. Or he could just be a guy who valued his privacy. His crowd could have preferred to stay in the shadows. That was when inspiration struck me. I snagged the phone. A quick check of the calendar confirmed she'd be in St. Louis this week.

"Hello, Jamie," Vera cooed. "Are you calling to say Bert misses me?"

"I'm sure he does. How's the exhibit going?"

"Delightful. The museum has done a wonderful job promoting the event. There are some lovely people here."

Vera was traveling to each city with the sampling of Peter's art. Working together with the director and curator for the Detroit Institute of Art, along with Peter's attorney, we'd put together a list of appropriate larger cities. In addition to security, a customized truck was arranged to properly transport the sculptures to each location. Vera had been expanding her high-society contacts. Friends loaned her their private jets to go to each new stop on the tour. She was being wined and dined, staying in posh hotels or luxurious mansions. Vera loved to travel and be pampered. To say she was having the time of her life was simply an understatement of the same caliber as saying Tom Brady is an average-looking guy and a decent quarterback.

She gave me the rundown on some of the stars from St. Louis. The exhibit was on display until Sunday evening. Then everything would be packed up and hauled to Kansas City.

"Lincoln Banning called me last night. He's still getting requests from other museums to schedule visits. This was originally going to be a twelve-city tour. We may have to expand it," Vera said.

Banning was the attorney who handled Peter's estate. He had become the point person for all things related to the tour. I knew she was whining, but truth be told, Vera loved the attention. Meeting new members of society's cream was an added benefit.

"Jamie, you and Malone should fly to Denver next

month. There are some wonderful people there who'd be thrilled to meet you."

I hesitated. Next month would be just after our anniversary. Would Malone even remember it? Vera was probably expecting an immediate answer. That wasn't going to happen.

"Let me think about it and discuss it with him. But that's not why I'm calling. I just sent you a photo. Do you know this guy?" Earlier, I had cropped the picture so that it only showed Bellamy.

"Hold on. I need my glasses."

The fact that she admitted this wasn't lost on me. This was a glimpse of the human side of her that she rarely let others see. Vera and I had become quite a bit closer over the last few months. I waited while she checked the screen.

"Should I know him, Jamie? He doesn't look familiar."

I blew out a breath in frustration. "No reason. Just grasping at straws here. I'm trying to put a name to that face and just keep coming up empty."

"I'm sure you'll figure it out. Now I simply must run. The stylist is here to fix my hair. Tonight's the official opening of the exhibit and I honestly want to look my best."

"Have fun, Vera."

"I will. Give Bert a kiss for me when you see him." She paused then added, "I love you, Jamie."

"I love you, Mom. We'll talk soon."

Just that quickly, she was gone. The "I love you" part was something new. We'd been talking a couple of times a week. In the past, months could go by between calls or visits. And the love between mother and daughter was always implied, but rarely spoken. Perhaps we were growing closer at this age than we had ever been before. Maybe we were just growing up, getting more accustomed to how our lives were intertwined and would always be connected.

The alarm on my phone chimed. It was time to get ready for my quote-unquote dinner date with Randy. Earlier, he'd sent a text with the location and the time. The smartass had even included a picture of a young woman in a slinky little black dress with the notation "this would be good" followed by a bunch of smiley-face emoticons.

I checked the name of the restaurant and clicked on their website. He'd done well, picking a fancy place in Bloomfield Hills. I was tempted to go in my current attire but didn't want to make the situation any more uncomfortable than it was going to be. After all, I was a surprise guest.

CHAPTER SEVEN

Randy was waiting in the parking lot. I couldn't swear that he'd been pacing, but he did seem to bubble with a bit of nervous energy. I stepped up and gave him a quick hug.

"Thanks for doing this, Jamie."

I linked my arm through his. "You're buying me dinner. I should warn you, the menu on the website looks very appealing."

"It's the least I can do for your help. So how do we handle the introductions? Are you using a cover name?"

"Nope. Let's keep it simple. Just introduce me with my first name. You can say we met in South Haven while I was on vacation a couple of years ago and we bumped into each other yesterday at the coffee shop."

"That's all true," Randy said. He seemed relieved that it wasn't a complicated plan.

"Be attentive, but not too attentive. We don't want your mother to think there's anything more between us than simply old friends getting together."

Inside the restaurant there was a coat room. The evening had cooled quickly once the sun dropped below the horizon. The end of October was just a couple of weeks away. November's cold temperatures were hovering around the corner. I was wearing a lined trench coat with a silk scarf at the throat. Randy checked his coat, then turned to help me with mine. My back was to him as I slipped it off my shoulders.

"Holy crap!"

I glanced back and gave him a flirty look. "Something wrong?"

"Not a thing. Wow! It's just that I just never pictured you all dressed up before." He handed my coat to the young woman behind the counter, then moved alongside me with a grin. "That is a beautiful dress for a beautiful lady."

Just to mess with his mind, I'd picked out a body-hugging dark red dress. It almost reached the middle of my thigh. Almost. With black nylons and heels, I felt like a true adult. I'd added a pair of dangling silver earrings and a simple silver necklace. A faint spritz of perfume behind the ears and the backs of my wrists was the finishing touch. Linda would have been pleased that I'd worn makeup again. Two nights in a row. What was the world coming to?

"It seemed like a good idea to fit in with the patrons. This is a classy place." I stood in front of Randy and adjusted his necktie. "Besides, I want to see what kind of reaction Bellamy gives me."

Randy took my hand as the hostess guided us to our table. "Showtime."

There was a moment of hesitation as Allison looked up, seeing the two of us approach. Bellamy had been in deep conversation with her. When he saw us, he bounded to his feet in a fluid motion. His gaze flicked up and down my body as if I were a treat on the dessert menu.

"Randy! This is such a great surprise," Bellamy said, pumping Randy's hand in a friendly manner. "And you didn't tell us you were bringing a date." Bellamy voice was scratchy, as if he were a smoker, or had been for a long time. There was a definite rasp to it.

"Another part of the surprise," Randy said smoothly. "This is Jamie. She's a good friend I bumped into last night.

Jamie, this is Nicholas Bellamy. And this lovely lady is Allison Brooks. My mom."

I shook hands with them. Allison was even prettier in person. There was a warmth in her expression, in her eyes, that couldn't be faked. She winked at me, then turned to her son.

"Suddenly, beautiful women find you attractive," she said playfully. "There must be something in the water in South Haven that causes this. Maybe you should have it analyzed."

"It's more likely the women feel sorry for him," I said, returning her wink.

"Do you know Liz and Gracie?" she asked.

"I haven't had the pleasure yet. But Randy showed me their pictures."

Allison raised her right hand and extended the pinky finger. "Right there. That's where Gracie has him wrapped up. It wouldn't surprise me if she gets a pony for Christmas!"

Randy was shaking his head in dismay. She had read the situation perfectly.

We chatted while perusing the menus. Bellamy caught the waiter's attention and drinks were ordered. No one commented on my request for plain tonic water with a lime. Bellamy and Randy conferred about appetizers. They decided we could share a couple of orders of deviled crab and a smoked salmon flatbread. Bellamy ordered some of the most expensive dishes on the menu. Was this normal, or just because Randy was buying? Once the appetizers, which were delicious, were gone, it was time to get to work. Randy and Allison were talking quietly.

"Randy tells me you're an entrepreneur, Mr. Bellamy."

"Nick. Please, Jamie, call me Nick. We're all friends here."

"Thank you, Nick. What kind of business do you have?" I did my best to smile sweetly and keep my expression devoid of any skepticism.

"Boring stuff, really. I worked at a small manufacturing company for a long time. Parts that were primarily for the automotive industry. The owner became ill and several of us got together to buy the company." Bellamy shrugged. "About three years after the sale was final, a national firm approached us. They wanted to purchase the operation. It all started with that."

"Did you sell the business recently?"

"No, Jamie, that was quite a while ago. I made a nice profit on it. Still receive healthy dividend checks every year. Shares of stock in the national company was part of the package. Since then, I've invested in several different types of businesses."

Something in his eyes flickered. He was being polite, but less than forthright with his answers. I needed more.

"I've always been curious about entrepreneurs. An old friend has a little restaurant and she's been approached multiple times about expanding and even offering franchises. But I have no idea how that sort of thing works," I said.

"Franchises are a whole different animal," Bellamy said. He seemed to relax a bit with the new direction the conversation was taking.

"What types of businesses appealed to you?" I leaned a little closer. Bellamy did the same.

"I prefer smaller ones. Or ones that are a few years old and need an influx of capital to take it to the next level. There's a garden shop I'm considering. A wedding photographer approached me last month. I'm also looking at a specialty bakery, one that does wedding cakes and pastries for large events. Now that marijuana has been legalized in Michigan, they're considering opening a second shop that would provide cannabis-infused baked goods."

Time to play the innocent redhead card. "I wouldn't have a clue about any of those. However do you decide which one is a wise investment?"

"A well-written business plan makes a difference. If they

don't have one, it's not worth consideration. And of course, they should be able to make a good pitch," Bellamy confided, "although sometimes, I just listen to my gut. Instincts can help."

"That's fascinating. I'd like to hear more about the whole process," I said. "I never really thought about so many different opportunities to own a business."

Bellamy gave me a single nod. His expression remained passive. "Of course, it takes a while before you see any return on your investment. It's important to be patient. You can't rush these things."

I was about to respond when Allison put her hand on his arm. "Enough serious conversation. You two look so intent. Let's just relax and enjoy the ambience and this lovely meal."

"Of course, darling," Bellamy said. He covered her hand with his, then leaned over and kissed her cheek.

"My apologies," I offered, then decided on another tactic. "You make such a sweet couple. How long have you been together?"

Allison beamed a smile. "Just a few months now. We met at a fundraiser for the K-9 True Companion. Two single people placed at the same table. One thing led to another, and here we are."

"You make it sound so easy," I said.

"Maybe it was fate," Bellamy said, still holding Allison's hand.

I caught Randy's eye. Before he could respond I jumped back in. "Randy told me a little about that. He said there was an auction too. Did you bid on any prizes or donations?"

"I put my name on a couple of things at the silent auction. A trip to a spa and tickets to a Broadway musical that's coming to town. But I didn't win," Allison said. "The real excitement was with the live auction. A reporter from Channel Four was the auctioneer. She was excellent."

Bellamy nodded in agreement. "Yes, she was exceptionally good at cajoling more money out of the patrons. A very charming young lady."

"Nick actually made a bid on a few things as well," Allison said.

"That dinner cruise sounded like fun," he said, giving her a sweet smile.

Allison explained that once the bidding started, the competition grew quickly. As the numbers climbed, the action slowed. Even with a few encouraging words from the persistent auctioneer, there were still several people interested in the top prizes.

"I went as high as five thousand dollars for the cruise, before someone went to six thousand. That was too rich for my blood," Bellamy said.

"There was a painting too!" Allison exclaimed. "A lovely scene, done by a local artist. I thought for certain you were going to win that one."

Bellamy smiled. "It would have looked good at my condo. But there was a certain determined woman bidding against me. She was not going to stop. I gave up when it hit four thousand dollars." He shrugged. "The proceeds all go to such a great cause, and it was worth the money. I can probably find something just as good at one of the galleries around town."

The arrival of our meals interrupted the conversation. Everyone got busy eating. But in the back of my mind, a glimmer of an idea began to take root.

***

When Malone came home, I was still in my dinner ensemble. Guitarist Jesse Cook was playing on the stereo, softly filling the room with his moody rifts. There was one light on low in the corner. I'd been reading the latest John Sandford novel. As the back door of the house opened, I closed the book and stood to greet him.

"That's some dress," Malone said. He pulled me close for a kiss that lasted an hour or two. At least that's what it felt like.

"Glad you approve," I gasped.

Malone's left hand was holding my right. His right hand went to my waist and he started swaying, moving me with him in time to the music.

"A beautiful woman, wearing such a glamorous outfit, is quite a surprise to come home to."

"It's what I wore for dinner. Just thought you'd like to see it."

"Like isn't a strong enough word, Jamie."

He moved me about the living room. It was a good thing my heels were still in place, or he'd be towering over me. Malone drew me closer and brushed his lips against mine. Shivers ran through me.

"Perfume, too. Jamie, you're driving me crazy."

"That's a mutual feeling." I was anxious for him to throw me on the sofa or drag me to the bedroom. But Malone was enjoying the moment. Truth be told, so was I.

"Your legs look incredible in those stockings," he whispered in my ear.

"Seems to me you tore my pantyhose the last time I wore them."

He chuckled, still nuzzling me as we moved together. The stubble of his beard was giving me a chill of anticipation. "There was a run. It's not like you were ever going to wear that pair again."

"You shredded them, Malone!"

"A spur-of-the-moment action. The desire was too great to ignore. But that's really your fault."

I widened my eyes at that comment. "How is it possibly my fault?"

"That's the effect you have on me."

The song ended. We were in front of the window, backlit by the streetlights, the harvest moon and the little table lamp. It was impossible for me to take a deep breath. Malone is the only man who has ever had that impact on me.

"I did offer to buy you another pair of pantyhose," he said. The twinkle in his eyes was more evident in the moonlight.

"Which was very sweet. But I decided to take Linda's advice."

The next song started. He drew me closer somehow. "And what advice would your best friend have on this subject?"

"Forget pantyhose. Thigh-high stockings work just as well for displaying a shapely leg."

His eyes sparkled much stronger now. "So that's what you're currently wearing?"

"Yes. They're really very comfortable. And they make me feel sexy."

The kiss that followed stole the last of my breath away.

"Jamie, if you get any sexier, I'm liable to have a heart attack."

Malone turned me and shifted. The next thing I knew, my feet were off the floor. Instinctively, both of my arms went around his neck. His right arm was around my back now, with the left holding me behind the knees. Malone acted as if I was light as a feather as he carried me down the hall.

"Thigh-high stockings?" he whispered.

"Oh yeah. Wanna see them?"

"I think a slow-motion fashion show is in order."

"In this outfit, slow is my only speed."

Later, we collapsed on the bed. I dragged a heavy quilt over us and burrowed close. With my head on his chest, I could hear the vigorous thump of his heart as it slowed. My heels had gotten kicked off when Malone picked me up. The dress was now in a heap, tossed beneath the bedroom window, mixed in with his gear. I was still wearing the earrings, necklace and the stockings. Nothing else.

"I suppose you're going to make me crawl out of this nice warm bed and go turn off the stereo and the lamp," Malone said. He was slowly running a hand down my back.

"No need. They're both on a timer. It's very important that we do our part to conserve our natural resources."

Malone chuckled. "Yes, it's good that you save energy for serious matters like what we just shared."

"That's a different type of energy." I tried to change the subject. "Want to hear about my evening?"

"Not tonight. I'd rather just be in this moment with you. Let's forget about everyone else until morning."

Who could argue with that logic? I smothered a yawn on his chest. "Fine with me."

"Remind me to send Linda a thank you note for her advice on the thigh-high stockings. Maybe some roses too."

CHAPTER EIGHT

The high school required me to sign Ian out since he was leaving in the middle of the day. When the school year began, Terri had included Malone and me as authorized guardians. It was an odd feeling for me, having parental responsibilities for him. He was practically bouncing off the walls when I stopped in the office to pick him up. I thought he was going to race me out the door. In his infinite wisdom and a display of his vast knowledge of dealing with teenage boys, Malone had packed a cooler and stuck it in my car. There were two sandwiches with smoked turkey, bacon, gouda cheese and deli mustard, four red apples and a bag of sliced veggies. Four water bottles anchored the corners of the cooler. Ian spied it in the back seat and twisted around to grab something before I even pulled out of the parking lot.

"Don't you get a lunch break at school?"

"Yeah, but that happens at twelve-thirty. I'm starving."

I shook my head in disbelief. "And your darling mother didn't send you with a lunch to school?"

"Umm. Yeah, she did. I ate that around ten thirty. Maybe it's just nerves. I get hungry when I'm nervous. Mom sent peanut butter and jelly. That doesn't compare with a Malone feast!" He took an enormous bite out of the sandwich and groaned happily.

"Hey, keep in mind half that food is for me. And what possible reason do you have to be nervous?"

He shrugged. At least he had the courtesy not to talk with his mouth full. This time. "I'm just excited about working with Erica."

This would be the first official tutoring session. My laptop case was on the back seat as well. It was my intention to continue my research on Nick Bellamy. If I got stuck, there was always some actual writing, which I should be doing. There were a few details Nick had let slip last night during dinner. That would be my starting point this afternoon.

Erica Morehouse was in the parking lot when we arrived. Apparently, Ian wasn't the only one excited about the lessons.

"Hope you haven't been waiting long," I said.

"Not even five minutes. I wasn't sure about traffic this time of day, so I left a bit early." Erica turned to Ian. "Ready to get started?"

He grinned. "It's practically the only thing I've been thinking about."

"I wish all my students were this eager to learn," Erica said.

"I'm sure Ian maintains the same level of interest in all of his classes," I said with a straight face. He just laughed and shook his head.

Ian grabbed the cooler and his backpack. With my laptop in hand, I went ahead and unlocked the studio. On Saturday, Ian, Malone and I had discussed the idea of letting his tutor, whoever that may be, see the rest of Peter's collection in the adjoining storeroom. Malone and I agreed that this should remain locked, especially in the beginning. On the drive home, Ian had broached the subject once again. I told him that Erica's focus should be on him. Malone suggested that after the first month, if things were going well, we could reconsider showing her the rest of his artwork. Besides, all the art was packed away. It wouldn't be easy to open the crates so Erica could get a firsthand look. Maybe she'd be satisfied watching the videos we'd created last summer.

"Think of it as a bonus," he told Ian. "If Ms. Morehouse is doing well and you're learning a lot, this could be a nice surprise."

"I guess," he mumbled.

"So whenever we go downtown and Erica is going to be there, you'll stay in the studio," Malone said.

"You're the boss."

We were at a red light. Malone had glanced at me with a low-voltage smile. I turned in my seat to look Ian right in the eye. "Actually, I'm the boss on this. So don't mess with me, Junior, or you'll lose those art lessons."

Both guys started laughing.

Nobody takes me seriously!

I unlocked the studio and let them in. Ian lugged the cooler over to the back wall and set it beside the rolltop desk. Erica grabbed one of the extra stools and carried it over to what I was already thinking of as Ian's corner. They quickly settled in.

I booted up the computer and began reviewing my meager files on Nicholas Bellamy. There were a few things I'd picked up on last night, but it was still a long way from easy to find out more. Talking with Malone that morning had given me a couple of ideas as well. If I were a real P.I., I could have snagged his cocktail glass last night and sent it in for fingerprints. Maybe there was a legitimate reason why Bellamy's history was so vague. Maybe he was in witness protection. Maybe he was a retired spy. Maybe he was studying a role for a new cable series. Maybe he was a wealthy foreign dignitary who preferred to live incognito.

I was getting punchy. Leaning back, I watched Erica and Ian work. She'd brought a couple of books along. These were spread out on the table before them. They weren't whispering, just talking in normal tones. But the distance between us was large. I walked across the room and stopped in front of *Grace*, a stonework sculpture. It still amazed me that my father was so talented and had used so many different materials in his art. This was one of my favorites, which was why I liked it on display where I could see it every time at the studio.

Looking at this fantastic piece reminded me of another detail worth investigating. And it gave me an excuse to walk away from the computer for a bit. I closed the lid and grabbed my purse.

"If you two are good, I'm going up to talk with Krip for a bit."

Erica gave me a sweet smile. "We'll be fine. Tell him I said hello."

"Will do." I glanced at Ian. He nodded in agreement. "Remember the rule. This door stays locked. I don't want any snoopy reporters or treasure hunters trying to sneak in."

"You're the boss." There was a mischievous glint in his eye.

I leaned in and whispered in his ear. "Yes, I am. And I'm also the resident smartass. So don't get sassy."

He surprised me by slipping off his stool and kissing my cheek. "Understood, Jamie. Erica will keep me busy."

Krip was rocked back in an ancient chair, his feet propped up on the arm of the sofa. There was a coffee mug forgotten on the floor beside him. He appeared lost in thought. Whether concentration or memory, I couldn't tell. I rapped a knuckle on the doorframe.

"Got a minute or ten?"

"Jamie! For you, I can spare an hour. Or five. Isn't today when young Rembrandt has his first lesson?"

"He's still beaming after that impromptu session on Saturday. Then he talked my ear off all the way here about what he's discovering." I walked over and flopped on the other end of his couch.

"That's good to hear. I'm sure Erica can keep him

interested. She's a good teacher. And a pretty good artist herself." He smiled. Maybe he liked more about Erica than her talent with a paintbrush. "What brings you by on this dreary, windswept day?"

"I want to ask you about a painting you donated for the K-9 True Companion auction last summer."

Krip leaned back and laced his fingers behind his head. "K-9 what? Are you sure that was me?"

"It had your name on the program. A river scene, with a wooded background. Something titled *The Tug of the Current*. I'm sure the photo in the program didn't do it justice."

The old bear of a man grinned. Eyes dancing with amusement, he dropped his feet to the floor and got up. After rummaging in a file cabinet, Krip returned and settled beside me on the sofa. He smelled of coffee and paint, with just a hint of lavender. Flipping open the file, he showed me a picture.

"If *Tug of the Current* was in fact donated, it must have been done so indirectly. I sold that canvas in June, just a few weeks before you and I became reacquainted. When did this auction take place?"

"The middle of July. Do you know who bought it?"

"I have the credit card information. It was part of the showing here in the building that we have each month." Krip's forehead was now wrinkled in concern. "But what's this all about? Do you think whoever bought my painting had it taken from them? Tell me you're not delving into another stolen art caper!"

I put a hand on his shoulder to reassure him. "Slow down, Krip. There's no reason to think it's been stolen. And it's easy to clear this up. Would you be comfortable calling the person who bought it? Maybe it was their intention all along to donate it for the charity fundraiser."

"It would be my pleasure to contact her. Perhaps she changed her mind about the piece. Who knows, she may even be in need of something…else."

"Why am I not surprised this customer is female?"

He gave me a playful look, as if he were momentarily offended by the idea. "Jamie, I'll have you know that men often buy my work. It just so happens this purchase was made by a woman. A very dear woman."

"Maybe a frequent customer?" I teased.

"Well, she does enjoy visiting the gallery here."

Krip went to his desk, where the landline telephone sat. He punched in the number rapidly. He was just far enough away that I couldn't eavesdrop. I tried. The dirty old man saw me lean forward. So he turned his back on me and lowered his voice. How rude could he be?

Ten minutes later he ended the call. With a smug look on his face, he came back to the sofa.

"Was the lady in question happy to hear from you?" I asked.

"Naturally. She's a patron of the arts. And it turns out, she's quite savvy with her support of nonprofit organizations. Especially when it can be tax deductible." Krip winked at me. "She bought that painting with the express intent to donate it to the charity. It was her way of supporting both my work and that of the nonprofit."

"Well, shit," I muttered. Krip was chuckling. There was something in his expression that had me curious. "So is this patron in need of another landscape for her library? Maybe something that would be hung above the mantle, and visible from the comfort of her chaise lounge?"

"As a matter of fact, Jamie, she did ask if I'd be interested in painting a portrait. It would require me to travel to her home for several sittings." The merriment in his eyes was priceless.

"Odon Krippendore, why do I get the impression this is part painting and part booty call?"

That earned me a roar of laughter. "You've just given me the title for that painting. At least, that's how I'll refer to it in my files!"

With that question answered, I left him and went back to the studio.

It still didn't put me any closer to getting a fix on Nicholas Bellamy.

Who was this guy?

Ian and Erica were having an animated conversation. She had taken him over to *Grace* and was having him sketch it from different angles. Her voice was full of encouragement. I settled back at the old rolltop desk and spent some time working on the next book. Pushing thoughts of Nicholas Bellamy from my mind for a few minutes might even trigger something in my subconscious that I was overlooking. It had happened before.

It was almost time for the tutoring session to end. I called Ian over and asked him to start putting everything away.

"We still have twenty minutes," he grumbled.

"I told Erica she could take some pictures of Peter's work. And you can talk with her about each piece." I inclined my head toward the file cabinet. Ian knew Peter had kept detailed notes on each one.

"She may need better lighting. A couple of those are in the shadows at this time of day," he said.

My elbows were on the desk. I propped my chin on the heel of my hand. "Listen to you, mister 'she needs better lighting.' If that's what's Erica requires, go take care of it. You know where all the switches are."

He started laughing. "Yes, boss."

Another smartass comment. Maybe the kid was getting too familiar with me. It could be he was picking up my attitude.

***

Malone was working Wednesday night. After the lesson with Erica, the plan was that I'd take Ian directly home. At least, that was the original plan. I should have known better when diabolical teenagers were involved. I packed up my computer as Ian walked Erica out to her car. It wasn't quite dark yet, but the sky was overcast and ominous looking. The kid was humming as he came back into the studio, checking messages on his phone. Apparently, one text in particular had captivated his attention.

"Do you have to take me to my mom's house?"

"I'm not leaving you here. Grab your backpack and the cooler."

He smirked at me. "Could you take me to your house instead? Brittany's family is having pizza and they invited me. I haven't seen her since Sunday."

"What's your mom say about this?"

"Ummm. I didn't ask her. But I guess she'll be fine with it."

Somehow, I was now mimicking Linda's stern-momma pose with my hands on my hips. "Don't guess. This is the first day I've been responsible for you. She may already have plans for you to eat with her and Caitlin. Call her."

"Aw man," he grumbled.

"Call your mom and see what she says. If she's okay with it, I'll take you to my place, then run you home after dinner. Otherwise, I'm taking you straight home from here."

He slumped on the top of the cooler. "Mom won't be happy. She thinks I've been spending too much time with Brit as it is. Mom likes her and all, but she worries about me."

"You do realize that it's her job as a parent to worry about you. And Caitlin. She only wants what is best for you." I left my bag on the desk and stepped in front of him, resting my hands on his shoulders. "Your mom is not the enemy. I'll bet she remembers what it was like to be in high school and dating cute boys."

"Well, she was a cheerleader in high school. I've seen the pictures. And she was very pretty." He glanced up at me. "Caitlin looks a lot like she did back then. Only taller. Wait! You think I'm cute?"

"Don't try and change the subject. Call Terri and ask her."

Reluctantly, he hit the speed-dial number for his mom. While it was ringing, he put it on speaker mode. Terri answered on the third ring. Ian explained the offer to have dinner with Brittany's family.

"What's Jamie think about this?" Terri asked.

"It's not a problem for me," I said. "We can give him twenty minutes to eat pizza and then I'll bring him to your place."

"Twenty minutes!" Ian yelped. "What's the point of even going?"

Terri's laughter was perfectly timed. "Obviously, she's seen you eat. And it is a school night. Which means homework. You also need to spend a little time with me and your sister. If Jamie doesn't mind it, you can go. But I want you home at eight."

Ian thrust a fist in the air in triumph. "Yes! You're the best, Mom."

"Be good. Thanks for putting up with this, Jamie."

"It's no problem. See you at eight."

Ian ended the call and beamed a smile. He sent a quick text to Brittany and we headed out to the car. I locked the studio and made sure the security cameras were still on. When we'd arrived, I didn't mention it to Ian but I kept the cameras rolling. There was no reason to think badly of Erica Morehouse, but my cynical mind opted to be cautious.

CHAPTER NINE

Ian was back in plenty of time for me to drive him home. There was a smear of gloss on his lip, which I pointed out to save him a little grief. Brittany had walked him to my place before running back to do her own homework.

It was late. I was still at my desk. My mind kept shifting gears, like a truck driver hauling a heavy load up a long, mountain road. I had worked for an hour on the new book, then spent an hour on Nick Bellamy's background research. Then another hour on the book.

"You're at it pretty late." Malone spoke softly from the doorway. I'd been so engrossed in the work that I didn't even hear him enter the house.

"My mind is a jumble. That's a good time to quit." I shut down the computer and came around for a warm embrace.

He held me for a while, lightly stroking my back. "I was starting to get used to seeing you in makeup and dolled up," Malone said.

"You know I'm a jeans and sweater girl."

"True. It was merely an observation. And it made me realize something."

"What's that?" I asked, pulling back enough to see his face.

"That we need to get fancy and go out on a real date occasionally. Pick a nice restaurant, get dressed up and go out for a great meal. Maybe see a play or a concert. We don't do that very often."

"Will you wear a suit?" I teased. Malone spent his workdays in uniform. I would think the last thing he'd want to do was put on a suit and tie.

"Of course. Especially if you're wearing an outfit like the one you had on last night. Including the stockings."

That surprised me. There were only a handful of times where we'd gone out on a date like what he was describing. For some reason, it reminded me of Vera's conversation yesterday and her suggestion. I hesitated, not sure how Malone would react to the idea.

"Vera and the art collection will be in Denver next month. She'd like us to join her for a few days. We could make it a mini-vacation."

Malone didn't even hesitate. "That might be a good idea. We'll have to check the dates."

I noticed the rest of the house was dark. Malone slipped a hand down and flipped off the lights in my office. Then he guided me across the hall to our bedroom. My brain was now focused on dressing up for a date night. The trip to Denver would be an excuse to leave the jeans at home. He moved behind me. Malone grabbed the bottom of my sweater and lifted it up. As he inched the garment up, he managed to unhook my bra and take it along for the ride. My hands were in the air above my head as he pulled the clothing free. Just that quickly his arms were wrapped around me again, drawing my back to his chest.

"When you work this late, you get tense." He brushed his lips on my neck, which made me shiver. "I'm going to help you relax. Lie down on your stomach and I'll massage your back and shoulders."

Malone loosened his grip and nudged me toward the bed. I flopped on top of the covers, with my arms at my sides. He switched the small lamp on the night table on low.

I could feel my bones sink into the mattress. Malone grabbed a clip from the table and gathered up my hair to get it out of the way. Then he took a healthy dollop of body lotion and began to work it into my neck and shoulders.

"Should I tell you about my day?" I mumbled. Already I could feel the tension easing out of my muscles.

"Nope. I want you to clear your mind, Jay. Don't talk. Just let me take care of you. Relax."

"Umm. My mind is always working on something."

"No talking. Think about getting dressed up and going out for an evening. Think about where you'd like to go. Think about what you'll wear. Or think about going to Denver. Just. Don't. Talk."

Malone's strong fingers were working therapeutic magic, his thumbs on my spine as he moved slowly down below my shoulder blades. I groaned. Groaning is not talking. He didn't seem to mind that. My mind danced along from romantic nights out to the possibility of a trip to Denver. I had a feeling Vera would persuade one of her high-society friends to put us up in a top-flight hotel room. Malone's hands stopped at my waist. For a nanosecond, I was disappointed, thinking the massage was over.

Not a chance.

"I think your arms need a little attention too," Malone said softly, his lips brushing my ear. "Just lie still and relax."

"Mm mm." That's still not talking. It was just a moan of contentment. First, he rubbed my left arm, then the right, from the shoulders down to the fingertips. Malone spent a fair amount of time on the insides of my wrists and elbows. The muscles might be relaxing, but my soul was starting to quiver. Then he surprised me once again. Malone dipped a hand beneath me, unsnapped my jeans and ran the zipper down. He shifted off the bed, grabbed the fabric around my ankles and yanked the jeans off my legs like a Vegas magician. Somehow, my panties were still in place.

"Malone!"

"Hush. *No talking.* I can't do a proper massage on your

legs when they're covered. And stop wiggling."

Yeah, like that was going to happen.

He paused long enough to get more lotion, then proceeded to rub my legs, starting with the backs of the thighs. My body was in the throes of contradiction. The muscles were indeed relaxing as he rubbed the tension away. But this was so sensual, it was arousing the hell out of me. There wasn't a doubt in my mind that Malone knew exactly what he was doing. When his slippery fingers grazed the backs of my knees, I squealed.

His face appeared in front of mine. "No talking." He kissed me. "Close your eyes and just breathe."

"I'm trying," I whispered. Either he'd moved away and didn't hear me, or Malone chose to ignore it.

Now he was rubbing lotion on my calves. What had I possibly done today to make them so tight? Ballroom dancing while wearing stilettos? A lengthy hike in the woods? Nothing came to mind. Malone shifted, massaging my ankles and the soles of my feet. Holy shit! The fact that he could do this without tickling me just added to my confusion.

His voice came softly from the foot of the bed. "You have two choices, Jay. I can stop now, throw a blanket over you, and let sleep claim you. Or you can roll over and I'll massage your…front side."

"Those are my only options?"

"Yep."

I was hoping he'd discover one more. Not ready to let the massage end, I flipped onto my back. Maybe the sight of my near nakedness would give him an idea. Or an urge. I had to fight the impulse to leap up and grab him. Malone's gaze was down, his attention on my shins as he worked the lotion into my skin.

"Close your eyes."

"Malone…"

"No talking. Close your eyes. Let your mind drift. Take slow, deep breaths. Just let your body relax."

He was driving me crazy! And he damn well knew it. But I didn't want to break the spell. So I did as he instructed. Malone was not to be rushed. Gradually, he moved up to my knees. As Linda had commented the other night, patience was not one of my virtues. The minute Malone's fingers grazed my thighs, I was moving. I wrapped him up with my arms and legs and pulled him on top of me.

"Jamie…"

"Shut up. My mind and body are in sync." I started kissing him.

He kissed me right back.

Later, we were curled up beneath a light blanket, gasping for breath as our racing hearts calmed down. A relaxing massage. Yeah, right. Malone knew damn well that his attentions to my body were not going to result in me dozing off, with visions of palm trees and white, sandy beaches. The rat probably had this in mind all along. Not that I was complaining. He'd been surprising me like this for a long time now.

Nearly a year!

It was getting closer to a year every day. Maybe I should call the Guinness Book of World Records. Or at least, the local news.

That was the last thing to cross my mind as sleep overtook me.

***

I was down at Peter's studio. No matter how much time passed since he worked here, or what had gone on since then, I will always think of it as Peter's studio. This was supposed to be writing time. Working on the new book. Fleshing out the characters, twisting the plot and the subplots. Developing the conflict. That was what I was supposed to be doing. So why couldn't I stop thinking about Randy and his concerns for his mother?

Another look at the K-9 True Companion website gave

me the details for the event where Allison and Nick Bellamy met. It included the name of the television reporter who had been the auctioneer. Olivia Sholtis. She was part of the team at Channel Four and had a reputation of delivering strong stories. On a hunch, I called the station. It was eleven in the morning. There was a chance she was out in the field on assignment. Luck was on my side. She picked up on the second ring.

"This is Olivia." Her voice was just as bright and sunny as when she was on camera. I wondered if it was natural, or practiced.

"Hi. My name is Jamie Richmond and—"

"Jamie Richmond, the mystery author?"

That caught me by surprise. "Umm. Yeah."

"This is so cool! I really enjoyed your first two books. I'm saving the third one for my vacation." There was a pause as she switched back into reporter mode. "So what can I do for you?"

There was no plan. I was simply making this up as I went. "I'd like to meet you for coffee or lunch, if you have some time. There's a story idea I'm chasing, and you may be able to fill in a few details for me. It involves that charity where you served as the auctioneer."

Olivia took a moment to consider the offer. "I'm scheduled to do a segment in the studio for the noon broadcast. After that, I'm free for a few hours. Is this something I need a cameraman for?"

That got a laugh out of me. "Oh hell no! How about lunch at the Elwood Bar & Grille? By the stadiums?"

"They have the best food! I'll see you at one." She clicked off.

Hey, Malone hadn't fed me breakfast. Right now the thought of one of their special lamb burgers was making my stomach growl.

I was in a booth near the front when Olivia walked in. She was a little shorter than I imagined. Dressed in a navy skirt and blazer with an ivory blouse, she looked ready for the cameras. Chestnut-brown hair with a couple of blond highlights reached for her shoulders. I recalled that she cut it short during the heat of the summer. Olivia paused to wave a greeting to the owner before sliding onto the bench across from me. We agreed to order first. Burgers and Diet Cokes for both of us. And of course, their homemade French fries!

"That will be lunch and dinner for me," I admitted.

She flashed a big smile. "I've got two apples on my desk. That will be my dinner. These burgers are worth it. Now, before we go any further, I have a confession to make."

"Oh?"

"Jamie, after you called, I did an internet search and pulled up a few of your old articles. You had quite a track record of unraveling some complicated features. That's the kind of investigative journalism I want to do."

Such flattery. But Olivia seemed sincere. "Thanks. I've seen many of your reports. You've covered a variety of stories. Even a crime or two."

Olivia leaned closer, as if afraid someone might overhear. "I'd love to get a crime beat. But Channel Four prefers to rotate those around. I'm building relationships with a couple of cops. Sometimes, they even share information."

We chatted for a bit about some acquaintances we had in common. Then Olivia laced her fingers together and looked directly at me. Her eyes were as brown as her hair, almost like chocolate chips.

"You mentioned the charity fundraiser. Is this research for another book?" she asked quietly.

"Not exactly. But it could be. Stranger things than this have given me ideas for a story." I paused to sip my drink. She was more direct than I'd expected. Which, I recalled, was an indication of a good reporter. "Do you remember a lot about that night?"

Olivia flashed me a big smile. "It was a blast. That was just the second time I've been the auctioneer. A couple of the board members introduced me to many of the patrons during the evening. They wanted to point me to the ones who would be the most generous. Then during the auction, I called on a few and weaseled a bit more money out of those deep pockets."

"All for a good cause," I said.

"That it was."

My phone was on the table. I pulled up pictures of Bellamy and passed it over to her. "Any chance you remember this guy?"

"Sure. That's Mr. Close," Olivia said.

"Who?"

She laughed and returned my phone. "That's just how I thought of him. No idea what his real name was. He was memorable because he kept on bidding, but he never took home the prize. Like he was close to being the winner."

"His name is Nicholas Bellamy. Did it bother him not to win?"

Olivia shook her head. "On the contrary. He was a good sport about it. I even called him out a couple of times, tried to get him to raise his bid. He'd give me a big smile and raise his hands in surrender."

"So he didn't have his heart set on winning that painting, or the dinner cruise?" I asked.

"Nah. Although he seemed really interested in that two-year lease for the Tesla sedan. For a while I thought he might have been a plant, whose job was to get other people to raise their bids. Which results in the charity making more money." Olivia shrugged. "Sometimes I get a little cynical."

Our food arrived. We both dug in. The conversation shifted to other subjects. I learned that Olivia was married to Charlie, her college sweetheart. She used her maiden name professionally. Charlie got a kick out of Olivia being recognized when they were out in public, and occasionally being referred to as Mr. Sholtis.

"He even gave an autograph that way one time," Oliva said, laughing at the memory. "Next thing you know, he'll be getting an entourage."

"Sounds like he has a good sense of humor."

"Definitely. He's a good guy. A landscape architect by trade, and he knows so much about botany that it could be intimidating. But he downplays it. He's also a musician. That's how we met. We were both in the marching band in college."

"You two are like a fairy tale. Or a happily-ever-after romance."

She laughed at the image. "He's not that romantic. Most guys aren't. But Charlie has his moments."

"I know exactly what you mean." My face went warm, recalling Malone's actions last night—and earlier this morning. Time to shift gears. "Anything else you can remember about that night?"

"Nothing really about this Bellamy guy. But there was one of the staff that seemed a little jumpy."

My spidey-senses were humming. "Who was that? And jumpy how? Just excited? Maybe a little nervous?"

"Wow, you haven't lost those journalistic skills, have you?" Olivia asked with a grin. "That's exactly the type of questions I'd be asking."

"So you know the kind of answers I'm looking for."

The food was gone. The waitress had kindly brought us refills of Diet Coke.

"There was a woman who I think was one of the employees. She seemed a little tense before the evening got started. During the auctions, I noticed she was a bit frantic. Maybe it was her first time working an event like this."

"Do you remember her name?"

Olivia shook her head. "Don't think I ever knew it. All the employees wore little pins on their blazers. She had one. But I don't recall if I ever got introduced to her or was close enough to see her name badge."

We were quiet for a minute. Maybe it was simply a coincidence. Maybe she was new to the job and didn't want to screw it up. Maybe she had been screwing up and this was her last chance to do well and keep her job. Maybe I was the reincarnation of Agatha Christie.

Olivia tapped a fingertip on the table. "Wanna know what she looked like?"

"What the hell! You were holding back!"

She giggled. "Charlie was at the event with me. He was off to the side, just watching the activity during the bidding. He shot a few pictures of me. I think she's in the background."

Olivia dug out her phone and went to the photo gallery. She scrolled through the pictures and found a couple from the night of the fundraiser. Leaning across the table, she pointed to a woman in the background. Using my fingertips, I zoomed in. Captured there was a young woman who appeared to be looking directly into the camera. It was a little pixelated, but I could see almost every feature of her face. She had mousy brown hair worn to her shoulders. The tips of her hair were dyed blue. Swiping the screen gave me another shot of her standing to the side of the stage. Perhaps she was watching the bidding, trying to identify the high rollers. That may have been part of her duties.

"Can you send me those?"

Olivia retrieved the phone and passed them along. She looked around the restaurant, making sure no one was close enough to overhear our conversation. I was caught up in the intrigue and leaned forward. Olivia did the same.

"Don't quote me on this, but I'd bet a hundred bucks her boobs aren't real."

I burst out laughing. "Seriously?"

"Yep. Charlie seemed to…notice that too. She's disproportionately built. Maybe it was just extra support in her bra. And Charlie did comment on a certain…bounce factor that made me question the padding. But it's a wonder she could walk upright without tipping over."

And they say men are bad!

Olivia sat back. She checked the time on her phone and tucked it in her purse. "I need to get back to the station. Will you let me know what this is all about? It might be nothing, but you of all people know how little issues like this can turn into a good story."

"When I've figured it out, I'll let you know."

"Thanks for lunch."

"My pleasure."

CHAPTER TEN

After my productive lunch meeting with Olivia, my background search took on a new direction. I checked the address for the K-9 True Companion office on my phone, then headed out there. It might have been prudent to call and make an appointment, but I was too wired. Besides, there was something to be said about the element of surprise.

The office was located in a large office building on Telegraph Road out in Oakland County. Once there, before going inside, I studied the photos Olivia sent. Then I switched my phone to record mode and tucked it into the interior pocket of my jacket. I wasn't expected but sensed that any charitable organization would welcome an impromptu visitor. You never could tell when such visitors would become volunteers or financial donors.

The building directory listed the various tenants. I found the correct office and took the elevator up. The hallways had been recently painted and the industrial tile was clean and well maintained. The landlord or the management company was doing a good job keeping up appearances. It must have been close to the time of year when they raised the rent.

A plump, older woman sat behind the reception counter. She greeted me with a warm smile. "How can I help you?"

"I was hoping to talk with someone about your organization." I was continuing with my concept of having no specific plan. It had worked out well, having lunch with Olivia. That was often the way I wrote, too. Just make it up as I went along. Outlines can be too restricting.

"Of course. Let me see if someone in Development is available." She pointed a beefy finger at a couple of chairs by the wall. "It may take a few minutes."

Dutifully, I took a seat. On the table was a cluster of promotional materials, local magazines and newspapers. Last year's annual report was front and center on the table. There were flyers for upcoming events, along with information about the organization. I snagged the annual report and flipped through it. The approaching click and thump of high heels caused me to look up. Another woman hesitated in front of me, her hands at her sides. I dropped the report back on the table and rose to greet her.

"I'm Carleen Barnett, Director of Development. Welcome to K-9 True Companion." Her voice was soft, as if she was unaccustomed to speaking loudly.

She shook my hand limply after I introduced myself. "A friend mentioned your organization recently. I must admit that I don't know anything about what you do here or how you operate," I said.

If I had to guess, I'd peg her around sixty, with a round figure that made me think her idea of exercise was walking to the nearest ice cream parlor for a triple hot fudge sundae. She was short and roly-poly. Carleen was wearing casual slacks and a frilly blouse, her feet clad in a blocky pair of pumps.

"What exactly does the Director of Development do?" I asked.

"Development is all about building relationships, whether that may be with sponsors, individuals, foundations or corporations. I'm in charge of all the fundraising efforts for the organization. That includes writing grant applications, sending out thank you letters to donors and sponsors, arranging any events and working closely with the president and the board members."

"That sounds like a lot of responsibility. And a vital part of the business."

Carleen nodded and preened a little, as if pleased that I recognized how important her work was. She pointed down the hall. "We do have a staff meeting starting shortly. I can give you a quick tour and talk about our programs for a few minutes."

"I'd appreciate that. It was a spur-of-the-moment decision to stop by. I was driving past and remembered hearing about the organization."

"Are you interested in volunteering? We always have a need for people who want to help." Carleen's voice got a little louder and just a shade friendlier.

"Perhaps. Although I might also be interested in making a financial donation to support the operation."

Her heels seemed to squeak loudly on the tile floor. In my jeans and sweater, I must not have looked like the stereotypical donor. Carleen took a moment to compose herself. I glanced down the hall.

The whole office area was small. Beyond the reception area, there was a short corridor with three offices on each side. At the end was what looked like a conference room. Beside that was an open area. This must have been the breakroom. There was a small refrigerator under the counter, with a microwave oven above it. On the counter beside it was one of those coffee pots where you put in a little plastic pod and your flavored coffee came steaming out into your mug.

The bulk of the business was apparently conducted offsite. This charity wasn't a national organization. It was local to the Detroit area. The focus was on dogs as service or support animals. They had programs to help raise the dogs and give them the training they needed to be successful working with people who had a variety of medical issues. I doubted there was any type of kennel or veterinarian service to be found within the building.

Carleen found her voice. "These are our administrative offices. We've been operating for eleven years now. We started out working with a few veterans suffering from PTSD. Then we expanded to reach more people."

"Are there many employees or do you mainly utilize volunteers?" I asked.

"We have fifteen employees. Many of them are at the kennel, where we work with the dogs. There are only six regular employees here."

My smartass mode kicked in before I could stop myself. "So does that mean you have some irregular employees?"

Carleen shot me a look that confirmed she had no sense of humor. "We have some temporary or occasional workers and a contractor. The six of us here are full-time. The rest only work part-time."

"No offense. It just sounded odd when you referred to everyone as a 'regular' employee." I wondered if she'd learned that glare from the nuns in an old Catholic school.

She veered into an office close to the conference room. Her name was etched on a plastic strip that was in a bracket by the door. There was an empty slot just beneath that. There was a workstation just inside the entrance with a desk cluttered with paperwork. An inner door extended into Carleen's domain. She scuttled that way, clearly expecting me to follow dutifully in her footsteps. I did. From a folder on her desk, she dug out a glossy pamphlet adorned with cute pictures of several different breeds of puppies and adult dogs.

"This will give you more detailed information about our operation," Carleen said. She made a show of glancing at the clock on the wall, then double checked the time with the clunky watch on her wrist. "I hate to cut this short, but unfortunately my meeting is about to start."

"I understand. I'll look over the material later."

Carleen thrust a business card at me. "Call me if you have any questions. Or you can always email me. That's probably easier."

"That's a good idea."

Turning for the door, I saw a young woman enter the outer part of the office. She was the one in the pictures Olivia shared. The mousy brown hair still showed a trace of the blue coloring on the ends. She darted behind the desk. There was a stack of mail she'd been going through. I saw some open envelopes with checks sticking out of them. As I moved in her direction, she yanked open a drawer and swept the whole stack of papers into it.

"Aldis, I'll be in my meeting for at least an hour," Carleen said. "Please have the deposit ready so I can take it to the bank after that."

The young woman nodded. "Should I prepare the thank you notes?"

"Of course." She acted surprised that I was still there. "Be so kind and show our guest out." Carleen turned to me and gave me another limp handshake. "So nice to meet you."

"Thank you for your time," I said.

Aldis guided me toward the reception area. She took very small steps, as if she didn't trust her legs to hold her up. Aldis was rail thin and probably five-three at best. Her clothing was loose, plain and nondescript. I had to bite my lip, thinking about the comment Olivia made regarding the young woman's breasts. They certainly looked inflated and didn't match the rest of her body's frame.

"Have you worked here very long?" I asked.

"Just a couple of months now. I only work here three days a week. Then I work two days at another place. I'm on contract with a staffing company," Aldis said. Her voice was soft and a little high-pitched.

I smiled and tried to be encouraging. "I did a few temp jobs myself. It's always a challenge getting comfortable with a new environment. Are you with one of the big national agencies?"

"No. It's a smaller firm that specializes in nonprofit companies. It's called Delaney and Associates."

We had reached the entrance. Aldis kept her hands clasped together. She nodded and gave me a tiny flash of a smile. I thanked her and left. I couldn't swear to it, but sensed she waited until I was in the elevator before walking back to her desk.

Curiouser and curiouser.

I pushed this odd encounter from my mind. Nothing I saw or heard provided me with any clues about Nicholas Bellamy. Maybe I was just spinning my wheels. Maybe there was nothing more to learn about him. Maybe Bellamy was really who he said he was. Maybe he just kept a low profile, didn't need the instant gratification of social media or the recognition from his peers. Maybe I should give it up and enroll in culinary school.

I did indeed give up, and headed for home.

***

There was one more possibility to draw Nick Bellamy out from the shadows. If he was the successful local businessman and entrepreneur he claimed to be, he may have been featured in one of the area papers. I no longer believed Bellamy was his real name. The idea of scrolling through decades of newspapers, hoping to see his picture, had no appeal. But there was another source.

Crain's Detroit Business was a weekly publication that had been around Motown forever. Well, maybe not since the dawn of the printing press, but they'd been part of a publishing operation since the 1960s. For more than thirty years, one of the big highlights had been a feature, "Forty Under 40." It cast a spotlight on different people within the community who excelled in their business operations. Each year there was a nice professional photo, a biography of the recipient and a luncheon. In my search for Nick Bellamy,

I'd never given Crain's a thought. But after seeing a copy among the magazines in the K-9 True Companion's reception area, my neurons started jumping.

From the comfort of my home office, I pulled up the archives on the Crain's website. No sense trying to guess how old Bellamy really was. I went to the first year of the awards, and slowly scrawled my way through the winners. With the screen enlarged, it was easy to search the photos. My phone was propped up beside the computer just in case I found someone who could be a match. I was staring so intently at the computer monitor that I lost track of time. When the doorbell rang, I almost jumped out of my skin! Linda.

"Two days and I don't hear from you?" She dropped her coat and purse on the rocker and sprawled on one end of the sofa.

"It's been busy. And I sent you a picture Tuesday night."

Linda gave me a devilish look. "Yes, you did. All dressed up for that dinner date. I'll bet you got his attention. Still, I'm surprised you didn't call me when you were safely back home."

"I got...sidetracked." My face was growing warm.

"Hmm. You were still wearing that dark red dress when Malone got home, weren't you?"

"Yes."

"With the heels and the thigh-high stockings."

I was blushing as red as a tomato. "Yes."

"No wonder you got...sidetracked. But I suppose you can be forgiven for not calling me when you were...occupied." She gave me a wicked smile.

"You're so kind, Linda."

"So how was Ian's first lesson yesterday? I expected an update."

"The kid was nervous, but he really hit it off with Erica. Then he conned me into taking him to Brittany's for dinner before driving him home."

Linda gave me a throaty laugh. "This kid is going to feel

like a stud, spending his afternoon and evening in the company of such beautiful women."

"I think he only has eyes for Brittany. At least, right now."

"Hmm. Better keep his window locked when he stays over. I get a feeling young Casanova might try to sneak out for a late-night kiss."

"Seriously? He's just a sweet kid. Why would you even think such a thing?" I asked.

Now it was her turn as a flush of color touched her cheeks. "Because that's what happened when I was his age."

"Linda!" My memory banks went into overdrive, trying to picture who she was dating at sixteen. "Was it Carlton Gray? Or Roger Cottrell? Or Jameson Knight? Maybe it was that guy Sam whats-his-name?"

Linda was laughing so hard now she could barely speak. I waited. She threw a pillow at me. "Unlike you, I'm not the kind of girl who kisses and tells."

"Bullshit! You tell me everything. You probably told me back then, but with so many admirers, it's hard to keep track of your romantic dalliances."

Linda straightened up and brushed the hair from her face with the backs of her hands. That was one of those signals she was about to change the subject. I let her get away with it. For now.

"Any progress on your quest for Randy?"

I filled her in on my efforts, which wasn't much. When I told her about my visit to the charity's office, Linda perked up.

"You saw something, didn't you? Something odd?"

Reluctantly, I nodded. "Two things gave me ideas to follow up on. I'm checking Crain's business paper, on the chance that Bellamy was once featured there. And there was something hinky about a woman in the fundraising office."

"Hinky? Are you saying the carpet doesn't match the drapes? Or maybe there is no carpet, just hardwood floors? Or space-age vinyl?" Linda asked, her eyes sparkling playfully.

"I said hinky, not kinky. Her behavior was odd. When I was talking with her boss by her office, she was very nervous. She hurriedly put a bunch of papers in her desk. Checks and stuff. It was obvious she was hiding something."

"Maybe she's not accustomed to pesky redheads," Linda said.

I was about to comment when she checked her watch and pushed off the sofa. "Vince is taking me out for dinner. I've got just enough time to run home, take Logan for a walk and get glamorous."

"You're already glamorous."

She flashed me a smile. "You're not so bad yourself."

We hugged before she slipped on her coat. "Have fun," I said.

"Don't spend all night staring at that computer. It will drive you crazy."

I shook my head in disgust at the admonishment. "Yes, Mother."

"Jamie, you can be such a smartass."

"It's one of my redeeming qualities."

CHAPTER ELEVEN

With a fresh mug of tea, I got back to my research. Randy had sent me a text earlier. All it consisted of was a question mark. I responded with one word: patience.

Perhaps he picked up on the irony, knowing how impatient I get. Focusing on the computer screen, I studied each year's group of award winners. The hours ticked by. There were so many people. And so many different types of businesses had been recognized over the years. Maybe it was hopeless. I was about to quit for the night when my eyes snapped wide open.

There he was.

In living color, a nice professional portrait. Bellamy had more hair back then and a few less wrinkles. His nose had been broken and had a little bend to it. A good plastic surgeon had since taken care of that. It was sixteen years ago when Bellamy was selected for his efforts with Maxson Manufacturing. Well, the face matched Bellamy's. But the name didn't. Matthias Dekker was Nick Bellamy's real name. Or at least the name he was using back then. I sent the details to the printer and proceeded to do a goofy happy dance toward the kitchen.

Headlights filled the front window. Malone was home. I

was able to contain myself long enough for him to enter through the side door. Then I jumped him, wrapped my arms and legs around his frame and covered his face with kisses. Somehow, he managed to remain upright with his arms squeezing me to him. Malone hooked a chair away from the kitchen table with his foot and sat with me on his lap. My kisses now found his mouth and lingered there for a while.

"If that's the new welcome greeting, I'll be racing home every night," he said softly as we came up for air.

"I found him. Not five minutes ago. Guess that got me excited." I was only able to speak in short, breathless gasps. "Thought you'd want to share in my discovery."

"Something tells me you're too wired up for sleep."

I gave him what I hoped was a sexy, exaggerated wink. "Don't you know that sleep is vastly overrated?"

"You probably got that one from Chene." Malone was referring to our friend, the police detective who suffers from insomnia. "Jamie, it's been a very long day." He managed to stifle a yawn. "Right now, I'd like to wind down. Grab a hot, steamy shower, turn my brain off and just call it a night."

In my excitement, I hadn't even asked how his shift had been. There were some nights when the mayhem was nonstop and Malone doesn't even get a chance for dinner, let alone a good cup of coffee. Apparently, this was one of those nights. I should have picked up on this before launching myself at him.

"Sounds like your evening was anything but quiet," I said.

"Lots of activity. Several accidents, a few drunk drivers, and a brawl outside a high school after a football game. That's just what immediately comes to mind." He squeezed my buns with both hands and yawned again.

I leaned close and rested my forehead against his. "It would be my pleasure to wash your back. Rinsing off the day's grime sounds like a good idea."

"What about your discovery?"

"It will keep."

Malone's physical strength surprised me once again. One moment, I was on his lap as he sat on a kitchen chair. The next instant, he was standing, carrying me over his shoulder, down the hall to our room. The fact that he could do this without banging my head on the wall or tearing any ligaments impressed me. Clothes were quickly removed. We showered together, standing under the steamy spray until the hot water ran out. Dried off and cozy under the covers, Malone drew me close.

"Maybe I'm too young for you," I said softly.

"Are you saying I'm old?"

"Not old. Just…older."

"Jamie."

"Yes?"

Malone rolled onto his back and pulled me on top of him. I guess the shower had revitalizing powers. The kisses and caresses that followed were certainly not those of an exhausted man. Not that I've ever done a survey, but there was a lot of energy in his actions.

A short while later, we were cuddled together. There was no need for conversation. Our bodies and our hearts had been speaking volumes. It surprised me that sleep overtook me while Malone was still gently stroking my back. Maybe he'd been faking his exhaustion with an ulterior motive.

***

Friday morning I treated Malone to brunch. We went to a local café that specialized in king-sized omelets, Belgian waffles, and other delicacies. Malone eyed me over the rim of his coffee mug.

"Want to tell me about the guy you found?"

"I thought you'd never ask."

"Well, I'd like to know who you're going to visit, since you're dolled up again." He sipped his coffee, with the steam floating before his eyes. "Not that I'm complaining. I could get used to seeing you dressed up."

That comment got me a little flustered. "I am not dressed up. This is simply slacks and a sweater." Okay, so the slacks were a little snug on the buns and the sweater was one of those bulky wool ones, in a shade of green that went well with my eyes. I didn't mention the black satin camisole beneath it. That would be a pleasant surprise for Malone later.

"It's a step up from jeans and sweatshirts," Malone said. He gave me one of those low-voltage smiles that weakens my knees. Good thing I was sitting down. "So who is this guy?"

"His real name is Matthias Dekker. I found the profile in an old copy of Crain's Detroit. The picture matches, except for a few wrinkles and gray hair." I had printed out both photos and slid them over to Malone. He compared them, nodded and passed them back.

"So, why the subterfuge?"

"I don't know yet. But I'm going to find out. An internet search with that name landed me a few more details. Dekker did run Maxson for a few more years after being recognized by Crain's. Then the company was acquired by a national operation. I think he cashed in his chips and decided to see what else appealed to him. Maybe he really is a semi-retired entrepreneur."

Malone was slowly running his forefinger across the back of my wrist. I had no doubt he was perfectly aware of what this little bit of contact did to me. "That still doesn't explain the name change. And I see that determined look in your eyes, Jamie. Which often leads you into trouble."

"I am the picture of innocence." Well, some of the time.

The arrival of our meals interrupted his laughter. We worked on coffee and ate. Belgian waffles and bacon for me. Malone had opted for the French toast stuffed with blueberries and a side of sausage. We talked about Ian's lesson and Linda's visit. He filled me in a little more on the action at work the night before. When the food was gone, Malone sat back. For a long couple of minutes, he didn't say a word. He just looked at me, studying my face as if he wanted to memorize every freckle. I tried to sit still. Then I winked and blew a kiss at him. Malone propped his elbows on the table and held his coffee mug in both hands.

"What's your plan with this Dekker guy?" he asked.

"I'm meeting him at a coffee shop in an hour, out close to where we had dinner on Tuesday. A nice busy, public place. He thinks I want to talk about small companies to invest in."

"And in reality?"

"I'm going to tell him who I really am and show him what my research has turned up. When I explain that Randy is just concerned about his mom, I'm hoping Bellamy, or Dekker, or whatever the hell his name is, will tell me the truth."

Malone frowned at me. "That's your plan? This guy could be a psycho with a history of violence. I'm not keen on you meeting this guy alone."

"I never said I was going alone. I'm hoping you'd have some free time before your shift to be my shadow. After all, I just fed you this lovely, healthy brunch."

"No wonder you were so eager to buy," he said with a grin.

"I know you don't like me taking chances. But I can't let this go. I just want some answers for Randy."

Malone was quiet, considering my plan. He knew me well enough to know that with him or without him, I was going to confront Bellamy. He finished his coffee, gently placed the mug on the table and nodded. "You're being a good friend, Jamie, for this vacation-romance character. Let's find out where this goes."

***

We took Malone's Jeep. He didn't say it, but I got the

impression Malone wouldn't leave me behind with Dekker, even if he proved to be a nice, saintly man with a perfectly logical reason for changing his name and no ulterior motives that involved harm to younger, redheaded women. Malone drove in that confident style of his. He parked at the far end of the lot. Then he drew me close for a long, lingering kiss, with his fingers running through my hair.

"Give me your phone," he said when we parted.

Right then I would have given him anything in the world. My phone was a little unexpected. "Whatever for?"

"So I can hear what's going on. If Bellamy…"

"Dekker."

He gave his shoulders a shrug. "Okay, Dekker. If he says something that makes you uncomfortable, just say Colorado and I'll be right there."

Malone had speed-dialed his number on my phone. When the connection was made and he muted his own phone, tapping a wireless earbud into place so he could hear. Ain't technology amazing?

He went inside and bought a simple cup of coffee. Then Malone found a spot at the back of the shop where he had a clear view of the room. He spread a copy of today's *Free Press* next to his cup. Once he was situated, I entered the cafe, bought a mug of tea and grabbed a table. My phone was upside down next to my place, with a copy of Crain's latest issue beside it. Five minutes passed. I glanced up and saw Bellamy enter. I stole a glance at Malone. He nodded once.

Bellamy picked up a coffee and joined me. He was casually decked out in slacks, a buttoned-down dress shirt and a camel-hair coat. It was a tasteful outfit. Bellamy obviously had money. Hopefully, it was his own.

"It's a pleasure to see you again, Jamie."

"Nice to see you too. I appreciate your taking the time to meet me on such short notice."

Bellamy took a tiny sip of his coffee. Then he folded his hand on the table. "What's on your mind? Are you really looking to invest in a growing business?"

"I'm ready to share the truth and I'm hoping you'll do the same."

He considered the comment and took another minute sip of his coffee. "What kind of truth might that be?"

Quietly, I explained about my background and the friendship with Randy. I described his concerns about Bellamy and Allison. His eyes widened in surprise when I mentioned the research. Then I slid the old picture of him out of the Crain's magazine. Nicholas Bellamy gave his head a slow shake and chuckled at the end of my narrative.

"Damn, Jamie, you are very good at what you do."

"Thank you, Nick. Or should I say, Matthias?"

He smiled. "Matthias no longer exists. I legally changed my name seven years ago. It seemed like the opportune time to put him to rest."

"Why?"

Bellamy leaned back and draped his left arm across the empty chair beside him. "I was tired. Tired of being pestered by people. Tired of having to look over my shoulder. Tired of having to be so cautious. Of not trusting anyone. Of suspecting everyone I encountered had some form of a hidden agenda."

I just looked at him quietly, waiting for more. Bellamy fiddled with his coffee cup, then set it aside.

"When I sold my shares in Maxson, I became an instant millionaire, several times over. After years of devoting all my energy to the business, suddenly I was free. Or so I thought. That job had cost me two marriages. It had consumed my life. All I wanted to do was see what else the world had to offer. But everywhere I went, that past followed. Both ex-wives tried to get more money from me. I never had children, but rapidly, shirttail relatives started popping up out of the woodwork. It was like someone winning a mega-million-dollar lottery. Overnight, you become very, very popular."

Bellamy went on to describe the impact. His home

address and phone numbers became public. People he hadn't seen in years, even those he had never met before, started to call. Proposals arrived in the mail. Some folks even camped out on the street in front of his house. They followed him to restaurants. One man even pursued him into the bathroom at a saloon, trying to make a pitch as they stood at the urinals.

"All I wanted was peace and quiet. Time to reflect and decide what to do next. But it wasn't happening. I'd meet a woman somewhere and any thoughts of a real relationship were destroyed by the third date. She'd start dropping hints about money. Expensive places to visit, cars and clothes, the finest restaurants. So I decided to disappear."

I was intrigued. "How did you manage that?"

He chuckled. "I have a good attorney. Tim Kiley is his name. Together we came up with a plan. I sold my house, the cars and just about everything, and set up a private corporation. All the proceeds went into that. The dividends from the national company would be deposited quarterly. Tim recommended a money manager. The bulk of it was invested in mutual funds and tax-free municipal bonds. Then I legally changed my name. Matthias Dekker ceased to exist."

"And Nicholas Bellamy was born?"

Bellamy smiled. "More like created. Then I just...vanished. Once my new identity papers were completed, along with credit cards, I decided to wander about. Left Michigan and headed west. I stayed away from the big cities. Bought a slightly used pickup truck with a camper. For four years, I wandered, crisscrossing the country. Read a lot of books, listened to music. Dined in little cafes, stopped in places hardly anyone knows about. I met quite a few wonderful people along the way. They had no idea about Matthias Dekker or the money that went along with that name." Bellamy had a dreamy look on his face. He must have been recalling some of the good times on the road.

"What brought you back?"

He shrugged. "I was ready. Found a lot of peace along the way. Tim was the only one here who knew the truth. We'd talk about once a month or so. A couple of times he flew out to join me, brought me updates and papers that needed to be signed. That's when I returned. Only this time, I kept a low profile. Discovered that part of me missed the excitement that can go hand in hand with owning a business and helping it grow."

Bellamy continued working with Tim Kiley to find a couple of small businesses that were looking for investors. He didn't want anything to do with manufacturing. Nicholas Bellamy found a struggling IT company that supported small to mid-sized businesses with maintaining their hardware and computer systems. He dipped his toe into the business as a limited partner, which minimized his liability if something went wrong. Bellamy only offered advice when asked.

He stopped mid-thought, a puzzled expression on his face. "Why am I telling you all this, Jamie?"

I'd been wondering the same thing. "I think you've been ready to tell someone for a while now. Which makes me wonder. Does Allison know?"

Nick gave his head a negative shake. "Not yet. But I've been considering explaining all of this to her soon. This may sound like a line, but I care for her. She's bright, beautiful, vivacious, funny and with such a generous spirit, that she makes me think there's hope for us."

"You should tell her the truth."

Bellamy scratched his cheek as he thought about it. "I haven't lied to her. My name really is Nicholas Bellamy. And I am semi-retired. I do invest in a few small businesses. Matthias Dekker no longer exists."

"So it's not a lie. It's a secret."

"We all have secrets, Jamie. Sometimes keeping them can make a big difference in a relationship." Now he laced his fingers together on the table in front of him and leaned a little closer. "What are you going to tell Randy?"

"I haven't decided yet."

Nicholas Bellamy considered that. Then he picked up his forgotten coffee cup and drained it. "Would he be satisfied if you reassured him that his mother is safe with me? That I'm not out to steal her savings or leave her heartbroken for a thirty-something gold digger of a Barbie doll? Or just disappear into the mist without an explanation?"

That made me hesitate. "Why would I put it that way?"

"Buy me a little time, Jamie. A personal favor. I give you my word that I would never hurt Allison in any way, shape or form. That will allow me to tell her in my own way. Then she can inform Randy."

"He's got a lot to worry about over the next few weeks. With the wedding, Allison, his job and the girls."

"Just a little time is all I ask."

I looked away from Bellamy while I debated his request. Across the room, Malone was watching me. Those blue eyes of his locked on to mine. His lips formed the word "trust." Then he winked at me. It was a struggle to keep a straight face as I looked back to Bellamy.

"Will you be attending the wedding in November?"

"Of course. Allison and I have already made plans. I've booked a hotel room. We've got a suite, so Gracie can stay with us on the wedding night."

"From what Randy said, that's a month from today. Four short weeks will go by quickly," I said.

"Before then," Bellamy said. "I will definitely tell Allison before then. This isn't bad news, Jamie. I just want to find the right moment to…tell her. I want to tell her everything."

"To tell her about your past?"

Bellamy nodded and a small smile touched his lips. "And to tell her I'm in love with her."

That admission rocked me. But there was no denying the look in his eyes or on his face. Who was I to interfere with such plans?

"I'll tell Randy not to worry. I'd imagine he will continue

to do so, to some extent anyway."

A wave of relief crossed Bellamy's face. "It will be soon, Jamie. I promise." Then he extended his hand. We shook. Nicholas Bellamy flashed a brilliant smile, stood up and strolled out the door.

Malone joined me on the way out. "He sounds sincere."

"That's quite a story he told me. But it makes a lot of sense." I checked my phone. Randy should already be driving back to South Haven. Once inside Malone's Jeep, I called him and put the phone on speaker mode. He answered on the first ring.

"Jamie! Did you have any luck?"

"You can relax. Nick's a nice guy. And he really cares about Allison. Stop worrying and focus on Liz and Gracie."

"So what did you find out?"

We weren't driving yet. Malone was turned in his seat, watching me. "He is what he claims to be. Semi-retired. A successful businessman, who does a little investing in startup operations."

"Jamie, I can't thank you enough. But there is something else I need."

Malone chuckled and shook his head. I ignored him. "A summer-vacation fling has a limit to the number of favors I'm willing to grant you, Blondie."

Randy's laughter echoed through the car. "This one's easy. I just need your address. Linda's too. So we can send the invitations. Liz and I talked about this again last night. We want you both to be there!"

Stunned, it took me a second to gather my wits. "I'll send them in an email. Drive safely."

"I will. Thank you again, Jamie." He clicked off without another word.

"What the hell was that?"

Malone just grinned at me. "I think you already provided his wedding gift."

CHAPTER TWELVE

Malone dropped me at home on his way to work. My good deed was accomplished. Utilizing my research and investigative skills, I'd learned who Nick Bellamy really was. After my conversation with him, I believed the story he told, and his intentions with Allison. I should have been happy. But there was an annoying tickle at the back of my brain, hinting that I was overlooking something. I put my heels up on the corner of my desk to consider it. The room was too quiet. With the remote, I switched on the stereo and a collection of Motown greats began to play. Marvin Gaye, Smokey Robinson, Aretha Franklin and more kept me company. I have never been good at working in silence. Somebody once told me music is essential to life. That, and dark chocolate.

What was I missing?

Linda would tell me that I was expecting some deep, dark secrets from Nicholas Bellamy's past, something sinister and criminal that would become good material for another novel. But I was satisfied with what I'd learned. He seemed real. Randy was happy. Learning that there was someone in his mother's life who cared for her would be a blessing. That reminded me to send him the email with our mailing addresses. I wasn't going to mention the invitation to Linda. She could use a surprise or two.

So what was I missing?

There's a line from Oscar Wilde: "No good deed goes unpunished." I'm sure others have used that saying but it seems to me he was the first. I'd done a good deed for Randy. It had cost me a bit of time, brain power and skill. Yet that little tickle just wouldn't go away.

It made me wonder what my punishment was going to be.

I stopped wondering and went to pick up Ian. That night, he was going to the football game with Brittany at her high school. My unofficial part-time little brother was going to be around most of the weekend. Somehow, he'd convinced his mother to let him stay here for the night.

Ian practically dove into my car. "Hey, Jamie!" In addition to his backpack of books he had a duffel bag.

"Hey, yourself. Are you moving in? Because I would be happy to start charging you rent. And give you some chores. A growing boy needs chores to learn the importance of responsibility."

He grinned. "It's just some extra clothes Mom insisted I bring. But I was gonna ask a favor."

Suddenly everyone wanted favors from me: Erica, Randy, Bellamy and now Ian. The car was moving, so I couldn't really take my eyes off the road. I waited until we got stuck at a red light to look at him. "What kind of favor?"

"Sort of a personal favor. But you've got to promise me that you won't tell anyone else!"

"What the hell do you have in mind?" I was hoping either Terri or Malone had had the birds-and-bees talk with him long ago. Didn't they teach this stuff in high school nowadays? This was not a subject I was at all comfortable discussing with a hormonally crazed sixteen-year-old man-child.

A horn sounded behind me. The light had changed to green. I pulled through the intersection, then swung into the parking lot of a party store. Stopping the car, I faced him.

"Jamie, it's not that bad." Ian began to fidget with the straps of his pack, which was on the floor between his feet.

"A personal favor. One you don't want me to tell anyone else about. Start talking. And don't worry about using big words. I'll understand them."

"It's just…" He faltered there, as if he'd run out of gas.

"Just what? Tell me, Ian!"

He couldn't look at me. With his gaze on the floor, he mumbled something. I couldn't hear it. I reached over and lifted his chin, then turned his head so he was forced to meet my eyes. "What is it?"

"Will you teach me how to dance?"

Of all the topics that had been jumping through my mind, that one hadn't even made the top ten.

"You have got to be shitting me!"

"C'mon, Jamie." He gave me the sad, puppy-dog eyes, pleading for help. "I don't want to look like a goof with Brittany. She'll think I'm worthless if I can't even dance with her."

I couldn't believe this. "You've got a kid sister and a mom who could easily show you how to dance. Why don't you ask them? Or Brittany?"

"I'm sort of…embarrassed. I know it's lame, but they probably assume that I can already dance."

Next weekend, Ian would be escorting Brittany to the Halloween dance Saturday night. The kids were going in costumes. He refused to tell me what his was. Terri planned on coming over to get pictures. She insisted on bringing dinner for everyone as well.

"You gonna tell me what your costume is?"

"Nah, Britt would punch me in the head if I did that. She wants it to be a surprise." He slumped down in the seat, as if all the air had just leaked out of him.

"Now, suddenly, it's important and you're ready to learn. And you have a little more than a week before you're supposed to take her dancing for Halloween."

He looked so sweet and innocent. It was hopeless. "Please. Even if it's just a dance or two. Some moves that make me look good."

"What time are you going to the football game?"

"The game starts at seven. Her folks invited me over for dinner, so I'm supposed to be there at five-thirty."

That gave me a couple of hours to show him a few of the basics. I didn't want the kid to embarrass himself, but I'm no choreographer. Driving out of the parking lot, I headed for home. "You're gonna owe me."

"Anything, Jamie."

"I'll show you some simple steps this afternoon. Then you'll have time to practice during the week before the dance."

As I stopped at another light, he leaned across the console and hugged me. "You're the best, Jamie."

Back at the house, Ian dropped his gear in the bedroom, then ran down to the basement. There was enough space at one end, away from the pool table, where we could make an impromptu dance floor. I had no clue if the kid had rhythm or any idea how to move. But he was athletic and played baseball like he was born to it. I cued up the little stereo in the corner and put on an oldies CD. Ian stood before me.

"I don't know anything about the current dance styles people your age might prefer, so I'll show you some easy steps. Pretty much everything is based on that."

"Sure, let's start there."

When I took his left hand and told him where to place the right one on my back, Ian's face went bright red.

"Don't be embarrassed. You've hugged me before. It's not like you're grabbing my ass."

Somehow, he got even more flustered. "Malone would kill me if I even thought about doing that!"

"He'd have to wait his turn. If you get this way with me, what are you going to do with Brittany in your arms?"

Ian closed his eyes, drew a deep breath and let it out slowly. That seemed to help calm him down. At least he wasn't shaking. I showed him how to do a simple box step and we moved together in time with the music. After the first song, he settled down a bit more. I talked him through a couple of turns. He didn't even step on my toes. It wasn't exactly graceful, but he stuck with it. After an hour, I told him to take a break.

"You're part of the tech generation. Get on your computer and find some introductory videos you can watch. There are probably several for the current dances. Just don't start jumping and bouncing off the walls. Got it?"

Ian nodded several times, then gave me another hug. "Thank you, Jamie."

"Scram."

He raced up the stairs. The stereo flipped over to some jazz instrumentals. I was about to turn it off, then had a change of heart. Instead I moved to the billiard table and racked the balls. Concentrating on shooting pool would let my mind wander. It was possible, that way, I could discover what was still tickling the back of my brain and coax it out into the light.

I didn't exactly run the table, but I scattered the billiard balls on the break and slowly worked my way through them. Bert had taught me how to shoot pool and we'd had many games over the years when I was growing up in his house. While lining up a combination, my mind shifted again. It wasn't about Bellamy. But it was something I'd seen while looking into his background. Something bothered me. So why couldn't I remember what it was? Maybe it was in my notes.

I sank the last ball and racked the cue.

Time to get back to work.

***

It had been more than a week since I'd seen or spoken to Bert. That was unusual. Although he wasn't my biological father, and Vera married several times after Peter's untimely death, he was the one I was closest to. It used to be I would introduce him and think of him as my stepfather. For some time now, I've thought of him as my father. He's always been there for me. He picked up on the second ring.

"Hello, daughter."

"Hi. I was meaning to call you earlier this week and get together for lunch or dinner, but everything went sideways."

He snorted what could have been either a sound of disgust or laughter. I opted to believe it was laughter. "It's not like I've been checked into the old folks' home, and you have to stop by to dust and water me each week."

"I have difficulty picturing you in such a setting. You're much too young and active to be even thinking such things."

"Flattery from my favorite redhead. You must want something," he said with another snort of laughter.

"Not really. Although I did speak with Vera earlier this week. She suspects that you miss her and told me to deliver a kiss when I see you."

"Now that's the kind of message I can look forward to."

"Free for dinner? I know it's short notice…"

"Jamie, that's no notice. Unfortunately I've already made plans. I was just leaving the post to meet a friend. How about dinner next week? Tuesday or Wednesday would be good for me."

"Either one works. I could cook something." I couldn't keep the grin from my face. Bert knows the best thing I make for dinner is reservations.

"Lord help me! Dinner will be my treat. I'll call you later."

"Love ya, Bert."

"Right back at you, daughter."

No wonder Vera fell in love with Bert. He's quite a catch.

Once again, I found myself at my desk with my heels propped on the corner. If I listened closely, I could hear music coming from Ian's room, despite his door being shut. I pictured him swaying and twisting to the beat, pretending

Brittany was in front of him. Something told me that no matter how good or bad he was, she would make the best of it.

I looked at the bookcase perpendicular from my desk. There were a few reference texts propped there, within easy reach of my chair. Mostly this unit held a collection of items that had special meaning to me. On the top shelf were copies of my novels, held in place by a set of carved wooden towers. A copy of the acceptance letter for my first novel was in a nice silver frame. I had been putting a few significant pictures here as well. Me and Linda. Vera with Bert. Peter and Vera at some gallery opening. Malone and me in formal attire from last month's display of Peter's work. There was one of Ian, surrounded by his mom, sister, Malone and Brittany. One of Brittany and Ian, looking sweet and innocent at the picnic table. Special stuff.

On the center shelf was the heavy brass stamp that Peter used to sign his work. Beside it was the wooden puzzle box he'd bought just before his death. He'd meant to give it to me for my eighth birthday. I'd found it during last summer's adventure but hadn't figured out how to open it yet. Now I plucked it off the shelf and absent-mindedly tried to slide the intricate panels, hoping to stumble upon the correct combination.

What was I missing?

I let my mind wander. It was something from this past week. I scrolled through the days, my memory like a video on a slow crawl. Whatever it was remained elusive. How was that possible? I was a trained observer, someone who paid attention to details, no matter how insignificant they may be. Bert was the one who first taught me a few observation tricks. Years of working as a reporter helped sharpen that skill. My gaze went to the picture of him and Vera. It was from the same event in September where Peter's discovered masterpieces had been publicly displayed for the first time. Vera and Bert might no longer be married, but there was no mistaking the love they shared.

I put the puzzle box back on the shelf. Turning to my computer, I pulled up the file with all the notes I'd written during the week. This was another old habit from my days as a journalist. While I often scribbled things down in my abbreviated shorthand, I would elaborate on those once I was within reach of my laptop. Sometimes I'd just enter in random observations or thoughts and points that I needed to follow up on.

This file had everything related to Randy's request. Just to be thorough, I entered in the details of my conversation with Nick Bellamy from earlier that afternoon. I even added a comment about his intention to tell Allison the truth within the next couple of weeks. Now, I resisted the temptation to just skim it. Instead, I took my time, reading every entry, starting with Randy's original email.

And there it was.

Just a single line from yesterday, following my visit to the K-9 True Companion office and meeting a few of the staff. In the excitement of discovering Bellamy's former identity, I'd forgotten all about this. That simple little moment.

Aldis said she was a temp, working for a company named Delaney and Associates, a staffing agency that was supposed to specialize in nonprofit organizations. I'd never heard of it, but that didn't mean anything. It wasn't like I was looking to hire people. At first glance, you wouldn't think a company that only worked with nonprofits would have a lot of potential customers. I was of the same mindset, until I did a quick internet search and discovered there were over 22,000 nonprofits in the metro Detroit area!

Now I was getting intrigued. Who knew there were so many? I rocked back to consider this for a moment. Perhaps Aldis was just naturally nervous. She certainly seemed anxious when I was coming out of Carleen Barnett's office. Other than the blue tips on the hair and the abundant breasts, she didn't stand out in the crowd. She was a person in the background. Aldis could be the type of person who was accustomed to simply following orders. And visitors to that office might not be very common. They might have some visitors, but no doubt people usually came by appointment.

Still…

It was something I needed to look a little closer at.

***

The house was quiet. Ian had come home just a few minutes ago. He was fighting back a series of yawns, to no avail. A long day after a long, eventful week was taking its toll. He and Brittany had cheered themselves silly at the game, then gone back to her house for hot cocoa and board games with her family. I was sitting on the sofa, reading the latest Stephen King novel.

"Think I'll go to bed," Ian said. He smothered another yawn in the process.

"That's a good idea. I've seen livelier zombies."

He grinned, then leaned down and hugged me. "'Night, Jamie."

"Good night, kid."

The hug didn't end. "Thank you, Jamie. For everything you and Malone do for me. I don't say this enough."

That choked me up. "You're welcome. We like having you around."

"I love you guys," he whispered in my ear. Then he placed a light kiss on my cheek.

"We love you, kid. Now go to bed."

He sniffled and released me. Were those tears he was holding back? Before I could ask, he went down the hall. A few minutes later he was in the spare bathroom, brushing his teeth and getting ready for bed.

I tried getting back to the book but must have read the same page three times without comprehending a single word. Marking the place, I set it on the table. I was debating about a cup of tea when headlights flared in the driveway.

Malone. I glanced down the hallway. The door to Ian's room was closed and everything was dark. Malone came through the side door and met me in the kitchen. I put a finger to his lips and hugged him. Hard. After a while he held me at arms' length. There was a single courtesy light in the kitchen, a lonely little bulb that we always leave on. My face was in shadows.

"Something wrong?" Malone asked quietly.

"No, the kid just surprised me. A good surprise. Hell, a great surprise."

"How great?"

I leaned in and kissed him, just a tender one. "Ian came right out and said he loves us. And he thanked us for everything we do for him."

"That's pretty good for a teen-age boy," Malone said with a gentle smile.

"That's the first time he's ever said it."

Malone took my hand and led me back to the sofa. As he was about to sit at the end, he spun me around like a dancer executing a pirouette so that I ended up on his lap with my arms around his neck.

"Ian's still getting used to life without his father," Malone said quietly. "He and Asa were tight. I got to witness that many times over the years. Guess that set the foundation for the way I interact with the kid."

"For the most part, I've followed your example. And during all the time he's been around, I can see how much he's grown."

Malone chuckled softly. "The kid's sprouting like a weed."

"He's growing in more ways than physically. I'd like to think we've all grown closer together too. Me and Ian and you and Ian."

"That's a good point. Terri keeps me informed. If he's misbehaving, giving her grief at home or not holding up his end of his chores, she puts her foot down. She's a strong woman." Malone slowly ran his fingers through my hair.

"Which kind of reminds me of someone else I know."

Smooth talker. That earned him another kiss.

"I can never replace his dad. It's not inconceivable that Terri might get married again. Someday. She's a beautiful, intelligent woman. So the kid could have a stepfather too. I like Ian. I care about him and the family. And I enjoy spending time with him."

"So do I, Malone. He's a part of our own little family. You and me and Linda and Vince and Bert and Vera. Terri and Caitlin too."

"Don't forget Logan. That dog thinks he's human."

Malone drew me a little closer somehow. We were quiet for a time, just being together there on the sofa.

"We never did get back to that talk about kids," I said.

"Having one of our own, you mean. That's a different type of commitment. A lifelong one. Although I get the sense Ian's not going anywhere. I think he sees us as an extension of his family. Honorary big brother and big sister."

This topic had been playing out in my mind for some time now. My voice was barely a whisper. "Malone, do you think we even need to be having this conversation?"

"I think we're good just the way we are. But if something magical happens and you were to become pregnant, I'm not going anywhere."

That was the answer I'd been hoping for. I wasn't planning to have a child right now, but even birth control pills are not infallible. Just knowing he'd be right there beside me gave me the sense of peace I wanted.

"If it ever happens, I know you'd make a great father."

He gave me another tender kiss. "You'll be an excellent mama someday. You're already getting a lot of practice with Ian."

"That's more like annoying big sister."

"Sometimes, it can work in your favor."

"I'll keep that in mind."

Now that the emotional stuff was out of the way, I was

yawning as much as Ian had been earlier. Despite any amorous intentions either of us had, sleep claimed me in a heartbeat. There were some nights we just curled up in each other's arms without having sex. Somehow that made our time together that much sweeter. Not that there's anything wrong with the sex. Oh boy!

CHAPTER THIRTEEN

It was the middle of Saturday afternoon before I had some time to myself. Malone was off to work. Brittany and Ian were supposed to be studying together down in the basement at her house. Part of me wondered how much studying was really being accomplished. That made me recall Linda's comment about the kid climbing out the window to go steal a kiss. I would not have been surprised if Brittany's dad had installed security cameras around the house about the same time his beautiful little girl hit puberty. Maybe even a Nanny Cam in the basement.

Bert once told me "There is no such thing as coincidence," which my skeptical mind has continued to believe. I was considering deceit and misdirection when my mind went back to the activities of last summer. During the evaluation of Peter's masterpieces, I'd made the acquaintance of an art expert who wasn't exactly what he appeared to be. Harrison Mundy was crafty. I didn't know if he was in the area and wondered for a moment if he would remember me. Of that I had no doubt. We'd met only a few times, but each occurrence was memorable. I thought he was traveling with his daughter, Jocelyn. His background as an art expert kept him in high demand whenever crimes of that nature occurred. Mundy could be anywhere in the world. He wouldn't be caught dead on social media. I didn't even have a contact number for him.

Or did I?

Last summer Jocelyn had managed to sneak a tracking program onto my phone. That turned out to be beneficial when Harry wanted to meet with me. It made me wonder if she'd done more than that.

I snagged my phone and started slowly going through the contact list. I went past it once, then started to laugh. A listing near the bottom read "Townsend Hotel." That was the place where I had first met Jocelyn and Mundy. I opened the contact and read the details. It wasn't a metro Detroit prefix. A quick peek at the hotel's website confirmed it wasn't their number. There was a long string of numbers. Turned out the prefix was for a satellite phone.

I pressed the button and almost instantly a phone began to ring, as if my call was expected. Mundy's cultured voice answered before the third tone. I wondered if he'd taken voice acting lessons in his youth.

"Greetings, Jamie. I hope you are well."

"I am, Mr. Mundy. You are one crafty, sly dog. How are you and your lovely daughter?"

"We are in excellent health, Ms. Richmond. I was under the impression we agreed to forego the formalities."

"We did, Harry. Just an old habit. So what part of the globe are you in?"

Mundy chuckled lightly. "We are sitting on a terrace on the Amalfi Coast, gazing down at the Tyrrhenian Sea. Jocelyn was just perusing the menu for our dinner reservations."

"Italy! Color me jealous. But I thought the Amalfi Coast overlooked the Mediterranean Sea."

"That is true, Jamie. However this location flows into the Mediterranean Sea. So theoretically, we are both correct." Mundy's voice came smoothly over the line. It was difficult to picture him in Europe when the phone connection made it feel as if he was across the room from me.

"Harry, that sounds remarkable. I will be putting it on my bucket list."

"Many people prefer to visit between May and September. Jocelyn and I choose the latter part of the year, where there are fewer tourists to contend with."

"Harry, why do I get the feeling that you would fit in anywhere and never look like a tourist?"

That comment earned me another gentle chuckle. Mundy must have switched the phone to speaker mode as I heard Jocelyn's voice next.

"Apparently you discovered my little addition to your contacts list. Were you merely calling to let us know you were aware of it, or is something else on your mind, Jamie?"

"I am curious about a situation back here. It may be nothing, but it has my attention. There is the possibility of some type of criminal activity at play." I realized that whenever I spoke with these two, I no longer used contractions or slang and spoke in full sentences. What the hell!

"Perhaps it would be beneficial for you to elaborate," Harrison Mundy said.

I took a few minutes to spell it out. The more I talked, the more I realized how what I was describing was possible. It also made me wonder if this was the product of my active imagination. Was this a result of being raised by a cop? Or living with one? Or all the years during my career spent looking for mischief behind every news story I'd covered? Or just my suspicious nature in general? Or did I really have spidey-sense instincts? There was a brief silence after I brought everything to a conclusion.

"Jamie, what you are describing could in fact be a variation of a confidence maneuver," Harry said.

"A con game?"

"Precisely. Although truth be told, it would not be one that would reap immediate rewards."

"What do you mean, Harry?"

There was a muffled conversation. Then Jocelyn took over. "This would be known as a long con, Jamie. The chances that any one nonprofit organization, especially one that is not a regional chapter affiliated with a national or international operation, would generate sufficient capital in a single fundraising event to justify the expense, are minimal. What you are describing could in fact be strategically planned for three to five years before the thieves would disappear with the consolidated funds."

"A long con," I muttered.

"Precisely," Harry said. "Of course, from what you have described, that time frame could be sooner, if in fact they targeted a sufficient number of smaller organizations and gathered all the funds collectively."

"Have you ever heard of anything like this?"

"We have not personally," Jocelyn said, "however, you realize our interests usually center on the world of art."

"Of course. But you have given me some ideas that are worth considering. Could it be possible in your travels, Harry, that you might have encountered a *reputable* confidence man?"

That won me another light chuckle. "What you are describing is certainly an oxymoron. A reputable confidence man! Jamie, your imagination continues to impress me."

"You cannot blame me for trying. Well, do you know someone?"

There was no immediate response. I had to check the phone to make sure the connection was intact. I waited impatiently. Jocelyn stepped back in.

"At the moment, neither of us is aware of anyone who would be appropriate for your situation. But I will review our files after dinner. Should I discover a possible ally, I will send you the pertinent information in an email."

"I would greatly appreciate that."

"Jamie, if your curiosity is getting the better of you, perhaps you could start by reviewing the security footage for the location of this particular event, if it would be available," Harry said.

"That is an excellent idea. Now I should sign off. Thank you both for your time. Enjoy your dinner."

"We shall," Harrison Mundy said. "It is always a delight conversing with you, Jamie."

"Right back atcha, Harry. Bye, Jocelyn." I ended the call. At least I managed to work one bit of slang into the conversation.

Harry's idea about checking the security footage from the hotel was just the inspiration I needed. It was easy to picture the two of them, sitting down to a scrumptious dinner at a fabulous Italian restaurant, while they compared notes about possible con men. There was no doubt Harry would know of someone, or several someones, who fit the bill. Whether they would be willing and able to talk with me was another story.

Flipping back through my notes, I found the listing for where the event had been held. It was a country club out in Oakland County. The place was the type that would have decent security. I sketched out a plan. All it took was a couple of phone calls to put things in motion. Then I jumped on the computer and started doing research. I wanted more background information on Delaney and Associates. The more I learned, the more my curiosity kicked in. Another point was added to my plan. It was beginning to look like a treasure map, with trails crisscrossing the page. I tried it again with a fresh sheet of paper, turning it into a flow chart. Now step one led to step two and so on.

Satisfied that my plan was taking shape, I was able to put it aside. Linda had invited Ian and me over for dinner. It was supposed to be just the three of us for a relaxing meal. That was, until Ian mentioned it to Brittany. Somehow, he had utilized his teenaged powers to persuade Linda into extending the invitation to include his girlfriend as well.

"It could have been worse," I teased her when we

arrived.

She smiled and hugged me. "Worse than chaperoning two romantically involved teenagers?"

"We could have brought her dog too." Brittany's family had a black German Shepherd named Lucy. She and Logan had become buddies last summer when I was puppy sitting while Linda and Vince were on vacation.

"The dogs would have helped keep an eye on the kids."

Linda was the perfect hostess. She already had dinner on the table. There was a marinated roast chicken, seasoned baked potato wedges, salad and homemade rolls. The conversation was light and filled with laughter. If Ian felt even a tiny bit uncomfortable having dinner with one of his teachers, he didn't show it. I remembered Linda's comment from Thursday, about him often being surrounded by beautiful women. Between his mother and sister, Brittany, me and Linda and now Erica Morehouse, his tutor, the kid was definitely in the company of women. Upon reflection, I added Brittany's mother, Bridget Murphy. It was obvious where Brittany got her looks. But Ian was attentive. He even showed brief flashes of charm. He did spend a fair amount of time with Malone and Vince. Odon Krippendore was also an occasional male influence. All three men could be charming. Ian was obviously a quick study.

"I understand you're going to a Halloween dance next week," Linda said as we finished dinner. She'd even made a caramel apple pie for dessert. Showoff!

"It's our first big dance," Brittany said. "I'm anxious to see what kind of costumes the other kids wear."

Linda tossed back her curls, then winked at me. "I'm sure your costumes will be a hit. What are you wearing?"

Ian started to open his mouth. Brittany reached over and clamped her hand across it. "No way. This is a *major-league secret*. It's going to be a big surprise."

Ian mumbled and nodded in agreement. Laughing, she pulled her hand away. "I was going to tell her the same thing," he said sheepishly.

"Sure you were," Brittany teased.

"Well, I won't be able to see your costumes in person," Linda said. "I expect pictures to be sent."

"I'll make sure we get some," I said. "Of course, it would be helpful to have an appropriate background for the pictures. You know, like a woodland scene if you're going as Robin Hood and Maid Marian."

Brittany started giggling. "Nice try, Jamie."

"It was just an innocent suggestion."

Now Linda was laughing. "Jamie, you and innocence aren't even in the same neighborhood."

"Hush. Let's not give the kids the wrong idea about me."

"I think they both know all there is about you," Linda said.

Ian shrugged. "I think that's my cue to clear the table and do the dishes. Want to help, Britt?"

"Sure. You wash, I'll dry."

Linda and I exchanged a surprised look. Now that I thought about it, Malone often had Ian help clean up after cooking meals. Maybe there was hope for the young man. Linda told the kids how to load the dishwasher and just stack the clean platters and pans on the counter for now. Then we moved into the living room. I noticed Logan stayed behind, probably sneaking scraps and ear rubs from Brittany and Ian.

"Did you ever get to the bottom of Randy's problem?"

"I did. He was right to be a little concerned, but there's nothing for him to be worried about with his mom."

Of course she wanted more. So I gave her the details about Nicholas Bellamy and his former life. Linda was intrigued. When she learned about Bellamy's declaration of love for Allison Brooks, Linda got a little misty-eyed.

"That is so sweet to hear. Love truly doesn't care about age or background or experience. It doesn't matter how many boyfriends or girlfriends you've had. Anyone is still capable of falling in love," Linda said. "Just look at Randy. First him and Liz, now his mother and Nick. That's really something special."

"Says the woman who's in love with her own special man," I teased.

She threw a pillow at me. "Like you should talk. You'd better be careful, or you might give young Romeo there some ideas."

I glanced toward the kitchen. Over the clatter of dishes, we could catch snatches of the conversation between the kids. Ian chose that moment to steal a kiss, buzzing Brittany on the cheek. She laughed and pushed him away halfheartedly. They really were an adorable pair.

Linda and I relaxed, each lost in our own thoughts for a bit. Ian announced the kitchen was ready for inspection and asked if he and Brittany could take Logan for a walk. As if by magic, the dog appeared beside him, bumping his leg. Linda agreed and outfitted them with a leash and a disposable bag.

"Jamie and I will set up the dominoes game. Be advised: I'm very competitive," Linda said. "And Jamie is a sore loser."

"I am not. Besides, I usually win."

The kids were laughing as they headed out. We arranged the game on the dining room table. Linda pulled out an old-fashioned percolator and filled it with apple cider. She put some nutmeg in the little basket on top, along with a couple of cinnamon sticks. It would be a perfect complement to the evening.

We played a long round of Mexican train dominoes. Brittany proved to be a fierce competitor and won handily. I finished in second place. Ian was so far behind he gave up trying. He did manage to sneak an extra slice of pie. Linda graced us all with hugs on our way out the door.

CHAPTER FOURTEEN

Monday morning I was ready to go. The drive to the country club gave me enough time to clear my head and brush away any confusion or doubts. I'd charmed my way into a meeting with their operations manager, who oversaw everything about the place, including the security systems. My luck of the Irish was working. He still had the footage from the event on record. The guy was waiting for me in the clubhouse dining area. He sat at a table by the windows, overlooking part of the course. A couple of diehard golfers were walking down the fairway. One of the staff brought me into the room.

"Welcome, Jamie. I'm Travis Kool," he said, standing up to shake my hand. He was about my height but stockier. I got the impression of muscles, not fat. Travis had dark brown hair swept back from his forehead. There was a trace of stubble, perhaps the start of a goatee on his chin.

"That's a great name."

He shrugged. "Kids in grammar school loved to poke fun at it. Many thought my first name should be Joe. But, what's in a name?"

"A golf guy who quotes Shakespeare. That's impressive."

He waved me into a chair. One of the staff brought over a pot of coffee and a pair of mugs. Travis poured. I took a sip, then laced my fingers together, resting my hands on the table before me.

"Well, you asking to view the security footage is a bit unusual."

I nodded. "I get that a lot."

"You're not a police officer, so I'm guessing there's no warrant involved or anything official to go with your request," Travis said.

"That's right. This is strictly unofficial. I learned about this event while doing a favor for a friend. It gets a little complicated, but there may be some crooks at play here. Perhaps some criminal activity."

"So favors are your business?" he asked with a smirk.

Just what my life needed. Another smartass. Maybe attracting them was one of my superpowers.

"Lately, it seems that all I'm doing is chasing favors. But if you're willing to let me view the security footage from that fundraising event, I'll owe *you* a favor."

Travis took another sip of his coffee and considered that. "Would that be like a journalistic favor, or maybe having a character named after me in your next book kind of favor?"

However did we ever survive before the internet? At times I forget how much information is out there about people. All Travis needed was my name and the geographic area we live in to get more information on me. Of course, I'd done the same thing in my recent efforts for Randy.

"I don't do much journalism nowadays. But I'd be happy to name one of my characters after you."

Travis nodded and set his coffee aside. "You can make me taller too, right? Maybe a bit more rugged."

I started laughing. "Sure, but then, you might be the bad guy."

"Good guy, bad guy, badass. It all works for me. Come on, let's go watch some video. You can bring your coffee if you'd like."

Travis led me down a corridor. There was a keypad as part of the doorknob and he quickly punched in his numbers. "Only three people have access to the server room. Each of us has a separate code. That way I can tell who has been in here and when. Keeps everything secure."

"Your insurance agent must love you."

He shrugged. "It's important. Our system oversees all the operating equipment, makes sure the freezers and refrigerators are working properly, along with monitoring all the important rooms and events. The only areas not under the eye of the cameras are the restrooms. Any events, such as that fundraiser, are monitored and recorded. Everything is backed up on the server here and automatically stored in the cloud."

"That's very efficient."

"Our members expect us to take good care of this property," Travis said.

The control room was not a stuffy closet, but almost fifteen-foot square. There was a section where all the servers were quietly humming away. He guided me to a desk with a keyboard and mouse. In front of me were eight good-sized computer monitors, currently showing different parts of the clubhouse. Travis settled into a chair beside me. He clicked the mouse and suddenly four screens right in the center of the display changed.

"This is the evening you asked about, Jamie."

I was tempted to bring up the photos on my phone of Aldis. But it would be better to view everything as the night went on. There was no rush. Despite my lack of patience, I knew there could be other actions or interactions that might be pertinent. There was one camera angle from the rear of the room, facing the podium. Two others were at the far corners, focused on the audience. Another was aimed from above and to the side, catching the activity behind the curtain that separated the dining area and dance floor from the kitchen.

"We have security in the kitchen as well, but didn't think you'd need that," Travis said.

"What's the best way to watch this?"

"We can start all four cameras rolling at once. Then if something catches your eye, we can isolate it and zoom in."

"How long was the event?"

Travis didn't even bother to check the log. "Guests started arriving at 6:00. Cocktails and mingling for an hour. They had that little auction thing going on, so quite a few people were checking out the goodies and making bids."

"I heard about that."

"Dinner was served just after seven, following a few remarks from the host. Then they announced the winners of first auction, followed by the live version. Afterwards, you had schmoozing, dancing, and drinking until a little after midnight," Travis said.

"You just so happen to remember all those pertinent details?"

He gave me a grin. "I reviewed the footage over the weekend after we talked. Noted the pertinent times."

"That's quite thorough. You might have just been elevated from creepy bad guy status."

"I can do creepy," he said with a laugh. "My kids will testify to that."

I dug the notebook and pen from my purse and opened it to a clean page. With a nod of approval, Travis clicked the mouse and started the video moving. For the first few minutes, it was just guests slowly coming into the ballroom. I recognized Allison and a bit later, Nick Bellamy. There were a few people from K-9 True Companion scurrying about. I spotted Carleen Barnett and Norma Rush, the president of the organization. I'd seen her picture on their website.

"Hang on a second," Travis said. He froze the action on the screens and pulled the keyboard closer. His fingers danced across the keys almost as rapidly as mine would. Then he pointed to another monitor beside the primary four. That screen changed to show a long table with two women sitting behind it, greeting the guests and signing them in.

"I should have thought of this before. You can see the people working the table as well as the patrons when they arrive."

"Thanks."

We watched the action on this screen. Aldis, the over-endowed temporary worker, sat behind this table. The other woman, perhaps a volunteer, was beside her, greeting people and checking them off the list. Rather than those tacky stickers with "Hi, My Name Is…" on them, each guest was given a small metal nameplate with a magnet behind it. These were not cheap, which surprised me. Most nonprofits would rather spend money on the operations. Maybe they thought this was a distinctive way to connect with the patrons.

Travis let this video run its course until all the attendees were checked in. I spotted Olivia from Channel 4 and her husband, Charlie, come through the line. She smiled when a few people fawned over her. With that segment completed, we turned our attention back to the action inside the ballroom.

I jotted down the times and spots where Aldis was working. Carleen Barnett stopped her more than once to give instructions or check in. Following the registration, Aldis moved to a little table set in the rear corner of the room. The patrons continued to mingle, cocktails in hand. We watched them weave in and out of the displays for the auction items. Many people jotted down a bid on the clipboard in front of the prizes.

Several times, we heard Norma Rush encourage the patrons to circle back to check on the status of their favorite prizes. Quite a few people kept returning to a particular item, increasing their bids as necessary.

"That's pretty good sound quality," I said.

Travis nodded. "The board considers it money well

spent. No sense having security cameras when you can't hear what's going on. Better to have the full package. Especially if any situations are brought to our attention after the fact."

"Like me?"

"Not sure if you're bringing me a situation, or just a coincidence."

I bit back the comment about there being no such thing as coincidence. My gaze remained locked on the screen where Aldis was featured. Maybe I was wrong about her. Maybe she was simply an innocent young woman trying to make the most of the job or jobs she had. Maybe my overactive imagination was always creating nefarious criminal scenarios. Maybe Santa Claus and the Easter Bunny share a condominium in Jamaica. Maybe...

Norma Rush announced the end of the silent auction and encouraged everyone to their assigned seats. Each table was numbered and there was a little sticker on the nameplates the patrons had been given with their table number. I picked out Allison Brooks circling her table, chatting with a few people obviously she knew. As she took her seat, Nicholas Bellamy appeared. The look they exchanged was polite, but there was a flash of interest on her face. Cupid must have been busy that night.

Movement on another screen got my attention. We watched Aldis go to the tables where the open auction items were displayed. She gathered up each clipboard and returned to her little station in the rear. As the staff began serving dinner, Aldis started making a list of the highest bidders.

"Other than dinner, this looks like the only activity," Travis said, pointing a forefinger at the image of Aldis on the screen.

"She does appear to be the only one working." I looked around the room for Norma Rush and Carleen Barnett and the other three key people associated with the nonprofit. Each one was sitting at a separate table. Probably getting cozy with the donors who had the deepest pockets.

"Perhaps she's hoping her hard work will help make…her stand out," Travis said.

I glanced over to see his grin. "I'm sure it's her job performance that you were studying."

"I'm happily married with three kids," Travis said, "and there may be occasional…distractions at work. But my wife is a thousand times more beautiful than that girl and she's not liable to tip over walking down the hall."

I was laughing so hard he had to back up the footage on the screen. That made me remember Olivia's comments, which made it even more difficult to regain my composure. After several minutes I was able to focus again and concentrate on the activity.

Aldis took her list and pulled a typed page from a portfolio. She may have been matching the prize winners to a master list. Once everything was compiled, she darted out to the restroom. Returning to the banquet room, she caught Carleen's eye and got a nod of approval. Aldis approached and handed her the list, then stepped behind the curtain and chatted with one of the waitstaff. A meal was brought out and she ate standing up behind the curtain.

Travis watched this with a snort of disapproval. "That's no way to treat someone, regardless of their role."

"I agree. That doesn't make me want to support this organization."

"Makes me want to charge them a higher rate if they book their event here next year," he grumbled.

With the meal completed, Aldis moved back to her station. She sat primly with her hands folded in her lap. Norma, serving as the host, returned to the podium and announced all the winners from the silent auction. Polite applause followed. She then gestured toward Aldis and instructed the winners to visit with her before the end of the evening so they could make payment and collect their prizes. But there was no reason to rush off, because now the live auction was about to begin.

There were five big-ticket items in the live auction. Norma encouraged everyone to check out the program before the bidding started. Then she introduced Olivia Sholtis, who was serving as the auctioneer. We watched Aldis move over to a spot a little to the left side and behind the podium. From this vantage point she could see the patrons and monitor the bidding. On a clipboard she made notes, probably the item in question and the action.

Carleen came over and spoke to her as Olivia got the bidding started. There was a large screen in front of the curtain on the right side of the podium. Displayed now was a photograph of a white yacht out on the water. The first item was a dinner cruise on Lake St. Clair for twenty people. Olivia began a friendly patter with the guests. She cajoled a couple of people to increase their bids, reminding them the money was for a good cause. At one point she even offered to go along as the navigator.

"That reporter does a great job working the crowd," Travis said.

"Olivia's got the right personality for it. No wonder she does so well on her segments for the news."

"Give her a year and she'll be anchoring a broadcast on a regular basis."

I considered it. "That makes a lot of sense. She adapts to the stories she covers. Some are serious, others a bit more fun."

"I've noticed that too," Travis said.

In the background, Carleen stood beside Aldis. As the bidding ended, she bent closer and whispered in the young woman's ear. She was probably identifying the winning patron. I checked the other monitors but didn't see anything unusual. The big screen behind Olivia changed to show a large table elegantly set with a dozen bottles of wine on display.

We watched Olivia orchestrate the rest of the auction. Occasionally we caught a glimpse of Aldis and Carleen, conferring after the bidding ceased. When I saw Krip's painting brought out and placed on an easel, I felt a little tickle of recognition. Even on the video feed, I could tell this was one of his better works. Nicholas Bellamy did get involved in the action here, as he'd done with the cruise and the lease for the car, but he dropped out after a couple of rounds. I noticed that his chair was now closer to Allison's. Perhaps it just afforded him a better view of the projection screen and the action. Or it was a chance to get a little closer to the lovely Allison. It didn't really matter. She didn't seem to mind.

"Why do I get the feeling that we're finally getting to the good part?" Travis asked. He reached over and clicked the mouse, stopping the action.

"I have a theory. We're about to find out if I'm right or wrong."

"Want to clue me in on that?" he asked.

"No. If I say it out loud, it will sound foolish."

Travis studied me. "I doubt that. My money's on you."

"Thanks for the vote of confidence. You should know that I've been wrong as often as I'm right with my theories."

"Let's find out." He clicked the mouse again.

Aldis returned to her little table in the rear. The band, which had set up earlier, started playing some old favorites from the days of Frank Sinatra, Dean Martin, and Tony Bennett. Several couples got up to dance. I noticed Nicholas Bellamy escorting Allison Brooks onto the floor. They moved well together. I shifted my attention back to Aldis.

Slowly, different patrons came to her table to pay for their prizes. Travis and I were glued to the monitor. One lady wrote out a check and handed it over. Aldis thanked her and put the check in a little vinyl envelope that had a zipper on it. Next up was the couple who had won the dinner cruise. The man handed over a credit card with a flourish. Aldis picked up a tablet computer and entered in the information, then swiped his card through a little device attached to it. Just that easily, the money was charged to his account.

When she was processing payment from the third prize winner, I caught the difference. This was another credit card purchase. But just before that patron, a lovely, silver-haired matron, approached the table, Aldis slipped the tablet computer under the portfolio. She accepted the lady's credit card, then pulled her smartphone from the pocket of her blazer. Aldis keyed in the information, then swiped the card through a similar device attached to the phone. The lady used her fingertip to approve the purchase. We saw her give a negative shake of the head to Aldis, who closed out the app. The woman moved over to the display table to claim her prize.

"I'll be damned," Travis said. He stopped the video again.

CHAPTER FIFTEEN

"You saw it too!"

"Why would she use the tablet for some purchases, then use her personal phone for others? Unless that phone belongs to the organization."

"I doubt it. That young woman is from a temporary service. It doesn't make sense that K-9 True Companion would give her a company phone, especially when she's got that tablet to process payments," I said.

"My sister-in-law has one of those phone-swipe things. She makes pottery and sells it at a bunch of local art festivals. The device is linked to her phone, which is connected to her bank account. Charges that go through are usually credited to her account the next business day. Minus a small administrative fee, of course," Travis said.

"We just watched her use two different devices for processing payment. I'll bet one goes to the nonprofit and the other one goes into a dummy account."

"Ready to see the rest?"

I grinned. "Let's check out the instant replay."

Travis started the video. We were able to speed up the action when no one came to visit Aldis. Then whenever someone approached, I marked down the time and as much information as possible. After four more payments were made, we confirmed the pattern. Two more gave checks, which she tucked in the little envelope. When the winner of a live-auction item came forward, she used the tablet. With a credit card payment for one of the earlier items, Aldis used the phone. My page of notes was filling up quickly.

"You're on to something, Jamie?"

"Yes. She uses the tablet for the big-ticket items. The smaller ones, even though some of them garnered hundreds of dollars, are still small fish. But that's what she's running through her phone."

"Why not scam the big money?" Travis asked.

"Maybe this was a trial run. Or they were afraid it would raise suspicions if the proceeds from all those major items suddenly vanished."

We watched the rest of the action. At one point, everything was paid for except Krippendore's painting. Carleen stopped by to check on the progress, then hunted down the patrons and escorted them over to make payment. Aldis used the tablet to process their credit cards. Her phone was safely tucked back in her pocket. In the end, she handed the little zippered envelope to Carleen. Then she packed up her portfolio and the tablet and left. Travis was rocked back in his chair, studying me. The other screens showed the band still playing. People were mingling, dancing and drinking. The video showed it was a little after eleven. He reached over and clicked the mouse again, freezing the action.

"Tell me about your theory."

"I think this young woman…"

"Just her?"

"I think the temporary agency she works for trained her to skim some of the proceeds from this event. I think that any careful scrutiny of that organization's records will reveal that a bunch of money never made it to their bank accounts. This woman only works there part time. She would be the one to generate thank you letters for one of the bigwigs to sign. It wouldn't be that difficult to make some dummy ones up, with a slightly different address or post office box, to send to the people she scammed."

"Why bother with that?"

I waved a hand back and forth. "Maybe they didn't. If it was me, I wouldn't want a copy of that kind of letter in the files just in case someone wanted to compare thank you letters with the bank deposits."

"That's sneaky. You have a devious mind," Travis said with a grin.

"Goes with the territory."

"So now what do we do? Should I contact the client and let them know what we've seen?"

"Not yet. Can you make me a copy of everything we watched today?"

Travis hesitated. "Most of me wants to say yes. But I may need to talk to the president of the board first. Maybe the lawyers too. And they're going to want to know what you will do with a copy if we provide one."

"I'm going to put all the information together, wrap it up with a nice little bow, then hand it off to a couple of police officers I know."

"Think they'll listen to you?"

I winked at him. "I've got the inside track to getting their attention. But it would be helpful if you could at least print me a couple of photos. One where she's using the tablet and another when she's running the credit card on her phone."

"That I can do. You know, if you get enough for the police to take an interest in this, I'm sure management would cooperate fully with official representatives of law enforcement," Travis said.

"I like the sound of that."

"Thought you might."

***

The next logical step would be to pay a visit to Delaney

and Associates. According to their website, they had an office in one of the old buildings downtown, not far from the new sports arenas. Since their business focus was on small nonprofit organizations, I couldn't exactly walk in the door and bluff my way through a meeting. That was where the next part of my plan came into play.

An internet search for nonprofits in my area brought me to Seedlings Braille Books for Children. As the name implied, their entire operation focused on creating braille books for visually impaired kids. I'd been able to connect with Debra Bonde, the executive director and creator of Seedlings, through an exchange of emails over the weekend. We'd set up the meeting for early Monday afternoon. It turned out that the business was located within five miles of my house. Talk about convenient. Ms. Bonde was patiently awaiting my arrival. She was a slender woman who looked very comfortable in her surroundings.

"Thank you so much for agreeing to meet with me, Ms. Bonde."

"Please, call me Deb. I'm always happy to talk with people about our organization and the mission. Care for a tour?"

"I'd love that."

Deb showed me around. There were shelves with bound copies of books, printed in braille. Another row held actual picture books, with little adhesive strips of braille print that matched the dialogue. In the back of the building were two large machines, generating braille copies of the books. Deb explained that she started back in 1984 because there were few titles of braille books for kids and the ones that were available were very expensive. Through donations and fundraising efforts, they gave away roughly fifty percent of the books each year to blind children and sold the rest for under ten bucks a copy. She guided me into her office for a quiet conversation. We took the visitor's chairs in front of her desk.

"How many books do you create each year?"

Deb smiled proudly. "In 1985, I made 221 books, working in my basement on a machine my father built. In 2021, we printed over 35,000 books and articles in braille."

"That's incredible!"

"We have a small staff and a group of very loyal, dedicated volunteers."

"How do you handle fundraising?" I asked.

Deb gave me a gentle smile. "We've done different things in the past. Before the pandemic, we had an annual bowling tournament. Many local businesses and organizations would sponsor the event. We had a lot of raffle prizes and items people could bid on. A few years ago we started doing an online auction. Have you looked at our website?"

I admitted to checking it out over the weekend. There was a list of options, from regular donations, memorials to honor friends and family, holiday tribute cards, sponsoring the launch of a new title, and much more. There was even mention of an online auction, which was slated for next month.

"So the bowling tournament was your last big in-person event?" I asked.

"Yes. It took a great deal of time and energy to put it together."

"Have you ever considered something else? Maybe a dinner?"

Deb blinked a few times and leaned a little closer. "No, that's more appropriate for a larger organization. There are many additional expenses with something like that, which means you must raise a significantly larger amount in order to cover all the costs and reach your goal."

"Significantly more."

"Jamie, what are you getting at?

All weekend long, I'd been trying to figure out the best way to approach this. I could tell her it was all research for a story I was working on. Generally, people will answer my questions if they think it's a chance to expound on their expertise on a given subject. But I didn't want to do anything that could reflect poorly on this organization. Making braille books available for blind children tugged at my heart. It was time for the truth.

"Recently I stumbled upon a business that might not be all it claims to be. It could be nothing more than my overactive imagination. Or I could be right. Their business is all about helping smaller nonprofits with back-office functions, like marketing or accounting or staging special events. What I want to do is meet with them. If I claim to represent a local nonprofit, they're more likely to let me see who is at the controls behind the curtain."

Deb's smile widened. "Nice touch with that *Wizard of Oz* reference. So how would you go about this?"

"I'd schedule an appointment. Meet with one of their top people at their offices. Sort of like a fishing trip. Throw the line in the water and see what bites, or what reactions I get. But I don't want to just walk in without some connection to a real nonprofit business. Otherwise they might not let their guard down."

"Why pick Seedlings?" Deb asked.

"Proximity, for starters. I live nearby. And anything to do with books and reading is a natural connection for an author. You might inspire me to write a children's book."

We were quiet for a bit. Deb rubbed a finger on the arm of her chair. "We only have a small number of employees here. But we have quite a few volunteers who actively support the business in any number of ways. If you really were a volunteer, you could be checking out this business as a possible resource for our needs in the future."

"That would work."

"There's some paperwork you need to complete, so it's legitimate." Deb went behind her desk and withdrew a set of forms from a drawer. "How soon will you approach this other business?"

"With any luck, tomorrow or Wednesday at the latest. I want to move quickly on this."

After filling out the paperwork, Deb handed me a brochure with more information about Seedlings. I planned to study it well, along with a more thorough review of the information from the website just in case I was quizzed during the meeting.

"I really appreciate your help," I said, getting to my feet.

"If this business is truly taking advantage of nonprofits in some way, they need to be stopped. We do all our own marketing and accounting internally, but I can see how some smaller operations could find those services appealing. It may be easier to outsource such functions instead of hiring employees. Not every volunteer has the time or talents you need to do it all."

"What kind of items will you use for the online auction?"

Deb gave me that gentle smile again. "A wide variety of prizes. Gift cards, vacation rentals, gift certificates, tickets to sporting events. Those are often the type of things people would be interested in."

"How about an autographed copy of my books?"

"Done!"

I promised to drop off a set later in the week. And I was going to make a cash donation to the organization. Any operation that put books in the hands of kids got my support. Deb also gave me a couple of her own business cards. If anyone at Delaney wanted to check on me and my involvement with Seedlings, she'd backstop it for me.

My plan was proceeding smoothly. If things continued in this vein, I should have some answers. Which could lead to resolution. Or not. There had been times when the answers led to more questions: that turned into a vicious circle. Several times, back in my reporter days, I didn't like the answers. So I'd keep digging. This might turn out to be one of those situations. As a reporter, I had an editor to brainstorm ideas with. Nowadays I did most of my brainstorming alone, until I had a theory to bounce off Linda or Malone.

Back home, I entered my notes from the day's

excursions. Then I made the call to Delaney and Associates. The receptionist offered to schedule an appointment at the Seedlings office, which would be more convenient. But I wanted to meet them on their home turf, to get a better lay of the land. Maybe I'd even get a chance to see who the key people were. I explained that my business took me into the downtown area anyway. That was enough to set up a meeting on Tuesday morning.

Sometimes, it was just that easy.

CHAPTER SIXTEEN

Malone left early Tuesday. He was due in court, then planned to hit the gym before his shift. I still hadn't told him about my research into Delaney and Associates. It might turn out that the business was perfectly legit. If that was the case, then there was no sense getting him worried about me. I didn't want to overdo it, so I dressed in some black slacks with an ivory sweater. My hair was pulled back with a couple of clips. Just a simple touch of makeup around the eyes was all I needed. Linda would be chiding me about dressing like an adult once again. Maybe it really was time to give the blue jeans a rest.

My appointment at ten was with Sheldon Delaney at his office downtown. According to the company's site, Sheldon was the company's founder and chief executive officer. On the website, there was a page listing the primary people. That included a quick bio and a snapshot of Sheldon and one of Jillian Hess. Her title was Strategic Planning Officer. I had no idea what that meant. They were the only people included. The background information provided was fuzzy, without any real meat to it. That alone got my curiosity percolating.

I'd also noticed something missing from the site. Many

service-related businesses included a page for testimonials, or even had the logos of the companies they worked with on the bottom of the home page. This could be very helpful for potential customers in the form of referrals. Delaney and Associates had nothing like that at all.

Curiouser and curiouser.

The receptionist was a chunky, middle-aged woman who had given up dyeing her hair. This could have been a result of the pandemic, when beauty salons were shut down for the longest time. Her gray hair was pulled back into a loose ponytail. She confirmed my appointment, then led me to a conference room. I declined the offer of coffee and settled in for a brief wait.

Sheldon Delaney was a short, stocky man with a shaved head. His eyebrows were bushy and seemed to be doing their best to meet in the middle. At ten in the morning he sported a five-o'clock shadow. Or maybe this was his attempt at a manly stubble look. The suit he wore wasn't expensive. He carried a thick leather-bound portfolio and what looked like a plastic case of gum, about the size of a deck of playing cards.

"How can we be of service for you?" he asked, once we were settled in our chairs across the table.

"I'm a volunteer with Seedlings. I recently heard about your company and thought perhaps you'd have some ideas about an effective fundraising program."

Delaney sat a little taller in his chair. "Where did you hear about us?"

"A friend attended a dinner event for K-9 True Companion that you helped coordinate. He said it was a very enjoyable evening and they raised a lot of money. When he explained about your company's role in the evening, I thought it might be worth finding out more about it." I had my innocent-redhead face on now, complete with a little fluttering of the eyelashes.

"It's always nice to hear positive remarks about one of our efforts. That event was quite successful. Not only did they meet their financial goal, but I'm told they made several new connections, which is major coup for their development efforts. One never knows how those may pay off in the future. Development is all about the connections," he said.

"Are you familiar with Seedlings?"

Delaney shook his head. "There are so many nonprofit organizations in Michigan. Unfortunately, I don't know them all. In the few years that we've been operating, there are many that we've helped in one form or another."

That surprised me. If you had an appointment with a representative of a company, most people would at least do a little research before the meeting. Was this a sign of laziness, or cockiness? That raised my curiosity.

Delaney went on to describe some other recent efforts. I made a show of jotting a few things down in my own notebook. My phone was set to record the conversation, but that was nestled in my jacket's breast pocket.

"Tell me more about Seedlings," Delaney said. He opened his portfolio and slid the container of gum to the side. It was a little bigger than a cigarette pack. I noticed he was chewing some as he spoke. Maybe it was nicotine gum, the kind used by people who were quitting smoking. While we'd been talking, he kept running a finger over the plastic pack. Now it was next to his left hand. Delaney jotted a couple of notes. He wrote out entire words and sentences, instead of abbreviations or notes. Apparently, *he* wasn't recording the meeting.

"I recently started volunteering there. The idea of helping an organization create braille books for visually impaired children really appealed to me."

I gave him more details, combining what could be gleaned from the website with what I'd learned from my tour and the conversation with Deb Bonde. Delaney filled his page with notes, writing everything in a large, flowing script. With his head bowed over the page, I wondered if he shaved his skull daily. Maybe it was hereditary. Maybe it only needed a little fine-tuning at the end of the week. He continued to touch the case, moving it slightly.

"So you're interested in hosting an event?" he asked, looking up from his notes and making eye contact.

I gave him the innocent-redhead look again and a tiny shrug of the shoulders. "Right now, I'm just gathering information. Ms. Bonde gave me the impression that the board is considering different options."

"A strong board of directors understands that development can't be judged on the results of a single event. As I said earlier, development is all about building relationships. Those that last a long time will reap the greatest rewards." He sounded like a pompous teacher lecturing a class of distracted students.

"How did you get into this type of business?"

"I worked for several nonprofit organizations before deciding to start my own company. These were divisions of national operations, in places like Tennessee, Kentucky, Missouri and Indiana. I visited Detroit for a conference. It was obvious there was an opportunity here. A chance to help some of the smaller nonprofits to do great things." He straightened the portfolio and aligned his pen between it and the plastic box.

"What's with the gum?" I asked.

He flashed a brief smile that was devoid of any warmth. "Bad habit. But it's healthier than the cigarettes I used to smoke. Cleaner, too!"

"Your website mentions some other services in addition to helping coordinate events. How does that work?"

Delaney flashed me that quick, hard smile again. "Many of the smaller operations don't have the funds to hire someone to handle their financial matters. We have a number of contractors available, people experienced with accounting and bookkeeping and marketing. I'd be happy to put together some resumes, if this assistance would be of interest to the organization."

"Let me discuss this with the president and I will get

back to you." I closed my little notebook and tucked it in my purse.

"Don't hesitate to call me if you any questions," Delaney said.

He escorted me back to the reception area. The portfolio and the case were tucked in his left hand. Delaney gave me a fast handshake. It made me think of the kind a lame politician would use. Then he turned and headed back to his office.

I made a show of adjusting the strap on my purse. The office was smaller than I'd expected. There were only four private offices and the conference room. Besides Delaney's room at the end of the hall, I'd noticed only two of the other rooms were in use.

Curiouser and curiouser.

Not wanting to arouse suspicions, I headed for the elevator.

Down in the lobby, I noticed the directory for the building was less than half full. This wasn't one of the highly sought-after locations in the middle of the revitalization of downtown. That made me wonder how expensive the offices were. Perhaps Delaney chose this building because it was more affordable. It was possible that he met most of the agency's potential clients at their offices, rather than here. That could help convey the image that Delaney and Associates was larger than it really was. Something to investigate.

***

The Delaney office was not far from Peter's studio, so I'd brought my laptop and notebook with me. I was making the short drive over when my phone rang. Harrison Mundy's name popped up on the screen. I'd adjusted the contact list after speaking with him and Jocelyn the other night.

"Hello, Harry."

"Buongiorno, Jamie. I see you are in transit so this will be brief."

The old fox certainly knew how to get my attention. The device they put on my phone must have contained some type of GPS components.

"You are on the speaker, so I can drive and talk with you. I have been known to multitask."

"We have never doubted your abilities." Harry gave me one of his short chuckles. "Jocelyn has sent a picture. You should be receiving this shortly. We have discovered a former...colleague who may be able to assist you with that situation we previously discussed."

"Harry, you are a treasure. How will I reach him?"

There was noise in the background, then Jocelyn's voice filled the car. "Yakov will be in touch. I have included his information with the photograph. Luck must be on your side, Jamie. He happens to be in the neighborhood."

"It sounds rather noisy wherever you are. I thought the Amalfi Coast would be quiet and relaxing."

"We rarely stay in one place very long," Jocelyn said. "Right now we are at the train station in Venice. My father suddenly developed a hankering for Swiss chocolates. The train to Geneva leaves shortly."

This pair certainly knew how to live. I began to wonder if they had crossed paths with Vera during her wanderings.

"Take care, Jamie," Harry said.

"Thank you both. Enjoy your travels. Whenever you return to the Detroit area, I expect to see you."

"Addio," Jocelyn said with a giggle. The connection faded out.

I pulled into the lot beside the studio. The old manufacturing building had been converted to studios and galleries years before. There were only half a dozen cars in the lot this morning. Maybe the artists preferred to work later in the day when inspiration struck. Or the lighting was better. Or the hangover abated. Or...whatever.

After lugging my gear into the studio and securing the

door, I switched on the stereo to some instrumental music. Guitarist Earl Klugh, another great Detroit musician, was featured. His jazz and fusion songs were popular worldwide. I opened the file that Jocelyn had sent, not sure what to expect. There was a head-and-shoulders picture of a Black man, clean-shaven with a narrow moustache. His hair was clipped short and there were a couple spots of gray at the temples. He was wearing a white shirt with a gold tie, with what looked like a black or navy suit jacket. The details she provided were sketchy. About six feet tall, lean, somewhere between forty and fifty years old.

A double-tap knock sounded on the heavy hallway door. I was about to open it when something made me hesitate.

"Who is it?"

The European voice that responded surprised me. "I am seeking Miss Jamie Richmond. A mutual friend suggested we meet."

Unlocking the door, I pulled it partway open, blocking it with my hip. Standing there was the guy in the picture. Wearing the same duds. He must have sent her a selfie before she called me.

"What's your name?"

His eyes flicked back and forth mischievously. "Yakov."

"Yakov what?"

"Perhaps I am like Madonna and only use one name." The corners of his mouth curled up slightly. "Our friend sent me a picture of you as well, Miss Richmond. You were wearing something more formal. An evening gown, in a shade of green, perhaps. However, it is quite easy to recognize your lovely features and your red tresses."

That was the outfit I was wearing at the event, which was the last time I'd seen Harry and Jocelyn. This Yakov guy could give Harrison Mundy a run for his money in the suave department.

"C'mon in." I swung the door open wide. Yakov took two steps into the studio and froze in mid-stride. I secured the door behind him. Then I stepped alongside Yakov to make sure he was still breathing.

His eyes were locked on the display of sculptures. Yakov swallowed, then shifted his gaze to me. He laced his fingers together in front of his chest. "Would it be permissible to examine these? With my eyes only, of course."

"Go for it."

I went to the mini-fridge and pulled out two bottles of water, then settled on a stool next to the old drafting table. Yakov took his time studying each piece of art. Eventually he gave himself a shake and came to join me.

"Our mutual friend failed to inform me that I would be in the presence of such a priceless display of art. Your father was incredibly talented."

"I think so too." There were so many questions bouncing through my head. Maybe it would be best to start with an easy one. "Isn't Yakov a Russian name?"

He nodded. "Yes, it is."

"Oh."

"What, you have never heard of a Black Russian?"

"Well... I just...always pictured people from Russia in a certain way and..." I stopped talking, realizing he was laughing at me.

Yakov held up a hand. "In Russian, Yakov means 'supplanter.' Are you familiar with this word, Miss Richmond?"

"Call me Jamie. Seems to me it means someone who takes from another, or something like that."

"That is close enough. I must admit that the meaning fits well with my former occupation. Which is how I first was brought to the attention of our mutual friend."

"So you're a thief. How long have you known Harry?"

A puzzled expression crossed his face. "Who is Harry?"

"Our mutual friend. I thought that's who you were referring to."

"Ah, the old man. He too has many names. I know him as Jedrik, although he is no more Polish than I am."

Yakov explained that for many years, he'd been involved

with two other men who were thieves. They were successful as a team, but they operated on a small scale. It was important they stay within their abilities and under the radar of law enforcement. Things changed a decade earlier. His team disbanded after a close brush with the police. Then he became part of a gang of criminals that was leapfrogging its way around Europe. Some of their heists included art galleries and museums, as well as private collections. But theirs weren't simple smash-and-grab operations. There were several con games they worked as well. Some of their activities included stealing from various criminals, then disappearing without a trace. In Berlin they managed to abscond with five priceless sportscars from a collector. Yakov was the electronics wizard, able to identify alarm systems and methods of disabling or bypassing them. But he was also part of the strategic team who planned out the details for their capers.

Two years ago, he'd crossed paths with Harrison Mundy. Harry spotted several members of the group from witness sketches and surveillance videos obtained through Interpol. While the crew had started out cautiously, they had become sloppy in the most recent job. A night watchman had stumbled upon them as they were about the make their getaway. One of the gang members had clubbed him viciously and put the man in the hospital.

"Before this, we were never armed. I despise guns. Now the others all wanted to carry a weapon. And the job in Prague would be even riskier," Yakov said. "I was beginning to have doubts. However, no one left the team voluntarily."

"But you got out," I said.

He paused for a sip of water, then smoothed out his moustache with a long, narrow finger. "Jedrik convinced me. There was an opportunity to stop them once and for all. Our leader, Alexi, had drilled us all on one major point. If anyone stooped to cooperating with the authorities to bring the operation down, that person would be killed. And their family. And anyone they cared about. Yet Jedrik was able to persuade me. Together, we found a way."

"Harry tipped off the authorities and brought you out," I said breathlessly.

"Jedrik, or Harry as you call him, worked very closely with Interpol. He even arranged for me to be shot, so it appeared that I was dead to the other members of the crew. I had no known family. There is only one person whose safety is paramount to me."

"So how did you end up here? In Michigan, or even in the States?"

Yakov gave me a slow wink. "Jedrik, or Harry, made the arrangements. I was given a new identity. I am a consultant on crimes related to technology for several government agencies. My opinion is frequently sought on security systems for businesses, and individuals as well. The agreement allows me to move occasionally. I like the Midwest states. There is a significant population of Russian emigres in metropolitan Detroit, as well as Chicago, Minneapolis and of course, New York City. Washington D.C. is another region I enjoy. Montreal and Toronto appeal to me as well. There remains a very international flavor to those Canadian cities."

"And no one is looking for you?"

He shrugged. "Some of my features have been altered. And the others in my crew are in prisons in Europe. They all believe I am dead. I have no desire to return to the continent. Life goes on."

CHAPTER SEVENTEEN

"That's quite a story."

"It is ancient history." Yakov waved it away with a farewell gesture. "Jedrik only told me a portion of your...predicament. He simply asked me to visit you and offer advice. If that is possible."

I explained my concerns and suspicions about Delaney and Associates. Yakov listened without interruption. He simply folded his arms and propped them on the table. Even when I finished, he didn't comment for a beat or two.

"Harry referred to this as a long con. Is this something you have any previous experience with?"

"Not personally, but I have heard tales of such activity. The issue here is that the risk rarely matches the reward," Yakov said.

"What do you mean?"

"Most confidence maneuvers or scams focus on a single target. The idea is to take what you can from them or persuade them somehow to trust you with their possessions, while you quietly disappear. Perhaps you replace their valuable diamond necklace with a fake or something worth only an insignificant portion of the original. No experienced grifter would delay their departure, remain in the city after such actions," Yakov said.

"Grifter? Just another type of con man?"

"Yes. A scoundrel. A swindler or schemer, moving from one maneuver or game to the next."

"So if you were going to do this, how would you get your hands on the money? Aren't there safeguards in place?"

Yakov began to slowly rotate the water bottle on the table in front of him. "I can only speculate, but there are a few options that immediately come to mind. Are you familiar with the devices you can attach to your cellular phone that can read credit cards?"

"Of course. I've seen those frequently at art festivals. It's easier for the vendors, since many people don't carry cash, particularly at these events."

"Precisely," Yakov said with a nod. "This can easily be established. You connect the phone to a new bank account, one with a name very similar to that of an existing business. Many small businesses would utilize this method. A nonprofit organization could do the same at a fundraising event."

"So if a grifter had a second phone, they could be swiping credit card purchases, funneling the money into a bogus account. That's what I learned just yesterday while watching the video." I described the action and the use of two separate devices to process the credit cards.

Yakov cocked an eyebrow. "That is a bold move. I would have eliminated the video security system. Or possibly disabled it. In some cases, you can fool the system into believing it remains functioning, yet the recording is a simple duplication." He hesitated. "Perhaps being shortsighted would be a better answer. Perhaps these are arrogant people, assuming no one would be the wiser. Or that the person at the event was…disposable."

"Disposable?" I blanched at the image of Aldis being thrown away like yesterday's garbage.

"My apologies. That was a poor choice of words. What I meant was they could be expendable. If in fact they were caught, it would not be detrimental to their operation. The ones who orchestrated such a plan would not hesitate to leave this person behind."

I thought about Aldis. The young woman might have no idea what she was doing or the negative impact her actions could have on the different nonprofit organizations. While I was considering everything Yakov had explained, he rose and strolled around the studio. He stopped at Ian's corner. With a fingertip, Yakov lifted the cover of the sketchpad the kid had left behind last week.

"Did you inherit your father's artistic talents, Jamie?"

"Hardly. I'm a writer. That's the work of a young friend of mine."

Yakov carefully flipped a couple of pages. "This is impressive. With practice, he could become very successful. And quite popular."

"Are you an expert, Yakov?"

"Not at all. However, I know what I like." He closed the pad and rapped his knuckles on it. "Is there anything else I can tell you about this type of operation? The long con?"

I shook my head, making the tresses dance. "Nothing comes to mind. But I may be calling you."

"It would be a pleasure." He gently shook my hand and started to turn toward the door.

"Yakov, you said there is only one person whose safety is important to you. Who is that?"

He faced me and slowly shook his head back and forth, mirroring the gesture I had just used. "Jedrik warned me not to underestimate you. He said you were very observant."

I smiled sweetly at the compliment. "You didn't answer the question."

"Antonina. She is the only woman I have ever loved. But fate does not allow us to be together."

"That's a beautiful name."

"It befits a beautiful woman." What could have passed for a smitten look crossed his face. It's one I've seen on Ian frequently. "Wouldn't you agree?"

"Not sure I'm qualified to answer that."

"My apologies, Jamie. I assumed you must have met her. After all, she is the daughter of Jedrik."

I could feel the gears clicking into place. If Harrison Mundy was known to Yakov as Jedrik, then it made sense that Jocelyn was Antonina. I felt a little foolish not making the connection earlier.

"You're absolutely right, Yakov."

"I would do anything for Antonina." He nodded once. "Do svidaniya, Jamie."

"Later. Thank you for your assistance."

Once he was gone, I locked the door behind him. Jocelyn certainly had him under her spell. I wondered if he was the only one. Yakov had given me a lot to think about. His visit, right on the heels of my conversation with Sheldon Delaney, was causing my head to spin. I needed a break.

I rolled my desk chair over to sculptures. If there was a better way to clear my head, I hadn't found it yet. Well, unless Malone was around. His presence could always chase any issues from my mind. But that kind of distraction wasn't an option here.

Some people talk to themselves. I've heard they have the best conversations that way. Linda admits to doing this periodically, claiming it's therapeutic. She also claims to be the smartest person she knows, which means her conversations are always intelligent. I think she's just messing with my mind. But who is going to argue a point like that with their best friend?

Contemplating *Grace* got me wondering if there was a person Peter could bounce ideas around with. What would he think of my work? Would he be comfortable talking with me? Would Peter encourage me to keep digging? Or would he tell me to leave it alone?

With the discovery of the studio and the storage room, we also found seven journals Peter had kept. Each one was from a year of my young life. They were filled with stories, ideas and comments from moments we'd experienced together. Peter also included drawings and comments he wanted to share with me. It was a way to connect with him. More than once, reading those memories brought me to laughter or tears. Little memories that hovered in the clouds of my mind. I'd shared a few with Vera. She'd laughed, and cried too.

His work was another way to reconnect. I moved to *The Lovers*, a sandstone carving that I'd learned from his files had given him fits while he tried to coax the shape to life. Gently, I ran a finger along the work. Taking this time-out was helping. While I might not be speaking aloud to my father, it felt as if we were talking. Slowly, I worked my way around the studio. At one point I kicked the chair back to the desk and walked around. By the time I'd completed a second loop, my head was clear. I knew what to do. Time to get back to work.

"Thank you, Daddy."

***

Wednesday was supposed to be a quiet, uneventful day. This would be Ian's second tutoring session with Erica Morehouse. Since I was going to pick up the kid from school at noon, I decided to take care of some household chores during the morning. That included laundry, cleaning the kitchen and running a dust mop over the hardwood floors. Which somehow led to a brief session of wrestling with Malone as he was about to go meet a friend for a workout before his shift.

"Malone, are you telling me that my efforts to elevate your heart rate aren't sufficient to ensuring your good health?"

He chuckled and shook his head. "You know how to get my heart racing. But there are other aspects required for a full-body workout."

"Maybe you need to rethink your routine," I teased from the doorway.

He was sitting on the side of the bed, wearing sweatpants and a T shirt. He had been about to reach for his tennis shoes. Now Malone flashed me a wicked smile. Before I could move, he was off the bed, lifting me off my feet.

"Malone!"

"Hold still. I'm going to do a set of curls with you horizontally across my arms." He shifted his grip. One arm was beneath my knees. The other was under my shoulder blades.

"Don't drop me!" I started to reach for his neck.

"Keep your arms at your sides, Jay." He turned around now so that he was holding me over the bed.

Slowly he did a curl, rolling me in his arms as if his hands were reaching for his shoulders. To my amazement, Malone was able to do this twice. I'm slender, but no delicate ninety-pound Barbie doll. I struggled to keep my arms at my sides as he instructed. On the third curl, Malone dipped his head and kissed my stomach through my shirt. Then he released me, dropping me onto the mattress from shoulder height. I bounced, laughing in delight.

"We've just created a new exercise." He fell on the bed beside me.

"What are you going to call it?"

He gave it some thought. "Curling the vixen."

"I'm a vixen?"

Malone nodded. There were some serious sparks going on in his eyes.

"Hope that's one you're only going to do at home."

"Only with you, Jamie." He gave me a kiss that got my heart racing, then slid off the bed. "I gotta run."

"Sure, leave me all hot and bothered," I muttered.

Malone grabbed his shoes and went out the door. "To be continued."

"It damn well better be."

***

172

I packed my laptop in the case. Malone had already loaded the cooler with lunch in my car. As I reached for my purse, Erica called.

"I know we're supposed to work until five, but something has come up with one of my kids," she said after exchanging greetings. "I hate to cut it short, but I'd have to leave by three."

"That's fine. Even two hours of instruction for Ian is better than nothing. Is everything okay?"

She blew out a breath in frustration. "Yes. Now I have a meeting at the school with the principal at four. Apparently my ten-year-old son has professed his undying love to a girl in his class."

"At ten!"

"He's been acting strangely lately. I couldn't figure out what was going on. He's a lovesick puppy lately. Now I know why."

"If traffic's not bad, we should be at the studio by twelve-thirty."

"Great. Then we can start early. Thanks for being so flexible, Jamie."

Ian was waiting in the office. I signed him out and once we were in the car, explained about Erica's minor change in plans.

"So we'll leave the studio when Erica does and I'll drop you at home."

"I could go back to your house and stop by and surprise Brittany," he said.

With the abbreviated lesson, I had time to pursue something that had been bouncing around my brain for a couple of days now. "Not today, kid. Besides, you're going to see her Saturday."

He was about to try and work on my good side, but something about my expression or demeanor must have gotten through that I wasn't changing my mind.

"Well, at least I got out of school early. And I want to show Erica what I've been working on."

I hooked a thumb over my shoulder. "Malone sent some goodies. For both of us. But if you're not hungry…"

"Jamie, I'm always hungry!"

He pivoted around when I caught a red light. I could hear him rummage in the cooler. Ian spun back around with a sandwich wrapped in waxed paper and a hard-boiled egg in a plastic bag. "Roast beef with some kind of cheese and a white sauce on a Kaiser roll." He took a huge bite of the sandwich, and his eyes went big.

"Oh, that might be horseradish sauce and pepper Jack cheese. The combination can be a little strong."

Ian fumbled a water bottle from his backpack and drank half of it. "Now you tell me," he said when he could breathe and talk.

"Next time, take smaller bites."

We made good time getting to the studio. Erica was in the lot. Once we got inside, she had Ian set up an easel and instructed him to do a rough pencil sketch of any one of Peter's sculptures. I was just booting up the computer when she approached. Erica had a small bundle in her hands.

"Remember how I said being around all these treasures might inspire me?"

I nodded. "Has the same effect on me."

"I've had this in my workroom forever. But lately I kept thinking it needed my attention. I'm a painter, but every once in a while, I'll dabble with something different. No idea where I picked this up, or what I was going to do with it. Until last week."

Erica extended the small bundle to me. It was heavy, about the size of a baseball, and wrapped in a thick, cotton cloth.

"Go ahead."

I swiveled my chair so my hands were above the desk. Carefully I began to unwrap it. Inside the cloth was a shiny black sphere. There was an oblong-shaped hole in the center. Afraid that my klutz genes might kick in at any moment, I set it down gently on the cloth.

"I've never seen anything like this. What is it?"

Erica reached over and ran a fingertip across it. "Black obsidian crystal. It's volcanic rock. It was solid when I got it. Just a great big chunk. But after looking at these sculptures and the pictures I took, drilling the hole made sense. Then it was a matter of shaping, polishing it and smoothing out the rough edges."

"That's slick," Ian said, appearing beside her.

"It's gorgeous," I said.

Erica smiled at the compliment. "My husband said I can be like a carpenter, looking at a pile of lumber and letting the wood tell me what to do with it." Then she surprised me. "I want you to have that, Jamie."

"I couldn't possibly take it." I didn't want to insult her, but this was too generous by far.

"If you hadn't brought me on to work with Ian, I would never have seen Peter's work up close. That provided a psychic, swift kick in the ass to get me working on art again."

I kept glancing back and forth from the sculpture to Erica. She was serious. I was about to make an offer to pay her for it when Ian came through.

"What do you call it?" he asked.

She winked at him. "*Possibility*."

"That's perfect! We could just put it on display, like with Peter's work. It's still yours, Erica. It's just on loan from your collection. We can set it up over here, where it gets a lot of natural light," he said.

Delicately, he scooped up the sphere and carried it over to a spot near his table. Malone had installed a stereo speaker in each of the four corners of the studio. Ian went right to one of them. He arranged the cloth around it as a base, then rested the orb on it.

"That's perfect," Erica said. She was beaming a wide smile at both of us.

"I'll bet Malone can make a little wooden cradle for it," I said.

"I'd like that," Erica said. Satisfied that her gift had been well received, she turned to Ian. "C'mon, Rembrandt, let's see what you've got so far."

He took her over to the easel. From one of the drawers on his worktable, Ian had pulled a copy of the program from September's showing of the collection. He'd opened it to the page where *Fleeing Beauty* was pictured. That was without a doubt his favorite piece. He and Erica bent over his sketch. Slowly, she began to compare it to the photo.

I'd behaved yesterday. After the visit from Yakov, I updated all of my notes and transcribed the meeting with Delaney. Then I was able to focus on the book for three straight hours. Peter would have been proud of my dedication. I went back to my computer and pulled up the file on the nonprofits. A quick review was in order. Once I dropped Ian back at his house, I'd have just enough time to put my plan into action.

CHAPTER EIGHTEEN

Malone would have my ass if he knew what I was up to, and not in a pleasant or romantically satisfying way. Aldis had let slip which days she worked at the K-9 True Companion office so here I was, camped out with a good view of the primary entrance for the building. It was my hope that Aldis wouldn't go straight home, but if she did, I could confront her there.

Twenty-five minutes after selecting my spot, I saw not only Aldis exiting the building but also Carleen Barnett, the less-than-friendly development director I'd met last week. She didn't walk out so much as march, leaving the younger woman far behind. Aldis went to an old Chevy sedan and headed out. I let one car get between us and followed.

Aldis drove a few miles north on Telegraph Road, then headed east on Big Beaver. It was easy to tail her. She didn't speed or swerve about. I doubted she even looked in the mirror. After crossing into the city of Troy, Aldis signaled and entered the parking lot for The Somerset Collection. This upscale mall caters to the affluent, and those who want to be. She parked not far from the north entrance. I found a spot a couple of rows back and followed her inside.

Aldis went into a jewelry store and chatted briefly with

the manager. She handed over an envelope and picked up a gift bag. No money changed hands unless there was cash in that envelope. Curiouser and curiouser. Aldis tucked the gift bag into her purse and draped it over her shoulder. This purse was large enough it could have doubled as a backpack or an overnight bag. There was nothing stylish about it. Time to make my move.

I slowed my stride, arriving just at the entrance to the store as Aldis was coming out. Her eyes were down, watching how she placed her feet. I was struck again with the idea of balance issues to offset her sizeable chest.

"Hey, you're that girl from the animal place," I said, easing to a stop in front of her. Aldis looked a little surprised as she ground to a halt.

"I remember you, but I can't place your name," she said.

"It's Jamie. And you're…Alice?" I put a little uncertainty in my voice.

"Close. I'm Aldis. Do you shop out here very often?"

Time for a little white lie. "I was in the area and wanted to see what shops they have. Maybe grab a bite to eat. Anything you can recommend?"

Aldis gave a little shrug. "I'm not from around here. This is only the second time I've been to the mall. The prices here are way beyond my budget. I just came in to pick up some earrings for the next auction."

"Pricey stuff?"

She looked around to see if anyone was paying attention to us. I gently took her elbow and guided her to a bench a few spaces down from the jewelry store. Once seated, Aldis gave me a conspiratorial wink and dug the gift bag out of her purse. She opened the little box and turned it to catch the light. My breath caught in my throat.

"These are heart-shaped ruby and diamond earrings with a swirl drop style," Aldis said a little breathlessly. "This pair retails for around $1,800."

"Holy shit!"

"Exactly what I thought." She giggled. With a snap, she

closed the case and tucked it back in the gift bag. Then she returned the bag to her purse.

"K-9 True Companion is going to auction those off?"

Aldis nodded. "Ms. Barnett was supposed to pick these up earlier today. They want to get some photos done, so they can put these on the website as a big-ticket item for the auction. The plan is to have another fundraiser just after Thanksgiving, so they can get as much of the end-of-the-year contributions as possible. But she got tied up and told me to come get them."

"So do you get to take them home for the evening?"

"Yes. I don't normally work there tomorrow, but I can stop by to drop them off. I'll probably sleep with them under my pillow to make sure they're safe."

I looked around the mall. No one was paying any attention to us. I got the sense that Aldis didn't have many friends. Time to play a hunch.

"I'd bet those earrings would look sensational on you," I whispered.

Her eyes went big. "I couldn't possibly wear them! I'm clumsy. With my luck, I'd lose one down a drain." But I could tell the idea appealed to her.

"Come on. I'll help you."

There was a pub right near the entrance we'd used. I matched my stride with hers and guided Aldis inside. We got a booth near the back. It took very little persuasion to get her this far.

"Let's order some food. My treat," I said. "Unless you have dinner plans."

She shook her head. "No, I was going to make some ramen and watch an old movie. That was going to be the highlight of my evening."

We ordered an appetizer sampler. Aldis asked for a Cosmopolitan. She had to show her ID. I stuck with tonic water. Once the order was placed, I crooked a finger at her. "Bring the goodies."

She followed me into the ladies' room. I'd noticed earlier

that she wore a pair of little studs in her lobes. They may have been diamond chips, but I doubted it. I pulled a wad of paper towels from the dispenser and plugged the sink. Aldis giggled nervously but she tugged the gift bag out. I opened the little box and waited while she removed the stud from her left ear. She placed that on the counter, then carefully removed the ruby-and-diamond beauty.

"I can't believe I'm doing this," Aldis whispered.

"Why not? A pretty girl should have pretty things."

She ignored my comment and slipped the earring into place. Her gaze locked on the mirror. The harsh bathroom light made the jewels sparkle. Aldis was speechless. She turned her head to the side and swept back her hair so it wouldn't obscure the view.

"Wow. I mean…wow!"

"You should put the other one on too," I said.

There was a nanosecond of hesitation before she began removing the stud from her right ear. Carefully, Aldis hooked the other earring in place. Then she slowly turned back and forth at the waist, catching glimpses of the jewels dangling toward her neck. Tremors of excitement danced through her. After a minute or two, she blew out a breath.

"Maybe someday." She began to remove the one in her right ear. And what she said floored me.

"Your turn. These would look even better on you, with your hair color and complexion." Aldis extended the jewelry in my direction. Her face was aglow. How could I refuse?

I was wearing a pair of small, gold hoops. My fingers shook a little as I removed them and put the rubies in place. I never thought of myself as a material girl, but right then, that pair of earrings looked like they were exactly where they belonged. I gulped in surprise at how much I suddenly wanted them.

"I was right," Aldis said happily. "Those look perfect on you!"

"These are great. But we'd better return them to their velvet-lined box."

Reluctantly, I removed the earrings and we dutifully put them away. When we got back to our table, the appetizer sampler arrived. Aldis took a gulp of her cocktail and began to attack the Buffalo wings as if she hadn't eaten in a month. I opted for the chips and guacamole.

"We can order more if you want," I said.

"It's been a while since breakfast."

"Don't you get a lunch break?"

Aldis nodded. "I had just enough time to go to the coffee shop next door for a latte and a muffin."

"That's not enough to get you through the day."

She shrugged. "Some days are better. There was just a lot to do this afternoon and Ms. Barnett doesn't like it when I dawdle." Aldis giggled. "Dawdle. That's her word for me. I don't think she likes me much."

"I only met her that one time. But she didn't strike me as the friendliest person on the planet."

"She almost expects me to run." Aldis had a chicken drumstick in her right hand, with smears of sauce on her chin. Then she tilted her head down so her eyes were on her breasts. "That's not going to happen. I'd end up with black eyes! Or maybe a concussion!"

I had to clap my hand over my mouth to try and keep the laughter in. But it was pointless. Aldis dropped the drumstick on her plate, wiped her face and took another gulp of the Cosmopolitan. She was beyond giggling. The image she was describing was hilarious.

"Talk about unrealistic expectations," I said when the laughter subsided.

Aldis smiled at me. "A year ago, I could have run circles around that old cow. But my boyfriend kept pestering me to get the enhancement. He even paid for it. I just never expected them to be so...gigantic!"

I fumbled for a response. "That must have been quite an adjustment."

She speared a coconut shrimp and bit off a chunk. Aldis danced back and forth in her seat while she enjoyed it. I had a little more guacamole. As the waiter passed by, I ordered another round of drinks.

"This food is so good. I can't remember the last time I went to a place like this," Aldis said. Her face took on a dreamy look.

"Doesn't your boyfriend take you out to dinner and such?"

She gave me a negative shake. "We kind of keep things quiet. Mostly stay in at my place when we get together."

"I don't mean to pry." *In case you're keeping score, that's another little white lie.*

"It's no big deal. Kind of nice to have someone to talk to," Aldis said. "Mostly the only people I see are the ones I work with. And they're not all that social, since I'm just an 'occasional worker.'" She made little air quotes with her fingers when she said that part.

"Like Ms. Barnett," I said.

Aldis started to giggle again. "Yes, exactly like her. The other place I'm working at is with a bunch of church ladies. Old and wrinkled and smelling of cornstarch. They're probably whispering about me when I'm not there."

"No friends or family you can hang out with?"

She tried the chips and guacamole. "No. I'm not from around here. Just moved to town when my boyfriend talked me into it. That was right after he convinced me to have the boob job."

"There's a lot to see and do in Motown. Surely there's something you're interested in doing more than just hanging around at home," I said.

Aldis gave me a little shrug. "I've never been in a big city like this before. I grew up in a small, rural area of Indiana. Farm country. All I ever wanted to do was get away from pigs and chickens. And all the shit that goes with them."

"I try to avoid the chickenshit myself."

"Jamie!" She sputtered with laughter. "I'm going to use that line someday."

"Be my guest."

I was trying to think of a way to steer the conversation back to her job when Aldis did it for me.

"All I really do is work and stay around the apartment. That, and grocery shopping. Donnie likes it when I cook for him. That was one thing my mama taught me to do."

"At least you can cook. I'm a disaster in the kitchen."

"I'm no chef," Aldis said. "Just a few simple dishes from home."

I smiled at that image. "My mother wasn't much for cooking either. Whenever I offer to cook for my guy, he finds a way to change the subject."

"Are we still talking about food?" She had a silly grin on her face.

"Yes…well, mostly." It was my turn for a grin. Aldis was a sweet young woman, and I was finding it easy to like her.

The food was gone. Aldis pushed her plate away and used some extra napkins to wipe her fingers and face. She surprised me again with a serious question.

"Jamie, do you live with your guy?"

"Yes, for quite a while now. How about you?"

She gave her head a negative shake. "No. I only get to see Donnie a few nights a week. Sometimes he surprises me and just stops by. That's why I hang around the apartment most of the time."

Warning bells were sounding in my skull. This didn't sound good. "He shouldn't be upset if you went out. It doesn't sound like you two are exclusive."

"Well, he likes to think we are."

"There's more to life than work," I said. "However did you start working for Delaney and Associates?"

Aldis leaned back and gave me a sad smile. "Donnie set it up. There are so many companies looking for people right now, I could probably get a full-time job somewhere else. But since he spent all that money on my," she paused to roll her eyes, "enhancements, I just wanted to make him happy. Working there seemed to make sense."

The waiter stopped by to see if we needed anything else.

He had the audacity to bring a tray of desserts, which he dangled just above the table. This guy was good at his job.

"I couldn't possibly," Aldis said, although her gaze was locked on a thick slice of double chocolate torte. There was a drizzle of raspberry ganache across the top. It looked completely decadent.

"My treat," I reminded her.

With some effort she shifted her gaze to me. "Split it?"

"Well, if you insist."

"Oh yes, I insist!"

The waiter winked at me and hustled away. He came back a minute later with clean forks and two plates, each bearing half a slice of the torte. It took all my willpower to savor every tiny bite. I was tempted to ask for a glass of milk to wash it down. Aldis matched my pace and took her time with the dessert.

"Jamie, I've never been treated to such a great time."

"We'll have to do it again sometime."

"I'd really like that."

The restaurant was filling up with the dinner crowd. Time for us to go. We traded phone numbers while I paid the bill. I walked Aldis to her car.

"Take care of those earrings," I said.

She nodded. "Right beneath my pillow. Although I might have to put them on and take a selfie or two."

"You could show that to your boyfriend. Maybe he'll buy them for you."

Aldis shook her head. "I don't think he would like that. I'll just keep the picture for myself."

"You could always send it to me."

"I might do that. Thanks again, Jamie. This was fun."

"For me too."

Aldis stepped close and gave me a hug. This was a lonely girl who had just enjoyed a night out. Hopefully her boyfriend hadn't chosen tonight to stop by, while she was out. I waved as she drove away, and headed for my car.

During the drive home, I worked out the details from

our conversation. Whoever her boyfriend was, he was very controlling. The guy expected her to be at the apartment whenever he stopped by. And they didn't live together. Which seemed odd to me, especially if he was either paying for it or helping her with the rent. Unless the guy was married.

That could explain a lot.

CHAPTER NINETEEN

Friday afternoon was all about work. It had taken some effort, but I had diligently pushed any thoughts out of my head other than the current book. Scenes were starting to come together nicely. I'd just written an exchange of dialogue between my two main characters that flowed well. A little bit of sass, a bit of charm and a few flirtatious comments were traded. It felt right. I leaned back to savor it when my phone dinged with a reminder. Shit! I'd gotten so caught up in the writing that I nearly forgot to pick up Ian. I saved my work and headed out.

This was a little variation in the schedule. Originally Ian was going to be coming over Saturday, since he and Brittany were attending the Halloween dance at her school. That was before the kids realized there was a home football game Friday night at Ian's school. Brittany wanted to go. It took less than half an hour for her to persuade her parents to drive them to and from the game. Ian charmed Terri into getting permission to spend the night here. And he got Malone's approval as well. I willingly agreed. The kid is fun to have around.

Malone had been off work on Thursday, and he convinced me to take a "mental health" day. That resulted in our lounging about, going out for a leisurely brunch, wandering through the Edward Hines Park. It was a beautiful, relaxing day. It was a welcome change of pace, a day without any plans or pressures. Now it was up to me to grab the kid and bring him home.

He gave me a goofy grin as he climbed into the car. "Jamie, we need to make a little detour."

"What am I, your personal Uber driver?" Briefly, I faked a scowl.

"We just gotta swing by the house. I need to get my costume for tomorrow night's dance."

Now we were talking. "So that means I get to see it."

"Not a chance. Even my mom hasn't seen it yet. It will only take me a minute to grab it."

"Then your costume will be in your room while you guys are at the game."

His face went pale. "Please don't go peeking at it. Will you promise me that you won't look?"

"It is my house. Legally, I should be able to inspect any part of the house at any time, just to make sure there is nothing in the contents that would cause me any concerns or problems." Malone was right. I did enjoy messing with the kid.

"But it's a secret. And we want it to be a surprise! Besides, you won't get the whole effect until Britt's in her costume and she's there with me," Ian grumbled. Then he gave me that defeated, sad-puppy look. "I guess Mom could bring it over tomorrow, but she might forget part of it."

I rolled to a stop at a red light, reached over and messed up his hair. "Someday, kid, you're going to learn how to tell when I'm just giving you shit."

He slumped back in his seat. "Between you and Malone, I'm getting frequent lessons in that."

"So it should be easier to recognize when it's happening."

I waited in the car while he ran inside. Ian came back out with a garment bag and a big duffle. He carefully used the hangers sticking out of the garment bag to arrange it from the hook in the rear seat. Back at my place, that was the first thing he got out of the car and carried directly to his room. The kid didn't even stop to raid the refrigerator. That alone told me how seriously he was taking this. Tomorrow night was going to be special.

"Did I tell you that the Murphys invited me to dinner too?" Ian was hovering in the doorway to my office. He seemed to have relaxed a bit once he'd safely brought everything into his room.

"They are going to go broke feeding you."

"It was Mrs. Murphy's idea. Turkey burgers and salads tonight. Originally, I was just going to meet Britt at the game, but she talked her parents into doing the driving. One thing led to another and now, I get free dinner. I did buy the tickets."

I nodded. "That's good. And who paid for tomorrow's dance?"

"We split the cost. I've been saving up my allowance. And I still have some of the money I earned working for you during the summer."

My phone buzzed. Linda was calling. I shooed the kid away and answered.

"Are we still on for dinner?" she asked.

"Yes, indeed. Are you cooking another fabulous meal?"

She laughed heartily. "After five days of teaching, you'd be lucky to get peanut butter and jelly out of me. How about sushi? There's that place near my house. And we could go to the football game after."

"*You* want to go to the game?"

"I do go occasionally to show my support for the students. Besides, you told me last night about Romeo and Juliet manipulating the adults to fulfill their wishes. If we go to the game, we might just be able to keep an eye on them."

I considered that. "And I could bring the kids home afterwards and save the Murphy family a trip."

"You're such a thoughtful big sister," she said with a

laugh.

"That makes you the honorary auntie."

Linda made a rude noise. "Dress warmly. I'll see you shortly."

***

We had dinner at Shiro, a wonderful Japanese restaurant in Novi. It was early so we had no trouble getting seated and served quickly. The food and service were excellent.

"That sure beats the hell out of peanut butter and jelly," I said as we headed for the school.

"Actually, I'm out of jelly. Vince must have used the last of it this morning…on his toast."

I threw her a playful look. "Are you sure that's what he put it on? You always have strawberry preserves in the fridge."

"I'm not going to dignify that with an answer." Linda sat primly on the passenger seat, hands folded in her lap. But I could see little quivers at her mouth as she struggled to hold in the laughter.

"Whatever you say, Little Miss Innocent."

"That's Ms. Innocent to you." She adeptly changed the subject. "Did you set up a place to meet the kids after the game?"

"Yes, by the flagpole. Got the binoculars?"

"Of course. But those are meant for watching the game, not spying on Romeo and Juliet."

"I have no intention of spying on them. It's just possible that while I'm following the action on the field, I might happen upon them."

Linda giggled. "Just so long as you're not looking for the action in the stands. The kids will behave themselves."

We parked, and joined the crowd headed for the field. On the other side of the lot, a long stream of cars surrounded three buses from the Canton school system. It looked like they would be filling up the bleachers on their side of the field. Linda tugged a knit cap over her curls. We were bundled up in outdoor boots, jeans and heavy winter coats. I had a thick woolen scarf around my neck and a black knit cap on as well. The temperature was dropping rapidly. There was a little wind, but it wasn't strong enough to worry about.

"Think you can even spot the kids in this crowd?" I asked.

"If they're dressed for the cold as we are, all you might see are their noses."

Linda guided me to a section near the center of the stands, right about the fifty-yard line and halfway up. She greeted several other faculty members and school employees. Linda had been teaching here for almost a decade now and has always been well liked. She's also respected for her abilities to keep the students interested in the material.

My phone buzzed. Peeling off my gloves, I dug it out of my pocket.

"Trouble?" she asked.

"Just a text from Ian. He and Brittany spotted us. They're three rows from the field, on the right, about the twenty-five."

We both looked in that direction. The kids were standing up, facing us, waving their arms. I stood and waved back. Satisfied that the connection had been made, we all settled in to get ready for the game.

"You don't really think they're going to fool around here in the middle of the crowd, do you?" Linda asked.

I recalled Brittany's comments from our trip to the studio before Ian's birthday. She was more than capable of taking care of herself. I also believed that Ian was not the type of guy to try and push things. Malone would be reinforcing the concept of treating Brittany and any of the women in his life with respect. Brittany was not a timid little mouse, either. I relayed all of this to Linda.

"She's a brave, smart and beautiful young woman,"

Linda said. "I get the impression that if any guy tries something she's not ready for or agreeable to, she'll knock him on his ass."

"That probably comes from having two younger siblings. And caring parents. Brittany told me while they encourage her to participate in sports, they also have enrolled her in self-defense classes, since she was ten years old."

Linda nodded in agreement. "That's a smart move by her parents. Raising the awareness of the kids is a good idea. With any luck, she'll never have to use those skills."

"Still, it's good to know. Trouble doesn't always give you advance notice."

"Says the redheaded magnet for trouble." Linda wrapped me up in a quick embrace. "I'm just thankful that you don't turn your back whenever you see trouble brewing."

"Don't get soft and sentimental on me. Let's watch the game."

She released me and turned her attention to the field. But I noticed she wiped a few tears away with the back of her glove. Linda had come a long way in the six months since being kidnapped. I knew she occasionally had flashbacks of being held captive. Therapy was helping. And she had the support of those who love her. I considered her earlier comment about Brittany.

I leaned close to her ear, so she could hear me over the growing noise of the crowd as the game began. "You are a brave, smart and beautiful woman. You always have been."

Linda faced me. "Damn right! I learned it from you."

"I thought you taught me that."

"You are my best friend. You have been since we were seven years old." She leaned close, rested her forehead against mine. "I have loved you for every minute since we met. And I always will. You saved my life, Jamie. You are my life."

"That's what best friends are for." We both had tears

flowing now. "I love you, Linda. Now shut up and watch the game."

***

Late Saturday afternoon, Terri and Caitlin arrived. Malone was working and made me promise to save him a plate or two of whatever Terri brought for dinner. It took all four of us three trips to bring everything in from her car.

"Is there an army coming to dinner?" I asked, placing a large crock pot on the kitchen counter. She settled a second one on the opposite counter.

Terri popped the lid, gave the contents a quick stir, then covered it and plugged it in. She directed Caitlin to put the salads in the refrigerator, and place two large trays of rolls in the oven on low heat to warm them.

"We're feeding ten. So I wanted to make sure we wouldn't run out," Terri said. "I left the cakes and cookies in the trunk of the car for now."

"That's fine. Wait! What? You said we're feeding ten. What the hell?"

Ian had been standing by the hallway arch with his kid sister. Instinctively he turned, as if to sneak out of the room. He made the mistake of looking over his shoulder at me. I jabbed a forefinger in his direction. That stopped him cold.

Terri looked confused. "Ian told me ten. I thought it was only appropriate that we invite Brittany's family, since he's always mooching meals over there."

"You didn't think it was necessary to mention this to me?" I asked him with a scowl on my face.

"I talked about it with Malone," Ian muttered. "I thought he'd tell you."

"Malone never said bupkis about dinner for ten people. Where is everyone supposed to sit?"

Terri put her hand on my shoulder. "I didn't mean to cause trouble. It was just a way to thank the Murphy family for putting up with him."

I turned just enough so she could see me wink. Malone was right. I truly enjoyed tormenting Ian. It was time to give him a break.

"In the basement is an old kitchen table that Malone had in his apartment. Go down there, wipe it off. Set four chairs around it. There's a stool in the corner. And while you're at it, run a broom over the floor. We'll make that the kids table for dinner."

"I'll help!" Caitlin offered.

Ian's face relaxed and he made as if to hug me. I folded my arms across my chest and glared at him. Sensing my displeasure, he opted to hug his mom, then ran down the stairs with his sister on his heels.

"Malone never said anything?" Terri asked.

"He may have whispered it in my ear while I was sleeping. But I don't recall." I smiled. "It's just another opportunity to tease Ian. I don't mind Brittany's family joining us for dinner. Especially since you made all this food. They really are nice people."

Terri was grinning. "Malone warned me about your badass-big-sister approach with him. I really like that. Ian already takes you two for granted. Malone tries not to spoil him, but he means well."

"We both enjoy having him around. But he needs to be kept in check occasionally," I said. "Does that make us conspirators?"

That earned me a laugh. "It won't hurt him a bit. I'm always a little concerned that he might be getting cocky. After everything you two already do for him, I don't want him to get an attitude."

"Deep down, he's a good kid. That's a reflection on you and his dad."

Terri nodded. For a moment I was afraid that the mention of her late husband would trigger tears or some sadness. But she didn't flinch.

"Don't downplay it, Jamie. Both you and Malone get credit for keeping him grounded. It's good practice if you ever have kids of your own." She flashed me a wide smile. "I heard about the art tutor thinking he was yours."

Now it was my turn to laugh. "That took us all by surprise."

In the basement, the stereo kicked on. I could hear the kids moving about. Terri and I sat at the top of the stairs so we could watch them. The table was already set up. Caitlin was standing in front of Ian, slowly moving her hips, swaying to the beat. The kid watched her for a minute, then began to mimic her moves. There may be hope for Brittany's toes yet.

CHAPTER TWENTY

Dinner was a casual feast. Terri had made two gigantic crocks of spaghetti sauce, packed with mushrooms, peppers, slices of Italian sausage and homemade meatballs. There was plenty of pasta as well. Ian and Caitlin took a bowl of salad and a platter of rolls down to the basement for the kids. Tom and Bridget Murphy joined us in the kitchen, enjoying Terri's cooking. After dinner, there was a mad scramble as Brittany and her mother ran home so she could get into her costume. Caitlin went along to help.

Ian dashed into his room. Terri and I cleaned up the kitchen while Tom monitored his younger children shooting pool. I didn't have any video games or toys to keep them otherwise occupied.

"Do you know what the costumes are?" I asked.

"Not a clue. Ian has been very secretive about it. I could make a guess, but it's nothing more than that."

"Is there a particular theme for the dance?"

Terri shrugged and smiled. "Halloween. So just about anything could be on the table. I suggested Raggedy Ann and Andy."

"How'd that go over?" I couldn't help but laugh at the image of Ian in that type of getup.

"Not well."

We were enjoying mugs of tea in the living room when the girls returned. Brittany was bundled up in a long winter coat that draped to her ankles. A large hood covered her hair. Ian had been camped out in his room the entire time. Caitlin ran down the hall and banged on his door. There were some excited whispers traded back and forth. Caitlin returned, grabbed Brittany by the arm and led her to the bedroom. By now Tom, Bridget and the other kids had joined Terri and me in the living room. Everyone was chatting with guesses on the costumes.

Caitlin appeared, hands folded together, and stood perfectly still. As if a switch had been thrown, the room went quiet.

"Good evening, ladies and gentlemen. It is my esteemed pleasure to present Lady Cinderella and His Royal Highness, Prince Charming." Caitlin swept her arm toward the hall like a member of the royal court and gave a little bow.

Ian and Brittany entered. Her hand was on the crook of his arm. The winter coat was gone. She looked radiant, in a dark blue gown that flowed to the floor. The dress was cinched at the waist, to emphasize her figure. Brittany's long, dark hair had been curled and tied up with a red ribbon. Ian looked regal. He was wearing a double-breasted navy jacket, with plenty of medals, ribbons and shoulder epaulets. There was a red sash that ran diagonally across his chest. Hanging from his left hip was a silver scabbard. The plastic handle of a sword was visible. His trousers were tucked into black boots that had been polished to a brilliant shine. White gloves covered his hands.

Together they smiled and nodded at us like royalty from a fairy tale.

"Good evening one and all," Ian said in a deep voice. "It appears our arrival has caused the lady of the house to lose her ability to speak."

"She's not the only one," Caitlin muttered.

That broke the spell. Everyone started talking at once.

Bridget and Terri pulled out their phones and took several pictures of the kids together. Caitlin snagged one of the kitchen chairs and had Brittany perch on the edge of it. She posed Ian beside her, possessively resting one gloved hand on her shoulder.

Terri nudged me toward the kids. I curtsied to Ian. "Your Highness."

"Milady."

Soon the others lined up for pictures. Brittany was glowing at the attention from everyone. She seemed reluctant to leave when Tom declared it was time for him to drive them to the dance. Caitlin helped Brittany with her winter coat. Ian accepted kisses from me, Terri and even Bridget Murphy.

"How did you come up with the idea for the costumes?" I asked him.

"Linda called us that when we went to the exhibit in September," he said. "Brittany thought it would be perfect. It really wasn't that difficult to put the costumes together."

I could only shake my head in wonder. They were too cute for words.

The rest of the Murphy family returned home. Terri, Caitlin and I packed up the empty pots, pans and utensils. They were going home for a mother-daughter movie marathon. There was a sizeable portion of pasta tucked in the fridge for Malone, along with some salad and cake. Hopefully he'd be home before Ian returned. The kid was known to attack any leftovers with a vengeance.

Terri wrapped me up in a hug. "Thank you so much for everything, Jamie."

"It's my pleasure. And the spaghetti was great."

I hugged Caitlin too. In another year she'd be going to dances like this. Terri certainly had her work cut out for her, raising the two kids on her own.

And just like that, the house was empty.

I wandered around for a bit. It was an opportunity to do some work, but I had absolutely no motivation. My office remained dark. The idea of a movie marathon sounded perfect. There was nothing that caught my eye on any of the streaming services. From the cupboard, I dug out a couple of old favorites.

Linda and I have a long, running debate about who did the best portraying James Bond. I ranked them as Sean Connery number one, Pierce Brosnan number two and all the rest at number seventeen. While I didn't have any Bond movies on hand, I had other choices. So I watched *Entrapment* with Connery and followed that up with *The Thomas Crown Affair* with Brosnan.

My subconscious must have been at work. Out of all the films available, I picked two where the storylines were about heists. When I realized that, I recalled my recent conversations with Harrison and Jocelyn Mundy and Yakov. I vowed to put any thoughts of crooks and con men aside for the weekend. I sent Linda some pictures of the kids in their costumes. Malone would be home soon. He wouldn't notice if I snuck a bite from his cake. Would he?

CHAPTER TWENTY-ONE

Sunday evening, I was expecting to curl up on the sofa with Malone and watch the late football game. There was usually some good competition at this point in the season. The networks did their best to find a game that could impact the standings for the playoffs. Late afternoon, Malone drove Ian home. The kid was still floating on air after Saturday night's Halloween dance with Brittany. So I was a little surprised when Linda arrived at the front door with a garment bag dangling from her fingers.

"Jamie, you've got an hour to get ready. Let's go." She kicked the door shut with her boot heel. Her face was full of merriment.

"Get ready for what?"

"Your date! Come on, I've got your dress right here."

I stood in front of her with both hands raised. "Stop! What the hell! What date are you talking about?"

Linda pushed the garment bag into my hands and started toward the bedroom. I had no choice but to back up in that direction.

"Date night. Do you remember a couple of weeks ago when you got dolled up to meet Randy and his mom?"

"Of course. But what—"

"And Malone mentioned that you two should have a date night occasionally, where you get a little glamorous. Remember that?" Linda asked.

"Kind of." I hesitated. "But I don't recall telling you that."

"Psssh. Malone told me. That's when we went shopping." She marched past me into the closet and started digging through my shoe rack.

"Wait a minute. When did you and Malone go shopping?"

Exasperated, she faced me, with her hands on her hips. "Last week. He wanted my advice on a new dress for your date night. One that you could use a few times, like tonight and when you go to Denver. And maybe for Randy's wedding. Now will you stop stalling?"

I was frozen in place. What the hell was going on? She dropped the black high heels on the bed and took the garment bag from me. Linda turned and hung it on the top of the closet door, then slowly unzipped it and drew it off the hanger. Inside was a stunning black dress that would reach mid-calf on me. There was a slit to show off some leg. Dangling from another hanger was a small mesh bag. Linda pulled this free and pressed it into my hands.

"New lingerie for a new dress. I took the liberty of washing them for you."

"What the hell?" I whispered, opening the bag.

"One strapless black bra, one pair of black scanty panties, one pair of thigh-high stockings, nude in color. I was tempted to get a pair in red, but thought that would make a better Christmas present," Linda said.

"This is so unexpected," I said. My voice was still in whisper mode.

Linda gently took my shoulders. "You deserve it. Let me help you get ready. What should we do with your hair? You like that French twist style."

She was like a fairy godmother. Somehow Linda gently coaxed me to get moving. She styled my hair while I fumbled with makeup, perfume, stockings and the gown. It had tiny spaghetti straps on the shoulders and showed a little cleavage. Hence the need for the strapless bra. The bodice was just right for my meager curves. The skirt flared out. The slit was designed to flash most of my left leg, ending a couple of inches above the knee. Linda dug a simple gold chain from my jewelry box. It had a single emerald in a teardrop. The color was almost a perfect match for my eyes.

I was just stepping into the heels when there was a knock on the bedroom doorframe. Malone stood there, resplendent in a new black suit.

"Wow. Linda was right about that dress. Jamie, you're gorgeous."

My face went beet red. "Malone, I can't believe you set this up. I had no idea you were planning a night out." I moved close and planted a tender kiss on his lips. I would have put more into it but didn't want to smear my lip gloss. His tie was a brilliant shade of green. It was the same color as my emerald. There was a look of adoration in his eyes that made my heart beat a little faster.

Linda appeared at his shoulder. She had my wool winter coat and a colorful silk scarf draped over her arm. "I want a picture of you two before you go."

We moved to the living room. Linda took several shots with her phone, beaming a smile at us. Malone helped me on with my coat, kissed her on the cheek and guided me out the door. She promised to lock up.

Malone escorted me to the car. He refused to tell me where we were going. Instead, he lightly held my hand as we cruised toward downtown. The stereo was playing softly, but I couldn't remember a single song.

"I feel like a character in a fairy tale."

"That would be the gorgeous young princess, awaiting the arrival of the hero," Malone said.

"That's twice in a short while that you've called me gorgeous. Better be careful. It might leave a permanent boost on my ego."

Malone exited the freeway and coasted to a stop at the top of the ramp. "You are gorgeous, Jamie. No matter what you're wearing." He leaned in and nuzzled my neck with a kiss. "Or not wearing."

Fearing a smartass comment would pop out of my mouth, I refrained from answering. Malone steered through the light, early evening traffic and pulled into the valet stand at The Whitney. Originally a private mansion for a lumber baron, it had been converted into a restaurant and a bar years ago. Rumor had it that the ghosts of the original owners haunted the bar. This was one of Detroit's longest-standing gourmet restaurants, a landmark that had been around for more than a century. It was a favorite spot for Vince and Linda. I realized Malone and I had never been there. Truth be told, I'd never been here with anyone. Once inside, a young lady took our coats while another guided us to a table in the corner.

It dawned on me that Malone had only prepared light fare for our brunch. If I'd been paying attention, that might have been a clue. Usually he'd have something in the fridge or defrosting on the counter that he'd turn into dinner.

"Malone, did you rob a bank? This isn't a place for a cheeseburger after the game! Look at this menu!" You knew the establishment was ritzy when there was even a notice on the menu that cell phone usage was restricted to the lobby area.

"Relax. Don't look at the prices, look at the options."

"But, Malone, I—"

He reached over and squeezed my hand. "Hush." He had one of those low-voltage smiles going, with just a little spark at the corners of his eyes. Okay, maybe the voltage was a touch higher.

I gave in and studied the menu. It described a four-course meal, with an appetizer trio of shrimp cocktail, bruschetta with tomatoes, and beef tenderloin crostini for starters. Then there were options for the salads, the entrée and of course, dessert. No wonder he hadn't fed me earlier. My head was spinning at the choices. Malone opted for the pan-seared salmon, while I selected the sauteed shrimp and scallops. There was no rush to the meal. We talked about Ian and Brittany and how adorable they'd looked in their costumes for last night's dance. Over coffee, Malone confirmed that his request for the time off for the Denver trip was approved. At length, he paid the bill. The valet got a generous tip for having the heat cranked up when he brought the car.

"Are you enjoying our date night?" he asked.

"Malone, this whole evening is crazy. When we talked about a date night, I pictured wearing a dress from my closet. Not buying a brand-new gown. And the restaurant was over the top. Did you win the lottery?"

"Some people might believe it. But I don't gamble."

I was confused. "But if you don't gamble, how did you win?"

"I won because you're in my life, Jamie. There have been some tense moments, but those are far outweighed by the good times. For a year now."

"A year?"

A year! I'd been worried about it before but had lost track of time, getting wrapped up with Randy's problem and Ian's tutoring lessons and the Halloween Dance and the new book and…well, everything. But Malone knew.

He pulled to the side of the road. "One year ago tonight was our first date. Don't you remember?"

"A year?"

Malone removed his gloves, turned to me, and gently took my face in his hands. "One year ago. We went out to dinner at Dominic's, then went dancing."

"I remember." I valiantly tried to hide the shakiness of my voice. "And you didn't stay the night."

Malone nodded. "Seems to me we picked up on that theme the next day. But some things have changed in a year."

"Were you going to take me dancing tonight?"

"It's an option. There must be a club around here somewhere. Maybe a little jazz or something low key that we can dance to. Something not too crowded."

I leaned across and kissed him. "I know just the place. The perfect place."

He knew exactly what I had in mind. Malone drove to the studio. We ducked inside, turning off the security alarm and the video system. Over in the corner by the desk, he'd installed a compact stereo that could also be synched to my phone, computer, or one of the streaming services. That way, whenever I was here, music was available. He knew that music was an essential part of my life, especially when I was working. Malone removed my winter coat and draped it, along with his, over the chair by the desk.

He turned on a couple of small spotlights while I keyed up the stereo. I selected music from the late 1950s. It was perfect for dancing. He rolled Ian's drafting table and the stools against the wall, freeing up most of the floorspace. As the first song cued up, Malone gently took me into his arms.

"Happy anniversary, Jamie. I love you."

My heart did a little jig. That happened every time he said it. "I love you. Happy anniversary, Malone. I've never been with someone this long. I wasn't sure you'd remember."

He spun me away, then drew me back. "I remember. Just keep in mind that every date night isn't going to be this extravagant."

"My heart couldn't handle this very often. Maybe only once a year."

We swayed together. He guided me into a turn, drew me close again. "I was thinking more along the lines of once a month. But we'll plan it together."

"I can't believe you snuck out and went shopping with Linda. And that she was able to keep it a secret from me."

He chuckled. "Don't think of it as a secret. It was meant to be a surprise. She was a big help, especially with the…lingerie."

"Wait! Were you in the store with her when she bought everything?"

Malone nodded. "We were getting some very curious looks from the salespeople. It didn't take them long to realize the sizes Linda was selecting wouldn't quite fit her."

I spun slowly out of his arms, then let him draw me back again. "You realize that I expect you to go with me, the next time I'm shopping for lingerie. Were you uncomfortable in that kind of shop?"

"Nope." Then he grinned, amping up the voltage of that smile. "Well, maybe just a little bit.

The song ended. As the music faded, the kiss began.

"I think you'd better take this dress for our trip," Malone said quietly.

"Vera has mentioned that there have been some fancy parties at these different museums. She's been thoroughly enjoying herself."

"That's good to know."

I studied him for a bit. "Malone, what's going on? You're certainly full of surprises lately."

"I don't want you to get bored with me. Or start thinking that I take you for granted, Jay."

"That's not going to happen."

"Good to know."

I had no idea how long we danced. Malone guided me through the shadows between the spotlights. He made certain we didn't get close enough to any of the sculptures to bump into them. In some respects, I felt that Peter and his art were watching over us. Based on everything I'd learned about my father recently, it was a sure thing that he would have liked Malone.

He turned me again and drew me close as the song wound down.

A year!

Before the next song started, I snuck a kiss. That one lasted at least three minutes, since the song played all the way through before we started dancing again. How was this possible? I'd found a guy willing to put up with all aspects of my craziness, for a whole year. We kept dancing.

At some point later, Malone guided me to the corner where the stereo was. "Think it's time to take you home, gorgeous."

"This has been quite a way to celebrate our year together," I whispered in his ear, my arms around his neck.

"Seemed appropriate. Wanna try for two years?"

"Oh yeah."

We were quiet on the way home, lost in our own thoughts. It was after two in the morning. Malone lightly held my hand. I was able to lean over and rest my head on his shoulder. How was it possible that I'd become so comfortable with him? I couldn't imagine what my life would be like right now without Malone. If he wasn't around, there'd be no Ian. Or Brittany. Or Terri. Or Caitlin.

A year.

Back home, we still weren't talking. At least not verbally. But somehow, we were able to communicate. I think it showed a great deal of restraint on both our parts that we took the time to slowly undress and hang up our clothes before we crawled under the covers.

A year.

CHAPTER TWENTY-TWO

Usually, Malone's schedule gives him two days off in a row. I learned that in order to get Sunday night off to celebrate our anniversary, he'd been trading shifts with other sergeants. That meant he was on the job Monday. So after a morning spent leisurely in each other's arms, I had the late afternoon and evening free. I tried to focus on the new book but couldn't settle down. Nervous energy was flowing. Thought about doing some research, but no subject jumped out at me. I wandered around the house for a bit. Nothing was clicking. What's a girl to do?

Inspiration struck. I grabbed my phone and sent a text. Within a minute I had a response. After last night's glamorous ensemble, I was back in my usual attire of jeans, boots and a sweater. With the end of October, it was getting colder by the minute. Donning a heavy jacket and gloves, I locked up the house and headed out.

Traffic was thick. I hadn't realized it was almost five o'clock and the sun was already dropping low. Knowing the freeways would soon resemble a parking lot, I cut across on the main streets and soon got to Haggerty Road. This highway usually ran like a race track this time of day. I zoomed along with the commuters. Using my mad driving skills, I pulled into the parking lot of Antonio's Cucina Italiana with five minutes to spare.

Aldis was already there, so I parked beside her car. The wind had kicked up today, so we hustled inside where it was warm and cozy.

"This is a great surprise," she said. "I was thinking about picking up one of those discount pizzas on the way home. I'm sure the food here is a thousand times better and probably doesn't taste like cardboard."

"There's a full menu. And the pizza here is excellent. C'mon, let's get a table," I said.

The hostess guided us to a spot away from the door. We settled in. As if by magic, the waitress appeared. "Can I start you off with a glass of wine? Or maybe a bottle?"

"Have a glass if you'd like," I told Aldis.

"You don't mind? I noticed you didn't drink the other night."

"It's fine." I ordered a Diet Coke. Aldis opted for a glass of white wine.

"This looks like a great place. Do you come here often?"

"I've been here a few times. The food and the atmosphere are good. I skipped lunch. We can order some stuffed mushrooms for a starter, then take our time and look over the menu."

Aldis nodded in agreement. After the waitress returned with our drinks, I leaned back and studied Aldis closely. She fidgeted a little then lowered her eyes. I waited until she took a sip of her wine.

"Did you try those earrings on again?"

She burst out laughing. "How did you know?"

"Because it's the same thing I would have done."

Aldis pulled the phone from her purse and showed me a couple of selfies she'd taken while wearing those jewels. Her hair had been pulled back into a twist, so her neck was bare. "I haven't showed these to anyone. Just in case it would cause some trouble."

"And you returned them safely to their little, special

box?"

"Yes. That went right under my pillow all night. Then I was a good little worker bee and delivered them to the K-9 office Friday morning."

"Did your boyfriend get a chance to see them?" I asked.

Aldis shook her head. "No. He didn't call or stop by until yesterday. Donnie has been busy with work. I cooked dinner and we got to spend some time together."

"Why didn't you show him the pictures?"

"Donnie wouldn't like it. He wasn't thrilled when I had the tips of my hair dyed. Fortunately, it's almost all grown out. He likes me just the way I am." Her eyes dropped to her chest. "He liked me before, but says he likes me even better with the larger boobs."

I bit my tongue. The guy sounded pretty shallow to me. Aldis was a cute girl. She had nice facial features and soft, brown eyes. I'd known a few guys in the past who'd made comments about my small bust. If they only considered the size of a woman's chest to determine their beauty or worth, then I would never waste my time with them.

"Not all guys are obsessed with big boobs," I said.

Aldis gave a little shrug. "Wish I had your self-confidence. I'm guessing your man never tried talking you into something like that."

"You guessed right," I said. Thoughts of Malone's attentiveness to my body made me smile. "He likes my body just the way it is."

The appetizer arrived and we wasted no time making the mushrooms disappear. They were stuffed with shrimp and crab meat then topped with melted provolone cheese. Heavenly! Aldis convinced me to split a real pizza with her. We ordered the house special, which included cheese, pepperoni, mushrooms, ham, green peppers, bacon, onions *and* Italian sausage.

"Did you have a good day at work?" I asked.

"Mondays are always busy. The K-9 company gets a lot of mail over the weekends. Part of my job is to go through all the envelopes, open them, and separate the checks or credit card information. Then I'm supposed to process them and get the deposits ready. They have a form letter ready, so all I have to do is enter the name and address of the people who sent in the money."

"Did they train you how to do that?"

Aldis shook her head. "A little bit. But Jillian showed me how to work the devices for the credit cards. And how to enter the information into the databases."

"Devices? Is there more than one you use?" My Spider-Gwen senses were tingling big time. This must be part of Jillian Hess's duties as the Strategic Planning Officer. Some strategy!

"Sure. I use one on this tablet for K 9. There's another one that is hooked to my phone."

"Sounds like a duplication of work," I said.

Aldis nodded in agreement. "See, I always thought so too. Jillian said it's part of the service they provide. It's a way of monitoring the activity the business does, so they can make recommendations for improvements."

"Really? How does that work?"

"Well, the big donations, anything over $200, goes through the tablet if it's on a credit card. The smaller ones go to my phone. It's on a separate account, so Jillian can track it."

While I considered this, the pizza arrived. The waitress brought me another Diet Coke. Aldis ordered one too. Maybe the wine didn't agree with her. When the waitress left, I was ready with questions.

"Do people mail in their credit card information? That seems risky nowadays."

"The mail brings in checks. But they do get some people who use the K-9 website to make a donation and give all their credit card information there," Aldis said. She dug into a slice of pizza and rolled her eyes in happiness.

"That makes more sense. So then you use the tablet to process that donation on their credit card."

"Yes. I print those out so there's no problem with the numbers. Then I manually enter in the card numbers and the amount. I just do a squiggle for the person's signature, and it's done."

"A squiggle?"

Aldis extended her forefinger and waved it in the air, making a loop with a flourish. "A squiggle."

"That sounds easy."

"It is. Once Jillian showed me how. The first couple of times I was very nervous. Since then, it's been fun."

"So most of your job is processing the donations," I said.

"That's what I do first thing each morning. Then I log all the information into those two spreadsheets. Jamie, why do you have so many questions?"

I gave her one of my sweet, innocent smiles. "I'm just curious about your job. Working at a place like that, which helps people, sounds very rewarding."

Aldis considered it for a moment. "Well, I never looked at it that way."

"Why do you have two spreadsheets?"

Aldis made me wait while she finished her second slice of pizza. It was as good as I remembered. Between tonight's dinner and Terri's spaghetti feast from Saturday, I was getting my fill of Italian fare.

"One spreadsheet is a record for the K-9 people. The other one is for Delaney and Associates. That's how they keep track of the work I've done."

"How do you get the spreadsheet to Jillian?" I doubted that this was being printed out and transported back and forth.

Aldis rummaged in her purse and dug out a flash drive with a bright green cover. She held it up for a moment, then put it away. "After I enter all the information into the K-9 sheet, I just make a copy of it and save it here. The other sheet is where I list all the small donations that come in. Little checks, or those credit card notices that are for less than $200. You'd be surprised at how many small donations come in each week."

"What do you do with the small checks?"

"That's what the bank deposit is for. Jillian gave me a rubber stamp with the endorsement on it. I list them on a deposit slip. Then I give them to her with the flash drive the day after I work at K-9."

Now the part-time posting made more sense. Aldis worked at K-9 True Companion on Mondays, Wednesdays and Thursdays. She could easily drop off the deposit and the flash drive at the office on the days when she didn't work there, or early in the morning before going on her assignment. The big donations would go right in the proper accounts. The smaller ones were being skimmed. But if you added up enough small donations, that could result in significant money. Especially if you were doing this at many nonprofit organizations around town.

"That's an interesting way to do business," I said. "I don't understand how that can benefit the charities you're working for."

"Donnie says it will be a big help to the people at K-9 when he shows them all of the different ways he can help them manage their operations."

Confusion struck. "Donnie, your boyfriend works for Delaney too?"

"Sure. Didn't I tell you that?"

I shook my head. "Nope. You just said Donnie is your boyfriend and he got you a job there when you moved here."

"Well, it was pretty easy for me to get hired there." Aldis leaned a little closer and waved for me to do the same. "Does it make me a terrible person if I'm sleeping with the boss?"

"Donnie is your boss?" My brain was spinning.

"I know. It's not like I planned it or anything. I wasn't working for him when we met. Things just sort of happened."

"Does anyone else know?"

Aldis shook her head. "I don't think so. It's not like a big company. There are only a few people. Donnie's usually in the office, along with Jillian. Unless he's going out to meet with a new client."

I rocked back. What the hell!

"Sheldon Delaney is your boyfriend?" I managed to keep my voice low. "Donnie is Sheldon Delaney."

"Yeah. He doesn't really like the name Sheldon. That's why I call him Donnie. But I only do that when we're together."

CHAPTER TWENTY-THREE

This was my self-imposed deadline. I'd made up my mind last night. It was time to confront Delaney. I had put everything together in a file and left it on my desk. There was also a copy on the computer and loaded into the cloud as well. Yes, part of it was speculation, but it was filled with notes and recordings from my conversations with Aldis and that one with Delaney.

When I entered their office, it wasn't the image of calm professionalism. It was the picture of chaos. The receptionist had her back to the door and was jamming papers into a shredder. There were a couple of boxes next to her desk with files in them. Multiple phone lines were ringing but they went unanswered.

I marched past her desk and the receptionist went bug-eyed. She tried to get up and block my path. That wasn't going to happen. I was surprised to see Aldis standing timidly in the door of Delaney's conference room. Apparently, I'd caught him in mid-rant. I stepped a little closer.

"How could you be so stupid? You just rolled over like a freaking puppy dog, waiting for her to scratch your belly! I suppose you told her everything!" Delaney was repeatedly jabbing a forefinger in her direction, looking for all the world like he was going to poke her in the eye.

"She just kept asking me questions," Aldis said innocently. "I didn't think it was a problem answering them."

"You didn't think! That's an understatement!"

Aldis cowered back a step. Delaney closed the distance. So far, he hadn't noticed me in the hallway. The receptionist had returned to her station and started packing files into a cardboard box. For all intents and purposes, they were getting ready to bug out. I needed to know more.

"She was curious about my job." Aldis had reclaimed her voice. "I simply cleared up a little confusion."

"A little confusion? Christ, I'd hate to see a major screwup if this was just a little confusion!" Delaney backhanded her across the face. "How's that for a little confusion!" Aldis bounced off the wall and slumped to the floor. Delaney hovered above her, gearing up for another swing.

"Leave her alone!" I shouted.

Aldis caught a glimpse of me over her shoulder and scrambled out of the way. Only now did Delaney realize it wasn't one of his employees who'd dared to interrupt him.

"You bitch!"

Quickly I turned to Aldis. "Go!" I pointed down the hall. She scrambled to her feet and moved behind me.

Delaney grabbed my arm and dragged me into the conference room. This was no time for diplomacy. "Who the hell are you? Why are you here?"

"I just came by to talk about that scheduling that event," I said, wrenching my arm from his grip.

"Bullshit. You've been talking to Aldis. Asking all kinds of questions." He stomped around the conference room. I moved in the opposite direction, keeping the table between us. This wall was a set of glass panels, overlooking the hallway. Delaney was all the way in the room, back by the solid wall. Then he leaned his palms on the table and loomed across it in my direction. "Who the hell are you?"

"Someone looking for information. But if this isn't a good time, I can always come back."

Delaney sneered at me. "Sure, c'mon back next week. We'll be gone by then. Meanwhile just sit your ass down. I want answers."

Over his shoulder, I could see the chaos continuing. A frazzled-looking woman in heels stumbled out of an office with an armload of files. She dropped half of them as she hurried toward the receptionist. Just before she reached the counter, the outer door opened and two people entered. One was an attractive, dark-haired woman about my size and height. For some reason, it struck me as odd that she wasn't carrying a purse. She wore dark slacks and a woolen coat. But it was her companion who got my attention.

This guy was big. He had to be close to six-five. This was no beanpole, but a solid, sizeable guy. The weirdest thing was, he looked vaguely familiar. He wore his black hair long, dusting over the collar of his leather jacket. When our gazes met, he nudged the woman with him and hooked a thumb at the receptionist. He moved the other office worker aside and strode confidently down the hall toward the conference room.

"I want answers!" Delaney yelled, reaching across the table toward me.

"So do I!" I stepped back out of his reach. His leather portfolio was on the table. I grabbed it with both hands and swung at his face. It wasn't a homerun swing, but it felt damn good when I connected.

Delaney jumped back in surprise. His right hand came up to his eye. Apparently, I'd caught it with the corner of the book. "You bitch!"

He started throwing chairs out of the way so he could scramble across the table after me. I looked for another weapon, something with more substance, like a baseball bat or a hockey stick. From somewhere in the recesses of my mind, instincts took over. Linda and I had been taking kickboxing lessons at the local gym since the winter.

I was backed into a corner. He slithered across the table and was right in front me now, blocking the path to the door. The big guy was moving toward the conference room, but I didn't know if he was friend or foe. Delaney came forward. I planted my left boot, pulled back with my right and swung with what was hopefully my version of a game-winning field goal attempt in the Super Bowl. I connected with a satisfying shot right between his legs.

Delaney screamed and doubled over.

That one well-placed kick should have been satisfying. But my anger was up. The adrenaline was racing through my veins. The way he'd struck Aldis confirmed this bastard was no gentleman. As he bent forward, I brought my knee up fast and smashed his nose. Blood spurted everywhere. He even got some on my favorite jeans!

The big man barricaded the doorway. He took in the scene instantly. I was still crouched just beyond Delaney, my hands balled into fists, elbows tight to my sides. If he was part of Delaney's crew of grifters, I was in serious trouble. But nothing in the world could have prepared me for his reaction.

"Malone better not piss you off." His voice was low and deep.

That took a couple of seconds to register. "You know Malone?"

"You could say we play on the same team." He pulled the leather jacket back enough for me to see the badge on his belt.

Between us on the floor, Delaney was moaning. I took a deep breath, straightened up and shook out my hands, forcing the fingers to relax.

"Got any credentials to go with that?"

The big guy took a step forward, dug a leather wallet from his back pocket, flicked it open with a twist of his wrist and extended it to me. We were close enough that I could read the specifics and see his photo ID. Cameron

Kozlowski. Detective. Michigan State Police.

"Satisfied?" he asked.

"Yeah, thanks. You've got good timing."

He looked down at Delaney, who was cupping his crotch with one hand and his nose with the other. "Doesn't look like you needed my help. You wanna tell me what the hell's going on here?"

"Grifters stealing money from nonprofits. He runs the crew. They're destroying evidence. Hitting the highway." All of this came out in a rush. The adrenaline was still churning away at a fast pace.

Kozlowski bent forward and put a foot on Delaney's back, holding him in place on the floor. "That true, cupcake?"

"I need a doctor," he mumbled, still shielding his injured parts.

"The bleeding will stop eventually. The swelling will go away. Someday. Hope you got a good a lawyer."

The brunette who entered with Kozlowski hovered in the doorway. "I've got a crew coming in. Cyber unit is sending a team, along with somebody who can do a forensic audit of these computers. Downtown post is sending a couple of uniforms to help coordinate efforts."

"What about the other…associates?" he asked.

She flashed a dazzling smile. "Zip ties are so handy. Each one is secured in a separate room. Should I call for a medic?"

"Wouldn't hurt. I want to put the cuffs on this guy, but right now that would just be adding insult to his injuries."

"I'm guessing you work with this friendly giant," I said, feeling left out of the conversation.

"I'm Detective Laura Atwater," she said. "Koz didn't tell me your name."

"Jamie Richmond. Writer and unofficial pain in the ass."

She waved two fingers back and forth. "I know that name. You're a friend of Chene's. Don't you do some research for him occasionally?"

"Just as a favor. You could say I owe him one or two."
I realized I've been doing favors for so long it was becoming
my nature. Maybe I should get business cards printed up.
Jamie Richmond. Chasing favors is my specialty.

***

The rest of the morning was a blur. I sat at the end of
the conference table and watched the activity. A female
paramedic came in and stuffed cotton up Delaney's nose.
There was a good possibility it was broken. She dumped him
in a desk chair and slapped an ice pack on his swollen
crotch. His wrists were cuffed behind his back. After being
read the Miranda rights, Delaney asked for his lawyer.
Kozlowski let him simmer for a while, then had a couple of
uniformed troopers take him for booking and to meet with
his attorney. Meanwhile, Kozlowski and Atwater worked
each room, questioning the employees. From my seat, I
could hear the wails of the receptionist when she learned
about the possible charges she was facing. I doubted she
had much of a role in the business. But any penalties were
coming her way wasn't something for me to decide or to
worry about. More than that, I was worried about Aldis.

Technicians came in and began checking all the
computers. Two people were busy gathering up all the paper
files. One of the techs pulled Kozlowski aside as he was
exiting the last interview. They had a hushed conversation,
then turned toward me. The big guy filled the doorway. Uh
oh.

"Cyber guys are checking the computers. Odd thing is
the hard drives don't appear to be wiped, but there's little of
substance on them. Of course, they'll take it all into the shop
for a closer look. You happen to have any theories about
that?"

Somewhere along the line, Koz had found a couple of
Diet Cokes and sent me one. Perhaps it was his way of
indicating that he considered me to be on his side. I'd been

replaying my interactions with Delaney. Something still bothered me. I stood up and walked around the conference table, looking closely at the carpet, carefully stepping around the little, sticky puddle of blood.

"Lose an earring?" Koz asked.

"Is that a sexist or chauvinistic remark?"

He raised both hands and showed me his palms. "Neither. Just curiosity. Did you lose something in your tussle with that idiot?"

There it was. Down in the far corner against the wall. It looked like an innocent plastic container. On the counter was an old-fashioned coffee maker, the drip kind that brewed a full pot at a time. Beside it was a sleeve of cardboard cups and a stack of napkins. I snagged a napkin, then used it to retrieve the container. I turned to Kozlowski and set it on the table between us.

"I only met Delaney once before today, gathering information about their services, particularly about setting up an event to raise money for a nonprofit. He had this nice, expensive leather portfolio. And what seemed out of place was this plastic box of gum, about three inches square. He kept it right there next to his pad and pen."

"He could have a sweet tooth," Kozlowski said.

"And I could be a descendant of Sherlock Holmes."

He grinned. "Malone said you were a smartass. Not that there's anything wrong with that. Most of the people I work with seem to have that trait."

That earned him a smile. "What got my attention was the way he kept moving it with his hand, as if taking reassurance that it was right there. He didn't put it in his shirt pocket or in his coat. He kept it where he could see it and touch it. All the time."

"Sounds a little obsessive."

"When I came in here this morning, that case was sitting right on top of his portfolio. That's where it was until I grabbed the folder and smacked him in the face with it."

Kozlowski just stood there, watching me. From the

front pocket of my jeans, I dug out a thumb drive. I held it up, then set it right beside the case on the table.

"I'll be damned!"

"Nah, you're one of the good guys. But Delaney may be damned," I said.

Kozlowski called for one of the technicians. She photographed the box, then opened it. The inner lining still showed gum wrappers. But behind them were five identical thumb drives in different colors.

"How did you make that connection?" Kozlowski asked.

"I didn't, until you mentioned the fact that the computers were so clean. He could have used the cloud for storage, but Delaney didn't strike me as the trusting type. He'd want his information close at hand. What better way to keep all the records and information they'd swiped than on flash drives? I'll bet he's got the credit card information on the donors they ripped off too."

The tech sealed the case in a little evidence bag. Kozlowski pointed to a chair and dropped into one across from me. Detective Atwater joined us.

"You always happen to carry a flash drive in your pocket?" Atwater asked.

"When I'm working on a story, I always save it to my computer's hard drive, a flash drive and a file in the cloud. I usually keep the flash drive in my pocket whenever I'm traveling. The computer is in my car, locked in the trunk."

"Pretty smart move," she said.

"Thanks. I'd be upset if all my notes, research and the book accidentally got wiped out. Hence the multiple forms of backup."

"You're going to have to come out to the post and make an official statement," Kozlowski said.

"That's not a problem. But I do have a question."

"Go for it."

"I don't believe in coincidence. So how is it that I'm confronting this crook on a Tuesday morning and just when things are heating up, you two appear?"

Atwater and Kozlowski exchanged a look. He tipped a hand in her direction. She nodded and leaned forward.

"Our boss received a call late yesterday. An organization that he's fond of had used this Delaney company to help with some of their financial matters. They had a guy coming in to keep the books, record donations and process checks. This had been going on for almost six months."

"Bookkeeping was one of the services Delaney supposedly offered," I said.

She nodded again. "Yes. But the lady who runs that organization had done a little audit of her own. She just kept getting a creepy feeling that something wasn't right. Despite all their campaign efforts and a positive response, they had less money in the bank than a year ago. So she sweetly asked the boss if he'd mind taking a discreet look at everything."

"And your arrival today?"

"The boss asked us to stop by the office here and have a little chat with the people in charge. There was always the possibility that it was the finance guy acting on his own, ripping off the business," Atwater said.

Kozlowski laced his fingers behind his head and leaned back in a stretch. "Imagine our delight to walk in the door and discover everyone scurrying around like passengers on the Titanic. Then before I could even ask Delaney one simple question, you...dealt with him."

"He ticked me off. You didn't see him smack Aldis in the face."

He looked a little confused. "Aldis? Who is that?"

Atwater chuckled and punched him lightly on the shoulder. "She's the cleavage queen. As if you don't remember."

"Ah. The young woman." Kozlowski was able to maintain a straight face. "She is one of the temporary workers. This is the one you...bumped into."

"So what happens to the rest of them?" I asked.

"According to the personnel records we found, there were four temporary workers, plus the receptionist, Jillian

Hess, and Delaney. That was it. We interviewed Ms. Hess and Mavis, the receptionist. And we had a long talk with Aldis. We'll get warrants for the other three temps. It shouldn't be difficult to pick them up," Atwater said.

"Ready to go to the post and make that statement?" Kozlowski asked.

"Might as well. I can give you copies of my notes too, if that would be helpful. Of course, I might have to make a detour for some lunch."

Atwater smiled. "How about this? We can leave Koz here to clean up and you and I can stop at a deli for something to eat."

"Go ahead," Koz said. "I'll hang out here until these others are transported and booked. Then I'll meet you at the post. The techs can secure the office when they're done."

CHAPTER TWENTY-FOUR

All of that energy and adrenaline churning earlier must have resulted in an increase in hunger. When Laura Atwater and I stopped for lunch, I was ravenous. I devoured a roast beef and Swiss cheese sandwich that was twice the size of my normal portion. And a serving of potato salad. Atwater went for a smaller serving but didn't say a word about my appetite.

At the state police post, she took me into a small conference room. Atwater set it up to record the session. Realizing that this wasn't my first time giving an official statement made me hesitate. Not because I was nervous. My life had taken a curious turn in the last year or so.

"Is it safe to assume you know the routine?" Atwater asked.

"Yes. Ask your questions and I'll give you complete answers. But I need to know if you're going to charge me with anything."

"Why in the world would you be charged? And what for?"

I shrugged. "I did kick Delaney in the balls. And I probably broke his nose with my knee. Which, by the way, hurts like hell."

"Jamie, Koz saw everything. The hallway wall on that meeting room was one big window. He saw you trying to get away from Delaney, who was obviously threatening you. What you did was a textbook example of self-defense."

"Really?"

"Really. Some may say the bit with his nose was unnecessary, but in the heat of the moment, it was justified. Especially when you saw what he did to that young woman…"

"Aldis."

"That's right, Aldis. Her face was still red and swollen when I talked with her twenty minutes after Delaney hit her."

I shook my head. "Aldis is young and maybe a little gullible. But she's a nice girl once you get to know her. I hope she comes out of this all right."

Laura Atwater gave me a friendly smile. "When Koz and I talked with her, she was very forthcoming. Like you said, she's a little gullible. But Delaney had convinced her that it was all part of his business strategy. The idea was that she would do the 'double dip' running some purchases through her phone to process the payments. Then Delaney would later reveal to the clients how easy it was to skim a portion of the money from their events. Of course, he'd return the funds to them after the meeting. That's how he convinced her to play along."

"So if she cooperates with the rest of your investigation…"

"I doubt they will charge her with anything. But that's up to the attorneys."

Since I'd driven my car there, my laptop was on the table. Laura gave me a code so I could print out my notes. I'd separated these the other day, keeping my favor for Randy and the background search on Nicholas Bellamy out of it. The file included the dates and times of all the other conversations, along with my notes and research. I forwarded the audio files of the conversations to her phone.

"Not sure if these are legal or not, since they didn't know you were recording them," Laura said.

"Last I heard, Michigan is a one-party state. Since I was one party in the conversation, I didn't need their consent."

Laura was surprised. "That's interesting. Where did you pick up that tidbit?"

"I was an investigative reporter for years. Recording people during interviews was part of my normal process. Attorneys for the paper confirmed I could do it."

She made a note on the file. Then Detective Atwater went through her questions. I answered everything, trying to be as concise as possible. She walked me through the timeline. At the end, I suggested she contact Travis Kool to get a copy of the video from the event. Atwater nodded, then stopped the recording and set Kozlowski a text with the information.

"Between this report, the recordings and your notes, I'd say the state will have a very strong case against Sheldon Delaney and Jillian Hess," Atwater said.

"I didn't get a chance to interview her. What's her role in this?"

Atwater leaned back in her chair. "Turns out Jillian Hess is one of her aliases. Her real name is Dolores Krum. She's been arrested and convicted several times, usually misdemeanors. Pickpocket, mail fraud, prostitution. She's Delaney's ex-wife. Or maybe, his current wife. The record's a little fuzzy on that."

"What the hell!"

"That guy Delaney is no choirboy, either. He's been arrested several times as well. Three convictions for larceny, but it was always at a number that kept him out of prison for any length of time. His real name is Francis Sheldon."

"So while he was posing as her boyfriend, he was actually cheating on Aldis with this Jillian witch."

"Probably. That's why he wasn't around all the time."

I glanced to make sure her recorder was off. "I should have kicked him in the crotch twice."

***

After completing the report with Laura Atwater, I stayed in the interview room for a little privacy. It was time to face the music. Malone had half an hour before his shift started. He answered on the first ring.

"Are you all right?" he asked gruffly.

"Yes. What have you heard?" I was already tense. His tone added to it.

"Kozlowski called me. Thought I should know you kicked the crap out another bad guy. Have things calmed down yet?"

"Still feeling a little wired. But I think I'm okay. The bad guy never laid a hand on me."

"Jamie, you could have told me about this." The concern in his voice tugged at my heart. "You don't have to keep taking chances like this on your own."

"I know. But I just felt that it was something I had to figure out. Once I knew for sure, I was going to tell you everything."

He was quiet for a beat or two. "I'm not trying to change you. I just want you to be around."

"I appreciate that, Malone. Maybe I am just a redhead magnet for trouble like Linda said."

He chuckled. "That's a very accurate description. But I'm still worried about you. Sure you're okay?"

"Yes. But I could use a reassuring hug if you happen to have one hanging around there."

"That can be delivered. Wanna stop by or wait until after my shift?"

"Sooner is better. Malone…"

"Yeah?"

"I love you."

"I love you, Jamie. See you soon."

He ended the call. I sat for a minute, feeling the warm glow radiating from my core. One year and counting and

Malone was sticking around. Then I packed up my laptop, grabbed my coat and left.

***

It was late afternoon and the rush-hour traffic was already rocking. With a mixture of feelings, I cut across town. Relief, exhilaration, happiness, and a sense of satisfaction were all bouncing around, just to name a few. I'd figured out what the crooks were doing and found a way to stop them. No other nonprofits should be victims of their scams. Maybe the money they swiped would be recovered and returned. Maybe Aldis would be cleared and be able to start a new life. Maybe Malone wouldn't be mad at me forever.

I pulled off the highway and entered the parking lot for the post. This building was more modern than the one on the east side, where Kozlowski and Atwater worked. It was also much closer to home. I parked in the public lot out front and went inside.

Malone was at the reception desk, talking with one of the civilian staff. He caught a glimpse of me out of the corner of his eye. I slowed. Malone turned and led me to a small interview room.

"Malone, I…"

"Hush." Then he took me in his arms, pulled me close and kissed me forever. Okay, so it wasn't forever, but the intensity of it made me think it would last that long. My arms were wrapped around him, my fingers tangling with his hair. Eventually we separated. We were both gasping.

"Still want to try for two years?" he asked.

"Oh hell yes!"

"I know that curiosity and stubbornness are part of you. That's not going to change. I'm not going to try and change you, Jay. It's just…"

"Sometimes I take unnecessary chances," I said.

He nodded and took both of my hands. "Maybe you

could slow down on those chances a little."

I'd been thinking about this during my drive across town. It was dumb luck and good timing that Kozlowski and Atwater had arrived when they did. I didn't have my gun with me and if Delaney had pulled a weapon, things could have turned out very differently. Yeah, I do own a gun. Malone took me to the target range once a month for practice. But thinking about the gun now was getting me sidetracked.

"If there's a next time…"

Malone gave his head a negative shake. "You know damn well there's gonna be a next time. How about when there's a next time? Or just next time?"

I smiled. "Only a year and you already know me so well. Okay, *next time*, I tell you about it as things progress. And before I go confronting any potential bad guys, I'll bring you along."

"Guess I can live with that."

He pulled me close again. Being wrapped in Malone's arms, with my body pressed so tightly against his, chased away the last of my nervous energy. Malone sensed this was exactly what I wanted. What I needed.

"Didn't you tell me that you were having dinner with Bert tonight?"

I nodded. My voice was taking a momentary break since my heart was pounding with joy. Malone was staying with me. That was all I could hope for.

"I told him you might stop by this afternoon. He'd like to talk with you."

"Am I in trouble?"

"Kind of goes with the territory with you."

Malone escorted me down the hall to Bert's office. For some reason, I felt like this was a trip to the principal's office in high school and I was about to catch holy hell for flirting with a boy. Or making out behind the gym. Or something. Malone gave my hand a reassuring squeeze, then knocked on the door. Bert's rough voice called us in.

"She's all yours, Captain," Malone said.

"That remains debatable," Bert grumbled. But even from the distance, I could see the amusement in his expression.

He wasn't behind the desk. Instead, he was over to the side, where four gray-upholstered chairs formed a square. A lanky man got to his feet. He had sandy brown hair, desperately in need of a trim. I did a quick sartorial inventory. Casual slacks, shoes worn and in need of some polish, a dress shirt that was missing the top button and had seen better days. His hands were those of a laborer, or maybe a dockworker. Yet there was a sharpness to his demeanor. I got the impression he didn't miss much, if anything. He looked vaguely familiar. Some inner sense told me to be wary of this guy.

"Jamie, this is Captain Cantrell, from Squad Six."

Cantrell gently took my hand. "Y'all can call me Pappy. Ah ain't much on the formalities."

"It's a pleasure." Recognition kicked in. I tried unsuccessfully to place his accent, or drawl, to a specific part of the South. "I've heard a lot about you."

"Don'tcha go believin' half of it," Cantrell said with a grin. "They's mostly lies told by my crew. They expect people be 'fraid of me."

Bert motioned us to take a seat. He and Pappy were facing each other. I took a chair to Bert's right.

"Doesn't Squad Six handle the major cases?" I asked.

Pappy nodded. "Yep. Most of 'em cross the boundaries, from one city or county to 'nother. Seems to me y'all know Chene, and some of the rest."

My hunch was confirmed. "Chene saved my life. My best friend too. And I met Detectives Kozlowski and Atwater earlier today."

Cantrell nodded again. He had been watching me closely. Now he cut his eyes to Bert and gave him a grin.

Bert cleared his throat. "Jamie has the uncanny ability to find trouble. Or maybe it finds her. This latest is a perfect example."

"Mebbe yer daughter picked up her detective skills from you," Pappy said. "She helped us nail dem grifters. From what Kozlowski says, Jamie done the heavy liftin'. They got there in time to wrap it all up."

"Delaney and Hess, or whatever their real names are, were running the show. They had a few people working at the actual businesses, sneaking off with the money," I said. "They were using different approaches to fit their needs."

"Exactly. We might have caught up to 'em eventually. Y'all did us a favor, diggin' into what they was up to," Pappy Cantrell said.

Bert winked at me. "You have developed a knack for crime. Maybe you should become a consultant. Get a fancy office, schedule meetings with local departments and share some of your wisdom."

"Tease me all you want, but these crooks would still be on the loose if I hadn't started nosing around."

"Ah, for one, am glad y'all did. But ah do have a favor to ask," Cantrell said.

Again with the favors. Maybe I should ban that word from my vocabulary. "Name it."

"Next time y'all get a feeling, tell ol' Bert here about it."

Everyone's a smartass. We should form a chapter for this region and have quarterly meetings.

EPILOGUE

Almost a week had passed since the conflict at the Delaney office. We were at the Detroit Metropolitan Airport, waiting near the gate for our flight to be called. Linda had helped me pack for the trip to Denver. There were no jeans or bulky sweatshirts in my bag. I was wearing a pair of gray woolen slacks over some ankle-high boots and a cowl-neck cashmere sweater in a soft lavender shade. Malone had not seen me get dressed. It was my intention that he would be pleasantly surprised later by the lingerie beneath it all.

"Vera is going to meet us at the hotel in Denver," I said as he settled beside me. Malone handed me a latte. He wore a navy blazer, dress slacks and a white turtleneck sweater. Malone could have been a model in a fashion catalog.

"She really got us a room at the Four Seasons?"

I sipped the coffee and winked at him over the top of the container. "Nope. She got us a suite. Nice mountain view. And the hotel's only about fifteen minutes away from the Denver Art Museum."

"A suite in a five-star hotel."

"That's right."

"I can feel the credit card melting in my wallet."

"Nope. Friends of Vera's are footing the bill. They're hoping we'll be able to convince her to keep the collection in Denver for an extra week."

Malone must have realized it was hopeless to argue with Vera and her friends. She could be a real force of nature when she sets her mind to it. "Do you think Rembrandt will survive the week without a tutoring session?"

"He'll be fine. Erica has given him a project that will keep him busy. He brought home an easel, a canvas and some acrylic paints. Terri made him promise to keep it all in the basement, until he can go back to the studio."

"Ian's graduating to paint?" Malone asked, raising a skeptical eyebrow.

"Erica feels the time is right. She's going to do a video chat with him on Wednesday, so she can see how it's coming along. I really like her. Erica is keeping Ian excited about his art."

"She's the right person to challenge him. What's he painting? A landscape or a portrait?"

I shook my head. "The brat wouldn't tell me. Erica gave him options. He could use one of his sketches as a starting point. Or he might use an old one at home. She even suggested he try it with a model."

"Brittany's parents might not be comfortable with that."

"He may try and work from a photograph instead. Or maybe a photo online from one of the social media sites. I wouldn't be surprised if he has Brittany pose during a video call. Whatever way he chooses, it will be a good experiment."

Malone was about to comment when my phone buzzed. I dug it out and glanced at the screen. Kozlowski. I accepted the call and put it on speaker. There was no one else sitting within thirty feet of us.

"What's up, Koz? Malone is with me so you're on speaker."

"That's appropriate. Atwater is here too. We just had a meeting with the prosecuting attorneys on the Delaney case."

"Any good news?" I asked.

Laura Atwater chimed in. "Yes indeed. The prosecutors have agreed to drop all charges on Aldis, in exchange for her testimony against Delaney and Hess. The three other occasional workers might be looking at some similar deals."

"Don't tell me they used the old prisoner's dilemma routine," Malone said with a grin.

Kozlowski answered that. "Hey, if it ain't broke, don't fix it."

I'd heard of this gambit before. Multiple prisoners or in this case, criminals, were offered a deal by the authorities in the form of a reduction in charges in exchange for testifying against the others. It was an effective way of pitting the bad guys against each other. The first one to make the move got the best deal. Sometimes, it was the only deal.

"Whatever happened to honor among thieves?" I asked.

"You've been reading too many mobster novels," Koz said. "That kind of thing went out in the last century."

Atwater got back to the matter at hand. "The prosecutor wants to go big on Delaney, so he's looking at a decade or more in federal prison. Hess may do a little less. Her attorney is clamoring to make a deal."

"Clamoring?" Malone said with a laugh. "Imagine that. A noisy attorney."

"That's right," Koz said. "He's loudly doing his best to prove his client is innocent, or that she had a lack of complete knowledge of Delaney's criminal activities and strategies."

"But Aldis told me that Jillian Hess was the one who trained her on how to process payments on both devices," I said.

"Nobody ever accused this Jillian woman of being smart," Koz said. "Anyway, we wanted to let you know about Aldis."

"Thanks for sharing the good news," I said. "Will there be a trial?"

"Yes. Unless Delaney goes for a plea deal," Atwater said. "But at the rate the system moves, it may be six months before that happens. Meanwhile, Delaney's trying to put together enough money to get out on bail."

"The state froze all of his assets and accounts," Koz said. "Guy ain't got enough money on hand to buy a Happy Meal."

"Anything more on Aldis?" I asked.

"She's going back to Indiana. Not exactly where her family lives, but a larger town nearby. It turns out a girl she went to high school with reached out when she saw Aldis on the news. Aldis can share her apartment and she's already got a job lined up," Atwater said.

"A fresh start," Malone said thoughtfully.

Koz promised to keep me informed of any future developments. If it did go to trial, I would be expected to testify. That didn't bother me. He ended the call. I slipped the phone back into my purse.

"You should feel pretty good about that," Malone said.

I nodded. "Aldis was just an innocent kid. Maybe a little gullible. She believed Delaney and his line of bullshit. With any luck, she'll put him and this entire experience behind her."

"Captain Cantrell looked pretty good at that press conference last night," Malone said. "It sounds like the investigation has uncovered even more clients who got swindled by Delaney."

"There could be a lengthy court battle to see if any money can be returned to those organizations."

"That reporter from Channel Four seemed to know just what questions to ask Pappy Cantrell," Malone mused.

I'd kept my promise to Olivia and called her after my meeting with Bert and Cantrell last week. She'd been able to use the information to get a scoop on the other local stations. Olivia even persuaded Kozlowski and Atwater to be interviewed on camera and give her some good context and comments. Fortunately they made no reference to a certain stubborn redhead.

Late yesterday, I had a call from Randy. His mother had called to give him the news about her relationship with Nicholas Bellamy. True to his word, Nick told her everything about his past, just before declaring his love for Allison. Randy was both happy and relieved that things were working out so well.

Malone finished his coffee and glanced at me out of the corner of his eye. He waited until I took the last gulp of my latte, then took my cup and dropped both cups in the trash. The gate attendant called our flight. We waited until a lot of other people had already boarded before joining the queue.

Our bags had been checked. We would be spending four days and three nights in Denver. Malone had enough seniority and vacation days racked up that he could take the time off. He would return to duty Friday and work seven days straight. We'd leave the following Friday for South Haven, and Randy's wedding. Vera had informed me that Bert had succumbed to her charms and would be flying out to meet her in Denver on Friday morning.

Malone stood slightly behind me as we went down the jetway toward the plane. We were both carrying our winter coats, expecting snow in Denver. He slid an arm around my waist and gave me a squeeze as we waited for our fellow passengers to board.

"I never saw the boarding passes, Jamie. Where are our seats?"

I turned and snuck a quick peck on his cheek. "They're close."

"Close to what?"

It was our turn to enter the plane. I pulled the passes from my bag and showed them to the flight attendant. He smiled and gestured to the left. "Row 3. Enjoy your flight."

"Thank you."

I guided Malone to our seats and ducked in by the window.

"First class?"

"Yep. C'mon, Malone, you're blocking the aisle."

He dropped into the comfy seat beside me. "Don't let me forget to thank Vera for the upgrade. I'm not used to the first-class treatment."

The attendants were getting the last of the passengers on board. Moments later, the plane was pushed back from the gate and we trundled out to the runway for takeoff. I reached over and took his hand.

"Last time we flew, it was to Florida for a little spontaneous vacation."

Malone nodded. "That's the only other time we've flown together."

"That was vacation. This time it's a combination of business and pleasure."

"What business?"

I gave him a sweet smile. "Estate business. Since we're going out to view the collection and help to promote it and all, we're technically going on business. So, Vera didn't pay for our tickets. Lincoln Banning did." Banning is the lawyer who oversees Peter's estate.

"Jamie…"

Quickly I put a finger to his lips. "Don't be mad. I know we can afford to buy our own plane tickets and hotel accommodations. I was going to pay for the upgrade myself. When Lincoln found out we were going, he made the arrangements. I didn't realize they were first class until we got to the airport."

Malone gave me one of those low-voltage smiles. Then he kissed my finger. "Heaven help me. I'm in love with a rich broad."

A tingle raced through my heart. "What the hell. I'm in love with a cop. What in the world shall we do?"

"Guess we'll just have to make the most of it."

"That's a good answer, Malone."

The End

ACKNOWLEDGEMENTS

No man is an island. And no worthwhile author writes a story without a little help from others. That definitely includes me. I've been fortunate to meet or know people who can share their expertise with me on a variety of topics. For this story, I turned to a good friend, Debra Bonde.

Deb is the founder and president of Seedlings Braille Books for Children. I had the pleasure to work alongside her years ago, first as a volunteer, then as a board member. Deb's information tied in well with Jamie's curiosity and her investigation. You can learn more about Seedlings and the fantastic work they do by clicking this link. http://www.seedlings.org/

I've also had pleasure to know a few dedicated people who enjoy my stories and are willing to act as beta readers. This stalwart bunch doesn't pull punches and gives me honest feedback that is essential to making my stories better. Special thanks to Jerry Sorn, Mary Morehouse and Helene Love Snell.

I'd also like to express my thanks to the wonderful team at Inkspell Publishing. The ongoing support helps me bring these stories of Jamie's to life. From the artist who created the cover, to the editor and Melissa, our leader, they all worked tirelessly to make this book so much better.

Don't Miss these Jamie Richmond Mysteries

DEVIOUS

Jamie Richmond, reporter turned author, is doing research for her next book. Attempting to capture the realism of a police officer's duties while on patrol, she manages to tag along for a shift with a state police trooper. A few traffic stops and a high speed chase later, Jamie's ride takes an unexpected turn when she witnesses the trooper being shot.

Although it is not a fatal injury, Jamie becomes obsessed with unraveling the facts behind this violent act. While she is trying to sort out this puzzle, she becomes romantically involved with Malone, another trooper with a few mysteries of his own. Now Jamie's attention is divided between a blooming romance and solving the crime which is haunting her.

Jamie begins to question the events that took place and

exactly who could be behind the shooting. It was a devious mind. But who?

EXCERPT:

Suddenly, I saw a flash of light and heard a muffled bang. Smitty pitched onto his back, his right hand clawing feebly at his holster as a loud roar reached my ears. The door of the truck was still open, a brown arm extended beyond the edge of the spotlight. A gun was clutched in the gloved hand. I watched in horror as the trigger was pulled back for another shot.

Everything that happened next must have been instinct. Or maybe it was merely a reaction. Or dumb luck. Or the Force. Yeah, maybe it was the Force. I don't think I'll ever know for sure.

I reached across and pounded on the horn with one hand, flipping the buttons Smitty had used to activate the siren with the other. The sudden noise startled the driver. His arm jerked back into the cab and the door slammed. Spraying stones and dust behind, the truck lurched onto the road and raced away.

Fumbling the microphone off the dash, I thumbed the button. "Kleinschmidt has been shot! Send an ambulance!" I dropped the microphone and managed to get my door open. The frame around the window clipped my forehead and knocked me back a step.

I'd forgotten to turn off the siren and its wail was splitting my eardrums. "Idiot," I muttered, "stay calm." This was easier to say than it ever was to do.

Reaching back inside, I switched the siren off then rushed around to the front of the car. Smitty was lying on his back on the edge of the road. Blood soaked the gravel beneath him. His eyes were closed, but I could see his chest moving.

I dropped to my knees beside him. "You're going to be okay, Smitty. I called for help."

VANISHING ACT

When Jamie's best friend vanishes, she'll do anything to find her and bring her home.

A new year marks new beginnings for Jamie Richmond. Not only has she moved into a cozy new house, but she's brought Malone along with her to fan the flames of their growing romance. When Jamie's best friend, Linda Davis, enters the picture, she thinks everything is right with the world.

Linda begins a May-September romance with Vincent Schulte, Jamie's doctor and good friend. But while Vince is sweeping Linda off her feet, she unknowingly has captured the attention of a stalker. The idyllic life suddenly takes a very bad turn when Linda disappears without a trace on a cold and snowy day. The police are scrambling to find a clue that will lead them to Linda.

Malone does his best to comfort Jamie and encourages her to let the professionals do their job. But if there's one thing he's learned in their time together, it's that nothing will stop this stubborn redhead from solving this mystery.

Jamie turns all of her attention on figuring out who took Linda and where she might be, regardless of the dangers she may face. Her efforts once again put her in harm's way. But will she find her best friend?

EXCERPT:

"So are you going to tell me what's going on, Linda? You've been beaming a thousand-watt smile."

I saw the color radiate on her cheeks. She lowered her eyes and took a sip of her coffee. Finally, she drew a deep breath and raised her face.

"I think I'm in love."

I sat back in amazement.

"Vince came over last night. After dinner, we moved to the sofa. The fire was lit and one light was on low. I had been in a rush when I came home, so I hadn't bothered to change."

"So we're just listening to music. And I mentioned that I had to get out of my boots. My feet were starting to cramp. That's when things got…different."

"What do you mean, different?"

"Vince told me to move to the other end of the sofa. Then he slowly unzipped my boots and pulled them off. My legs were on his lap. He started to massage my feet, chasing away the aches and pains. Then he moved up to my ankles. And the whole time, he just kept talking, keeping his voice very low and soft."

"What did he say?"

Linda shuddered with the memory. "He told me all of the things he was going to do to me, all the ways he wanted to please me. It was like I was hypnotized. He was in total control of me. I couldn't move."

No words found their way out of my mouth.

"I swear he touched on every fantasy, no matter how dark, I have ever considered. And the whole time, he just kept talking softly, massaging my legs. Jamie, by the time he finally undressed me, I was so far over the edge, I didn't think I'd ever make it back."

FLEEING BEAUTY

A discovery of priceless artwork leads Jamie on a collision course with danger.

Jamie Richmond used to live a nice, quiet life. But last fall she witnessed the shooting of a police officer and figured out who did it. Then this winter saw her best friend targeted by a stalker and kidnapped. Yep, Jamie solved that one and came to the rescue. Now it's summertime and the living is supposed to be easy. All she wants to do is write her novels and spend free time with Malone, the guy who has been by her side since all this craziness began. But that's not likely to happen.

Jamie's father was a very successful sculptor who tragically died more than twenty years ago when she was just a child. What she remembers about him is little more than bits and pieces. A storeroom filled with crates of his work is discovered in an old converted factory. This potential fortune in artwork has been waiting all these years.

Jamie recruits Malone and a few close friends to help her unpack the crates and bring her father's gifts out to the light of day. News of this discovery leads to a robbery. Now Jamie is determined to figure out who is behind the crime.

EXCERPT

This sculpture was titled "Fleeing Beauty".

It was a woman caught in the act of running. Tendrils of slender marble in various lengths and thicknesses extended from her head, as if they were locks of hair billowing out behind her. Part of her face was obscured, turned against her shoulder as if attempting to hide her features from whoever was chasing her. The woman's body was voluptuous, full of dangerous curves. There was something haunting about this piece. The guys became quiet, which was unusual. Linda slowly moved around it, taking pictures.

"Holy shit," Ian muttered.

"Watch your language," Malone said, cuffing him lightly on the back on the head.

"How did he do that?" Ian said, taking a step away. "She looks real."

"She looks alive," Malone said.

"Check the file," I suggested.

None of us could take our eyes off the sculpture.

We spread the file out on the worktable. There were pictures of a woman standing in front of a drop cloth. She was blonde, with an impish smile on her face. She could have been in her early to middle twenties. It was impossible to tell how tall she was. Her figure was eye catching, with a tiny waist and round hips. Most of the pictures showed her in a one piece bathing suit. There was one where she wore a sheer negligee. There were shots of her standing on a pedestal, others with her arms outstretched, and still others where she was looking over her shoulder. In a couple of photos he must have used a fan to blow her hair back.

"She's a doll," Ian said.

"Jamie, I think this is the most beautiful thing I've ever seen," Linda said softly.

"You'll get no argument from me."

STEALING HAVEN

After months of hard work, Jamie and her best friend, Linda, are on vacation. Lounging on the sandy beaches of South Haven, on the shore of Lake Michigan, the ladies *only* plan is *no* plan. No deadlines for Jamie, the investigative reporter. No papers to grade for Linda, the high school teacher. It's time to kick back and relax.

That lasted until lunchtime on Monday, when they shared a table with Jared, a local cop and Randy, a city official who only had eyes for Jamie. Casual conversation revealed a home invasion, which got Jamie's curiosity going.

While the two friends explore South Haven, Jamie discovered a pattern with the home invasions. Sharing her clues with Jared, it isn't long before Jamie and Linda are recruited to help catch the crooks.

Sand, sun, romance and a mystery to solve. Sounds like a perfect vacation for Jamie.

EXCERPT:

That earned me another kiss. This one lasted for about an hour. Well, maybe it was a minute or two. My hand tangled in his hair, keeping him close.

"Glad I'm different from most guys," he said quietly as we separated. His hands returning to the wheel.

Part of me was still locked on his kiss. Was this really happening? I looked back at Linda. She flashed a wide grin and made a show of slowly clapping her hands together. I wondered if she knew how to drive a boat so I could drag Randy to the cabin below deck. With an effort, I reined in such thoughts.

"So I'm supposed to believe you don't find young women out looking for fun on their vacation and charm them with that smile?"

"You like my smile? I always thought it was kind of lopsided."

I took his face in both hands and turned it toward me. "Maybe a little crooked. But that's part of the appeal." Now I initiated a kiss. His hands slid through my hair, then softly ran his fingers down my neck. Shivers of excitement coursed through me. A horn sounded nearby. He broke the kiss and turned to check the water. Another boat passed in the opposite direction. A man and woman were at the helm, mirroring our positions, caught in the moment and sensuality of being on the water. I bit down on my bottom lip in frustration. I longed for more than kisses but safety came first.

"We don't want to run into some sailboat out here," Randy said with a grin.

I scooted back onto the bench. Maybe a little distance was in order? It might help my racing hormones. "How fast are we going?"

"About thirty. Want to go faster?"

Was he talking about the boat, or the two of us? Randy shifted. His right hand had dropped to the controls, his left lightly holding the steering wheel. He watched me, his lopsided grin worked its magic.

AVAILABLE AT ALL BOOK RETAILERS IN EBOOK AND PRINT

ABOUT THE AUTHOR

Mark Love lived for many years in the metropolitan Detroit area, where crime and corruption are always prevalent. A former freelance reporter, Love honed his writing skills covering features and hard news. He is the author of the Jamie Richmond romance mysteries, **Devious, Vanishing Act, Fleeing Beauty**, and **Chasing Favors**, along with the novella **Stealing Haven**. His short story, **Don't Mess with the Gods**, was written with Elle Nina Castle and included in the *Magic & Mischief* anthology. Love also writes the Jefferson Chene mystery series, **WHY 319?, Your Turn to Die** and **The Wayward Path**. Love resides in west Michigan with his wife, Kim. He enjoys a wide variety of music, books, travel, cooking and exploring the great outdoors.

You can find him on the links below.

http://www.amazon.com/-/e/B009P7HVZQ

https://motownmysteries.blogspot.com/
https://www.facebook.com/MarkLoveAuthor
https://twitter.com/motownmysteries
https://www.instagram.com/motownmysteries